How to
Breathe
Underwater

How to Breathe Underwater

Vicky Skinner

Swoon
READS

SWOON READS | NEW YORK

A SWOON READS BOOK
An imprint of Feiwel and Friends and Macmillan Publishing Group, LLC
175 Fifth Avenue, New York, NY 10010

HOW TO BREATHE UNDERWATER.
Copyright © 2018 by Vicky Skinner. All rights reserved.
Printed in the United States of America.

Our books may be purchased in bulk for promotional, educational,
or business use. Please contact your local bookseller or the Macmillan
Corporate and Premium Sales Department at (800) 221-7945 ext. 5442
or by e-mail at MacmillanSpecialMarkets@macmillan.com.

Library of Congress Cataloging-in-Publication Data is available.
ISBN 978-1-250-13787-6 (hardcover) / ISBN 978-1-250-13611-4 (ebook)

Book design by Brad Mead

First edition, 2018

1 3 5 7 9 10 8 6 4 2

swoonreads.com

For Jeremy:

without you, I'd be drowning

How to
Breathe
Underwater

One

I could see the swimmer beside me every time I came up for air. His face was distorted slightly by the plastic separator that divided his lane from mine, but I could see him pushing, his arms pumping fast. I was faster. I was always faster. I pulled ahead, closing the distance between the wall and me until my fingertips touched, and I came up for a deep, refreshing breath of chlorine-scented air.

"God, Kate," Harris (short-distance butterfly and my best friend) said, and panted. He'd come up out of the water a whole four seconds behind me. He needed to get his time down if he was going to make it to State. "Give a guy a break."

I was sucking in air, too, but each breath seemed to scream out my accomplishment. Harris might have been bigger than I was, but he would never be faster. "Give you a break so you can get lazy? I don't think so."

He pressed his back to the wall and closed his eyes, sinking into the pool just enough for his chin to dip below the surface. "Thank God I'll never have to race you for real. That could really bruise my ego. Maybe if *my* dad had quit his desk job to coach the swim team, I'd be as good as you." He grinned over at me, and I splashed him with a handful of water.

I snorted. "Yeah, right. It's called natural talent. I was mastering the dolphin kick while you were still in floaties."

"Harris, out of the pool," Coach Judd (assistant girls' swim coach) called to us. "We need girls in first."

Harris held his arms in the air, dripping. "But Coach isn't even out here yet." He gestured toward the door behind us, where Coach Masterson (head coach for the girls' and boys' swim teams, and my father) had disappeared ten minutes earlier for a parent-teacher meeting with Jenny Carther's mom. We were two weeks away from the start of school, a month away from the start of the season, and he was already lecturing parents.

Coach Judd rolled his eyes. "Doesn't matter. He'll be ready to go any minute, and I need the girls ready to go, too. Out!"

Harris sent me an irritated look but did as Coach Judd asked. I did the same, splashing up out of the water and sitting on the edge of the pool, my legs still knee-deep. Everyone else was hanging out in the stands and on the side of the pool, their suits dry. Over by the bleachers, April (a master in all events, and Harris's girlfriend) blew him a kiss. Beside her, Jenny Carther rolled her eyes.

"Hey, Jenny!" Chuck (100-yard backstroke, bulkiest and slowest on the varsity team) yelled out. "When's Mommy gonna buy you implants so you can fill out your suit?"

Coach Judd made a disgruntled noise but didn't call Chuck out. Jenny Carther (breaststroke leg of the 200-yard medley relay and exceptionally self-conscious for someone who weighed one hundred and thirty pounds of almost pure muscle) bolted from her spot poolside and raced by me. I listened to her bare feet slapping the floor until she threw open the door to my father's office, probably to tattle on Chuck.

I didn't turn to watch the scene, instead massaging my sore calves in the warm pool water. But after a moment, everyone went quiet. I looked up at Harris to say something, but immediately forgot what it was when I realized that every member of the girls' and boys' swim teams was looking in the direction of Coach's office, like a car had just crashed into it.

I turned to look, and my mouth fell open.

Inside the office, Jenny Carther's mother and my father were making out against his trophy case, and it was embarrassing how long it took for them to realize that every athlete on the swim team was watching them.

Finally they broke apart, my father's eyes finding mine amid everyone's, and the horror on his face matched the horror that had settled in my chest.

Before the end of the day, the swim team had spread the word about my father's little slipup. It felt like everyone in Salem knew, and it didn't take long for my mother to get wind of it as well. A month later, my mother and I were moving to Portland to live near my sister, Lily, and my life was completely ruined.

◦ ◦ ◦

"Wait, 6A?" Harris bellowed in my ear. "You can't go to a 6A school. You won't be in our division. We won't even be competing together!"

I pressed my forehead against my window and peered down at the traffic below, my body finally exhausted after a day of moving, not to mention the emotional upheaval of abandoning the house I'd been living in since the day I was born. I sighed, watching my breath fog up the window.

"I'm painfully aware of that," I told him. "It's not like I have a choice. Most of the schools out here are 6A, and seeing as how I don't have a car, I'm not going to move to a 5A school that's four times farther from home just so I can swim in the same pool as you."

He laughed, but I felt something serious settle under my skin. I was going to have to go back to the pool. I was going to have to join a different team like nothing had even happened, and it felt unreal.

"So, how's Portland? It's been a while since I've been there. I hear it's gotten smoggier. Is it extra smoggy?"

"It's not any smoggier than usual."

Our new apartment, located on the third floor of a high-rise apartment building in downtown Portland, was actually pretty nice. According to the brochure my mother had given me when she broke the news that we were relocating, the place had a heated rooftop pool, an indoor serenity garden, and a fitness center. There was even a doorman.

Out my window, I got a great view of downtown. We were in the thick of things, close to the Willamette River. I could practically smell it through the glass. It was a black blob of shadow in the darkness. Sure, it was nice, but not exactly nice enough to make me forget that my parents' pending divorce was the reason I was here.

"God, this blows." I heard the crisp sound of a can popping open.

"Tell me about it." My carpet was covered in boxes, suitcases, tote bags. And right in the center of everything, not yet cemented to a spot, was my bed, bare and cold. "You better not be drinking a soda. You know it slows you down."

Without even being able to see him, I knew he rolled his eyes. "Calm down, Mom. It'll be long out of my system before I hit the pool again. I don't have one foot in the water at all times, like you."

I knew he meant it as a joke, but in the process of my father's affair being publicized, my parents splitting up, and our current migration, it had been a month since I'd been in the pool—an eternity. "What's going on with you?" I asked, desperate to change the subject.

"Oh, you know, the usual. April's bugging me about homecoming, like I actually plan on going. First meet in a few weeks, and if I can't get my stroke count down, Coach is going to suffocate me in my sleep—and my dad would provide the pillow."

I sat down on the floor, my back pressed against the windowsill. "Well, can't say I blame them. You're too distracted. You need to stop focusing so much on getting April to put out and spend more time doing drills."

"Not everyone can be a child prodigy, Katherine. Hey, let's video chat. I want to see your new place."

"Oh. Yeah. Okay." But just as he said it, my phone beeped, letting me know the battery was about to die. "Um," I said, pushing up off the floor and searching my room, phone still pressed to my ear.

But I was fairly certain my charger was still in the back seat of the car, where I'd tossed it in my haste. "Hey, I have to call you back. Battery's about to die. I'll call you when I'm plugged in." I didn't wait for him to answer, just hung up and tossed my phone on the bed on my way out the door.

We had a parking space underneath the building, in a parking garage. I wasn't a fan of elevators, so I took the stairs down to the lobby and then walked the two floors down to our parking space. I used the key fob to unlock the doors and reached into the back seat where, sure enough, my charger was sitting. I snatched it, ready to get back upstairs.

As I was locking the car, I heard a strange noise on the other side of the lot, like the air going out of a balloon, and then coughing. It wasn't the clearing of a throat, but a hacking, gagging struggle for breath.

On instinct, I tried to remember my CPR training. I'd gotten certified one summer so I could be a lifeguard, but it had been long enough now that I wasn't sure I could remember all the details if the person I could hear needed it.

Another series of coughs broke the silence, and when I got back to the building's entrance I stopped, just feet from the door. Parked in one of the first spots in the lot was an old station wagon, right under one of the overhead lights. The light shone down on a woman, probably in her fifties, sitting sideways in the driver's seat with her feet flat on the concrete. She was bent over at the waist, her long gray-spotted braid trailing down to her lap. Hovering beside the open door, stooping to be level with the woman, was a boy my age, a hand on her shoulder as the woman wheezed violently.

"Are you okay?" I asked.

The woman didn't appear to need CPR. She was breathing, and she was conscious—both encouraging. When the guy's eyes found mine in the shadows, all I saw was fear. I saw that his other hand was clutching the woman's. Neither of them said anything for a long moment, but I could hear the rattling of the woman's breath, the sounds of her lungs still struggling for air.

"Everything's fine," the guy finally said. "Thank you."

I turned my attention to the woman, thinking that maybe she would say something different. Maybe she would tell me to call an ambulance. But instead, she coughed hard, gasping between fits. I took a step forward, feeling helpless. There had to be something I could do, but the guy sent me a strange look that reminded me that this had nothing to do with me. So I backed away and went inside, moving slowly in case he called out after me for help. He didn't.

When I was back inside the bright lobby, Bobby, the evening doorman, looked at me with worried eyes.

"Everything okay?" he asked.

I was still watching what I could see of the boy and the woman through the glass doors. "There's a woman out there. She's having trouble breathing."

Bobby's eyes widened and he rushed to the door, but as soon as he caught sight of the two out in the garage, his progress lost its urgency. "Oh. That's Harriet. You don't need to worry about her. She's got a nasty case of emphysema. Consistent bronchitis. Gives her a lot of trouble. Years of smoking will do that to you. I'm sure she'll be fine. Her son will take good care of her. If she needs medical attention, he'll make sure she gets it."

———

7

I watched the woman's back lift and fall in deep breaths, her son still bent over her.

○ ○ ○

I jerked awake the next morning and groaned at the light spilling into my bedroom. I made a mental note to hang my blinds and curtains before the end of the day. I lay in bed for a second, trying to get used to the unfamiliar smell of the new apartment. It was cold, so much colder than my father had ever kept the house, and I wanted to stay under the warm covers forever.

As soon as I opened my door, I tripped over a sewing machine. "Motherf—!" I shouted when I lost my footing and slammed into the wall.

"Language!" my mom shouted from the kitchen. "I'm glad you're up," she said when I got to her. "I made breakfast. Eggs, bacon, and toast." She shoveled some onto a plate and set it in front of me at the table with a smile pasted on her face that was so fake, she looked like a plastic doll.

"Thanks, Mom."

She went back to the stove to make herself a plate. "How did you sleep?"

The truth was that I hadn't slept much at all. The traffic sounds outside my window all night had kept me awake, along with the noise from the apartment upstairs. I'd never lived in an apartment before, and I'd never lived in the center of a huge city like Portland. We'd lived in West Salem for as long as I'd been alive, a much quieter sector of an already relatively small city.

I didn't tell my mother any of that. "Good," I said, trying to sound optimistic. I didn't want my mother to have to worry about the fact that she had completely upturned my life by moving us out here, even if that's exactly what she'd done. It wasn't like she'd had a lot of options.

"Have a lot to do today," she said, munching on her toast. "I want to try to get a good number of the boxes in here and the living room unpacked." She finished her toast, the only thing on her plate, and rinsed her dish in the sink.

In Salem, every Sunday morning had been the same: a hard swim at sunup with dad, Mooney's Café for a recovery meal of pancakes and eggs, and a walk along the river in the late-morning sun.

This was our first Sunday without Dad in a long time, and it showed in the bags under my mother's eyes.

"I'm off to locate the trash chute," she said, picking up a bag of garbage.

"Why don't I take it?" I asked, leaving my breakfast behind to take the bag from her.

She gave a little sigh. "Are you sure?"

"Yeah, no problem."

I was still in my pajamas, a T-shirt and Superman boxers, but I decided to go right then anyway. I'd just made it to the front door when I saw the planner lying open on the entry table. I recognized it immediately. Every season, my father would put my meets, practices, and workouts in a planner so I wouldn't get behind. Pages and pages of swim-related activities. My mother must have found it in a box somewhere. I glanced over my shoulder at her. She was digging through a box in the kitchen, pulling out towels and pot holders. I reached out and snatched the planner off the table before opening the door.

I was standing hopelessly in the hallway with no clue where the trash chute was when the door directly across from me opened and someone joined me in the narrow hallway.

It took me a second to place the boy in front of me as the one I'd seen in the parking garage the day before, the one leaning over the woman with the bad lungs. Dark, messy hair that might have been styled to look that way or might have been subject to nervous fingers; dark eyes, the color of which I couldn't decipher with the length of the hall between us; the sleeves of his shirt bunched up around his elbows.

I wanted to ask him if his mom was okay, or maybe ask him his name, but I saw his eyes go first to my boxers and then to my garbage bag.

"Can you tell me where the trash chute is?"

He pointed to the end of the hall. "Take a left and then a right. Last door on the left."

"Thanks."

I hauled the garbage bag up but paused when he said, "Nice boxers."

Like an idiot, I said nothing. I just turned in the direction he'd indicated. At the end of the hall, before I rounded the corner, I couldn't stop myself from glancing over my shoulder for one last glimpse. He stood by the elevator, the button illuminated, and then he glanced over his shoulder, too, his eyes meeting mine down the hallway.

I looked away quickly, turning the corner. I almost forgot I had the planner in my hand when I pulled the door open to toss the trash in the chute. The bag fell from my hand, and I looked down

———

at the planner. It contained my entire life. Everything I was expected to do, everywhere I was expected to be. But now it was just as much trash as the garbage I'd thrown down. A new place meant a new swim schedule.

I pulled open the chute again and tossed the planner in.

Two

When I stood in front of my closet mirror before my first day of school, I looked like myself. Same face, same girl. But I felt different. It felt like the whole universe had tilted on its axis.

I swallowed down two bowls of cereal and watched my mother type away on her laptop at the kitchen table, a newspaper open beside her. My mother hadn't always been a stay-at-home mom. She was an office manager for a small dental practice when I was younger but quit not long after my father started coaching me.

I leaned forward to see what she had circled. *Administrative Assistant. Billing Coordinator. Claims Specialist.* I wasn't sure what most of those jobs were.

"Are you taking me to school today?" I knew she wasn't trying to ignore me. She had big things to take care of today and probably not a lot of time to figure it all out. But she'd barely looked at me through breakfast, and I was feeling a little anxious.

Mornings were usually busy: rushing to an early workout, getting through breakfast as fast as possible, jumping in the car and making it in time for Dad to prep before the first bell. I wasn't used to my mornings moving like a snail, the way this one was.

"Oh, I thought maybe you could take the school bus."

"What about the car?" I was sixteen and perfectly capable of taking myself to school. It would be a luxury after the years of riding with my father, who refused to get me my own car, saying that a car in the hands of a sixteen-year-old would only lead to drunkenness, teenage pregnancy, and the state penitentiary.

My mom shook her head, her eyes moving from computer screen to newspaper as she sipped her coffee. "I need the car for job hunting today. You'll be fine. You can take the bus." Gloom must have been written all over my face because she rolled her eyes. "Stop being so dramatic. It's just public transportation; I'm certain that you'll survive."

She smiled at me, and it almost looked real against her dirty-blond hair, wide mouth, and freckled skin. I tried to erase the disappointment from my face. I wanted to make this as easy as I could for her, and if that meant taking the bus to school, then I wasn't going to argue.

"Oh, by the way, I talked to your new coach on the phone yesterday evening, and I don't think we're going to have any issues getting you prepped with the team in time for the season. Their first practice is tomorrow, and she wants to meet you then. But you just focus on having a great first day."

My stomach turned, and for a second, I thought I was going to lose my breakfast. Until then, I'd almost been able to distract myself enough to forget about swimming, about joining a new team. I suddenly wished my mom was taking me to school just so I wouldn't have to be alone with my nerves.

"Oh, and you have your last dress fitting this afternoon."

How could I forget? Lily was getting married on Saturday, and I was the maid of honor. My sister was the one who had convinced my mother that moving to Portland to be closer to her made the most sense when my parents split. Lily had chosen to transfer to a college in Portland to follow Tom, the love of her life, when he was offered a job in the city.

"How long before the bus comes?"

"I think you've got time." Her eyes were unfocused in thought. I wasn't sure what I'd been expecting. What was she supposed to do, hold my hand and drop me off at my first class?

"I'll just go ahead and go down now," I told her. I didn't think I could stand another second of sitting there, listening to her fingers typing on her laptop. I picked up my bag and moved to the front door, my eyes on her, waiting for her to offer to walk me down or at least to the door.

"Okay, sweetie. I'll see you tonight. Maybe we can meet for dinner after the fitting? Somewhere nice to celebrate your first day."

"Yeah. Okay." I hesitated, my hand on the doorknob. "I'll see you tonight."

She looked up and smiled, and I tried to let that be enough for me for the moment, but once I left the apartment, I would be in a brand-new place with unfamiliar faces and unfamiliar streets. I fiddled with the doorknob, feeling the tips of my fingers start to sweat.

When I opened the door, my heart stopped.

I immediately recognized the boy standing in the hallway,

———

leaning against the door directly across from ours. I gasped and he straightened up, putting both hands out quickly, like I was a rabid dog he needed to persuade not to bite him. It was the boy that knew where the trash chute was.

"I'm sorry," he said. "I didn't mean to scare you. Um, your mom said I could just wait out here for you."

"My mom?" I heard my mother's chair scrape away from the table.

She rushed to my side. "I completely forgot. This is Michael." She gestured to the guy, who now had an uncomfortable tilt to his mouth. "He lives across the hall, and he rides the bus to school, so I thought the two of you could ride together."

I narrowed my eyes at her. How in the world had she had time to make friends already? We'd been in the building for a whole forty-eight hours.

She smiled at Michael and, as if she could read my mind, said, "We met in the lobby last night. It'll be nice to have a friend on your first day, won't it?"

Michael watched me, waiting. The truth was, I had eyes. Michael was cute, almost painfully so, like he was completely unaware of it. I noticed. It wouldn't kill me to be in close proximity to him long enough to get to school.

"Okay," I told them both and stepped out of the apartment.

Michael's face crept from hesitant to kind. He gestured to the elevator. "After you."

I hesitated. "I'm going to take the stairs. I can meet you down there."

He stood there, his arms hanging limply at his sides. My mother was still standing in the doorway. She laced her fingers together in front of her hips and sent me a sympathetic smile, like I was a kindergartner on my first day, throwing a fit in front of everyone.

"When Kate was really little, she wandered into an elevator by herself at a department store and got stuck between floors. She's had some trouble with them ever since."

I just stared at her. Was it completely necessary for her to divulge all my business to anyone within a two-mile radius?

Michael's eyes were fixed on his shoes, but the generous curve of his mouth made it obvious that he was holding back a smile. "No problem. I've always liked the stairs better."

We didn't speak the whole way down, but every few seconds, Michael glanced over his shoulder at me, probably to make sure I was still there.

Out the lobby windows, I saw that large storm clouds were building up in the sky like a vast army about to attack.

"Don't worry," Michael said as the doorman held the door for us. It wasn't Bobby. This was a guy who sent us a close-lipped smile and wished us a nice day without enthusiasm. "It rains way more here than it does in Salem, but it doesn't usually last very long."

He knew I was from Salem. What else had my mother told him? My Social Security number? The shape of the birthmark on my shoulder? Which, incidentally, Harris always said was shaped like Denmark.

When we reached the curb, I breathed in the moist air, closing my eyes and tilting my head back, like I could suck all of it into my pores if I tried hard enough. I loved the way the air smelled right before a storm. Wet and thick. I heard a whir and a click

———

16

beside me and opened my eyes just as another smell mixed in the air: the acrid, nauseating smell of cigarette smoke, pulling me out of my euphoric moment.

"God, who's smoking?" I said seconds before I realized that Michael, standing beside me at the stoplight, was the one who had lit up. He blew out a mouthful of smoke in the direction of the stoplight, but the wind blew it back in my face. I coughed.

"Man, I'm sorry. I didn't realize . . ." He trailed off as he walked around me to stand on my other side.

I focused on not gagging. The smell of cigarettes was the worst thing imaginable. It always got my stomach churning. How could someone so cute be a smoker? Didn't he know what it did to his lungs? I clamped down on that thought when I remembered the shape of his mother, bent over in her station wagon.

"I'm trying to quit," he told me, even though I hadn't asked. I glanced over at him and watched as his full lips closed around the cigarette. He pinched it between his fingers and noticed me staring. "Should I put it out?"

I waved the suggestion away. I didn't want to be *that* girl. "No, it's fine."

A silence passed between us, and then out of nowhere, he said, "Your mom told me you guys picked this building because your sister lives close by. That's pretty cool."

"Yeah, I guess." It certainly didn't feel cool. It's not cool when your dad is cheating on your mom, your parents are getting divorced, and you're being uprooted from your entire life. But I got the feeling he meant well.

"We really only live here because my uncle owns the building." He smiled, and I was caught for a second. The hand holding his cigarette was down at his side, and he looked like a photograph hanging on a blank wall in an art gallery, his body tipped slightly toward mine and smoke trailing up out of the cigarette into the humid air. Black jeans, olive-green thermal top, hair shining with the moisture in the air around us so thick I could almost touch it.

I wasn't really sure why he mentioned his uncle. It was completely irrational, but I felt like everyone was staring at us.

"I'm just trying to even the playing field a little," he told me, putting his cigarette out on a NO PARKING sign beside him and flicking the butt onto the street in front of us, where it was immediately crushed under the tire of a passing car. "You know, since your mom pretty much shared your entire life story with me last night." When I didn't say anything, he lifted a hand and scratched the spot where his hairline met the back of his neck. "My uncle set us up in this fancy place. Because my mom is . . ." He trailed off and looked away from me. "My uncle owns buildings from here to Seattle."

Over his shoulder, I saw the bus approaching, but I was still looking at Michael, who seemed to have lost some of his confidence. The bus came to a hissing stop in front of us and the door folded open. I hopped on quickly, Michael behind me.

I took the first empty seat I found, and Michael slid in beside me. He didn't greet anyone, didn't even *look* at anyone, just took the seat next to me like we'd known each other forever.

He turned to me as the bus started to move. "Your mom said you were some kind of famous swimmer."

I rolled my eyes. "It's not like that. I won a few races at the state championships last year. And I, uh, sort of set the state record in the 200-yard freestyle race. Not a big deal." Except, of course, that it was. I'd worked harder than anyone else on the team. I knew part of that had to do with my father always working me, always pushing to make me better, but at the end of the day, it was me. I'd won that race, I'd set the record, I'd taken the medal, and it had admittedly put me on a pedestal at my old school. But I wasn't sure I was ready for everyone at my new school to know about it.

He shrugged. "If you say so. Sounds like a big deal to me." He was so close I could see the sprinkling of freckles spread across his cheekbones like constellations.

We fell into silence, and the question that had been at the back of my mind rushed to the surface. "So, um, is your mom okay? Because the other night . . ."

He nodded, the corners of his mouth turning down slightly. "She's fine." He fell silent, looking out the front windshield, and I grasped for something to say, coming up empty. Maybe I'd gone a step too far, asking about his mom?

We sat in silence for a moment, but then I could feel Michael's eyes on me. "You nervous?" he asked.

"No," I lied, partly because of my pride and partly because I still wasn't so sure I wanted this guy to know *everything* about me.

"What's your first class?" he asked.

I reached into my backpack and pulled out my schedule. "Chemistry." He leaned in close to me, taking the other side of the paper in one hand so that we were looking at it together. Except

I wasn't looking at it at all. I was looking at the side of his neck, at his pulse beating there.

"Oh. Dr. Stewart," he said. "I had him last year." His eyes continued to scan the page. "Hey, we have American Lit together."

He looked away from the paper, at me, and I was inexplicably more nervous than I had been a second ago. "Is it a good class?"

He quirked an eyebrow at me. "If lit is your thing."

"Lit is pretty much my thing."

He grinned. "See, your mom didn't mention that to me. You still have plenty of your own secrets to divulge."

I knew he meant it as a joke, but I felt a weight in my chest at his words. Yeah, I had secrets. Like the fact that I hadn't been in a pool since that preseason practice, like a part of me was relieved to be away from my coach, like the last month still didn't feel real.

He had a strange, serious look on his face, so I turned away from him, shoving my schedule back in my bag.

We pulled up in front of the school, redbrick and separated into multiple buildings that were fanned out along the block. It was a little like a college campus, with buildings curving around each other and the streets on either side a labyrinth. According to my mom, they didn't have an on-campus pool.

I followed him into a building, and inside, Michael stopped and pointed across the open lobby. "Your classroom is down that hallway there. First one on the left." I nodded, and then we stood there in silence for a moment as students rushed past us. Maybe we'd just met, but he was officially the only person I knew in school, and the thought of being alone again made my palms sweat.

"I'll see you later?" he asked, already backing away from me.

"Okay." Once the sea had swallowed him up, I turned to the hallway he had directed me toward. I hovered awkwardly in the doorway of my classroom. No one noticed me, and I took that second of inattention to ground myself.

The bell sounded and the teacher spotted me. He was short, mostly bald, and wearing a maroon sweater-vest. "Oh, hello. Katherine Masterson? We still have a group that only has three right over here." He gestured toward a lab table at the front of the room, where two very pretty girls sat with a boy who had his head down on the table. When I took a seat beside him, the boy let out a quiet snore.

"That's Roger." One of the girls, whose long black hair was pulled into a ponytail, smiled at me. She was thin and had big, full lips that glittered with a layer of lip gloss. "He sleeps his way through first and last period. It's kind of his trademark. I'm Marisol, and this is Patrice." She nudged the girl beside her. I could tell even while they were sitting that she was almost a head shorter than Marisol. Patrice had a round face, curly brown hair, and a friendly smile.

With perfectly applied makeup, shiny dark hair, and brown skin, they were the kind of beautiful a boring girl like me dreamed of being. I crossed my arms over myself.

"I'm surprised Dr. Stewart even put you here," Marisol went on. "He wouldn't let anyone but Roger be in our group because he says we're a bad influence."

Patrice snorted. "Oh, please. He said *you* were a bad influence."

Marisol rolled her eyes, and then, like I was no longer there, they began speaking to each other in Spanish while I sat there feeling as relevant to the conversation as my buddy Roger.

"Ladies," Dr. Stewart sighed, "can we please start class?"

◦ ◦ ◦

I was on my way to second period with my nose buried in my map of the school when I heard someone call my name. It was a bit surprising, as I didn't really know anyone yet, but when I looked up, I spotted Michael's smiling face in the crowd. I maneuvered through the throng to get to him.

"Are you lost?" he asked.

"Um." I looked down at my map. "I don't think so. This is Building C, right?"

His mouth made a funny shape, and then he reached out and flipped my map around so that we were now in Building F.

"Okay, yes, I'm lost," I said.

He laughed. "Just go across the quad. The building directly across from this one." His phone beeped and he pulled it out, concentrating on sending a text before he looked back at me. "Is our campus really that much bigger than the school you went to in Salem?"

I looked down at the map, with its string of buildings and sharp turns. "I guess not. Just . . . different."

He held his hand out to me. "Here, let me put my number in your phone in case you need me."

I stared at his outstretched hand for a second before surrendering my phone. I'd never let a boy put his number in my phone before. He tapped away at it while I watched, and I knew the image would be burned in my brain forever.

o o o

There were four different lunch lines in the cafeteria, and as people shuffled past me, splitting off in different directions, I chose the one closest to me and got in line behind a girl I thought I recognized from second period.

I grabbed a peanut butter and jelly sandwich and then found myself staring at rows and rows of mostly full tables. I searched for an empty seat somewhere, but they were all surrounded by groups of intimidating strangers, and I was beginning to lose my nerve.

Back in Salem, the swim team always ate together, and it had been a long time since I'd been confronted with this many unfamiliar faces.

"Kate?"

I turned back to the line to find one of my lab partners a few people back. She smiled at me, and I took a step back to join her. "Patrice, right?" I asked as I slid alongside her. I'd met so many new people that I was having a hard time keeping them straight.

"Yeah. Chemistry." She reached for a container of yogurt and then smiled up at me. The sincerity of it stretched all the way to her dark eyes. "Sorry we got our first big assignment on your first day. Kinda sucks."

I shrugged. "That's okay. I'm actually glad. It's better than being tragically behind."

"True."

She paid for her food, and I was just about skulk off alone when she said, "Hey, do you want to sit with Marisol and me?"

She gestured to a table in the center of the room, where I recognized Marisol sitting by herself, doing something on her phone.

"Really?"

She grinned. "Of course. Lab partners have to stick together." She laced her arm through mine and led me to the table. "Look who I found," she said when we sat down.

Marisol's eyes found me across the table and she smiled. "Kate! Hey! Lunch buddies!"

She sounded so genuinely happy to see me that it made my stomach warm. Had I ever been this nice to a complete stranger in my entire life?

"What class do you have next?" Marisol asked, shoving a french fry in her mouth.

"American Lit, I think."

Marisol's eyes went wide. "With Hure? Or Johnson? Because everybody got Hure for Am Lit this year, *except* me and Patrice." She rolled her eyes. "She's the absolute best. Johnson is a walking ferret."

Patrice smacked her on the arm. "Calm down. You're scaring her."

I was feeling the complete opposite of scared. I felt comforted. I consulted my schedule. "Um. Yeah. Hure."

Marisol groaned. "*Everyone* got Hure. Even Patrice's boyfriend."

Patrice nodded, as if she needed to confirm the information.

"She's thinking about breaking up with him," Marisol said absently. I blinked at her, wondering if this word vomit was normal for her.

Patrice smacked her again. I felt like I was getting the

———

CliffsNotes version of their relationship. "I am not," she clarified in my direction. "Things are just weird right now."

Marisol chewed silently, but there was something judgmental about it. I never knew chewing could be judgmental.

Patrice groaned. "Shut up. It's not even a big deal. We're going to be fine." Her natural glow dimmed a little, but it only lasted a second before she was smiling up at me. "So where are you from?"

"Salem."

Patrice bounced a little in her seat. "Oh, I have a cousin in Salem. I like it out there." Her face scrunched adorably. "But I'm sure you'll love it here."

Marisol fluttered her eyelashes. "There isn't anyone as awesome as us in Salem."

Patrice nodded, agreeing solemnly. "It's true. And now you have the most awesome friends in Portland."

I had friends in Portland. I wasn't going to be completely alone. The thought was such a relief that I spent the rest of the lunch period listening to them talk and argue, and I knew that if I didn't like anything else about Portland, I liked them.

*　*　*

When I walked into American Lit and saw Michael sitting in the back of the class, I thought maybe my day had peaked.

He didn't notice me at first, his head down as he scribbled on a piece of paper, but then his head came up, and he smiled. My brain shorted for a second, and I snapped myself out of it. I'd known the boy less than the length of one school day.

"You must be Miss Masterson." A pretty woman with caramel-colored curls and dark skin who I assumed was Mrs. Hure grabbed a stack of supplies off the corner of her desk. "Textbook, syllabus, and reading list. Have a seat where you like."

There was an open seat beside Michael, so I took it before anyone else could, and as Mrs. Hure started to lecture on *The Great Gatsby*, Michael turned slightly in his seat to look at me. We were far enough in the back that he could lean over and whisper to me.

"Having a good day?" he asked, and I caught the faint smell of cigarette smoke on his clothes, clumsily covered by cologne.

I nodded and shrugged, a weird half-committed, casual gesture.

He leaned back to settle in his chair again.

"Has anyone already done the reading for Friday?" Mrs. Hure asked, and everyone chorused a resounding, "No."

Everyone but Michael, who said yes quietly enough that I thought maybe I was the only one who'd heard him. I bit my lip, but Michael still heard me laugh. He glanced over at me, and even though he didn't smile, there was amusement in his eyes.

In front of him, he had his book open, and I caught the color of pen marks in the margins, notes written up and down the page. Maybe they were his or maybe they were in the book when he got it, but either way, I was mesmerized by the way they seemed to devour every page as he flipped through his book during the lecture.

I tried to focus through the lesson, taking notes even though I'd already read the book last year, but my eyes kept finding their way back to him, and every once in a while, he caught me looking and I had to focus elsewhere.

When we were dismissed, we didn't speak to each other, but he lingered long enough for me to gather my stuff and we walked out together. In the hallway, he looked at me over his shoulder, already turned away from me.

"Know where you're going?" he asked with a teasing smile.

"Yeah," I said, but as he walked away from me, I wasn't so sure.

o o o

Waiting for the bus at the end of the day, I watched people gather, talking and laughing and meeting up with their friends. They moved in groups to get into cars—three, four, or five students piling into one four-door sedan. I checked my phone, but there were no messages from Harris to indicate how swim practice had gone.

Someone brushed my shoulder. When I turned, Michael was standing beside me, completely casual. *We do this every single day*, his posture seemed to say. In the afternoon sunshine, he somehow looked even better than he had in the gray morning.

He reached into his pocket and pulled out a pack of cigarettes. I watched him as he took one out, stuck it between his lips, and then froze, blinking off into the distance. He seemed to remember where he was: a school campus that definitely didn't allow smoking. He untucked the cigarette from his lips and put it back in the pack, coughing out a laugh. "Habit," he said, sticking the pack back in his pocket. He rocked back on his heels and smiled at me. He had great teeth and the kind of smile that came with dimples, and I had to stop staring at him.

I couldn't help noticing any time a cute boy was within ten yards of me. I liked their mouths and their arms and the way they held themselves. I liked their voices and their hands and the way their back muscles rippled every time they moved. I'd spent the majority of my life hanging around lean, muscular guys who wore little clothing and were always dripping pool water.

But my dad didn't like boys. *Any* boys. He didn't even particularly like Harris, and Harris and I had never been even remotely interested in each other romantically. My father had always been successful when it came to keeping guys away from me. No one was interested in going near Coach Masterson's daughter, especially not when she was too busy training her face off for District and State meets to focus on dating.

And now, here I was, standing next to an extremely attractive guy, and I wanted to say something. Anything. But I couldn't. Coach Masterson somehow struck again, and he wasn't even around to witness it.

"Kate!"

A line of cars had parked itself against the curb in front of the school, and there, right in the center, was my sister's Mercedes. She had her head poked out the window and was waving at me.

I waved at her and was already stepping off the curb when I remembered Michael. I turned back and his eyes were on Lily. "Dress fitting," I said, as if that explained everything, and took off toward her car.

When I hopped into the front seat, Lily wasn't even looking at me. "Who's he?" she asked.

I waited until we were out in traffic before I looked back. He had disappeared onto the bus. "His name is Michael."

"He's cute. Please tell me you batted your eyelashes at him."

I rolled my eyes. "Not everyone is interested in getting engaged at nineteen."

She shrugged. "Fine. Get engaged at sixteen. I'm not judging." She grinned over at me then and gave my shoulder a playful shove. "How are you?"

I waved off her question. "Excited for Saturday?"

She bit her lip. "I'm nervous. There are going to be so many people there! You know how Tom is. He wanted to invite everyone he knows, so there's going to be, like, two hundred people."

"Everything is going to be great. I used to get so nervous for big meets, but it was over so fast, it always made me feel a little ridiculous for worrying."

She snorted and flipped on her turn signal as we pulled into the parking lot of the little boutique dress shop where she'd gotten her gown and ordered all her bridesmaids' dresses. "Somehow I doubt I'll feel that way," she said, turning off the car. "But thank God, I get a big vacation afterward."

Three

The shop was a white-lace wonderland, with so many puffy and satiny dresses poking out from every corner that I could barely see where I was going. Then I was being whisked off to a dressing room in the back, where I was told to strip down to my underwear.

My dress was strapless and turquoise. Behind me, the sales lady was tugging on the fabric of the dress, pulling it tight and putting pins into it.

"Do you think you can have it ready by Friday?" Lily asked around the finger in her mouth. At the rate she was going, she wasn't going to need a manicure before her wedding because there would be no nails left. Pacing like she was, she looked just like our mother. Same crease between her eyebrows, same long, dishwater-blond hair, same tense posture.

The woman, pins sticking out of her mouth, hummed a little and then nodded.

Lily sighed. "You look great."

"Yeah, I'll have the crowd applauding my beauty. No one will even notice you."

She shrugged in a strange, artificially indifferent way and took a seat on the high-heel-shaped chair facing me. "Hey, can I ask you a question?"

I felt myself go rigid from my toenails to the roots of my hair. "Sure."

Lily bit the inside of her cheek, drummed her fingers on her knee, did everything but ask me the question.

Meanwhile, the saleswoman was trying to shimmy me out of the dress without sticking me with any of the pins. She wiggled it over my head, and I tried not get impatient as I stood on a platform in front of my sister in nothing but my underwear.

"Do you think I should uninvite Dad?" she finally asked without looking at me.

I went for my clothes, hurrying into my jeans and top before sitting next to Lily on the little pink seat. "I don't think you can do that." It wasn't what I wanted to say. I wanted to tell her to disown our father, to never speak to him again, to disinvite him and also tell him where he could shove it. But I couldn't. "He's our dad."

She balled her fists in her lap, clenching and unclenching them. "Aren't you mad?"

"Of course I'm mad. He cheated on Mom, at my school, at my *pool*. And then he kicked us out of our house. And now Mom is looking for a job, and I have to go to a new school, with a new swim team and a coach I don't even know, and boys who show up on my doorstep at seven in the morning, and I have to take the bus, and my lab partner sleeps through class, and it's all Dad's fault." I stopped talking and stared down at the carpet, aware of her eyes on me. Sure, I was mad. Of course I was mad. How could I *not* be mad? But what was I supposed to do about it? I'd already cut Dad out. I couldn't erase him from the planet completely, no matter how much I wished I could.

"But it's your wedding, and I think Dad has to be there." It was like poison on my tongue to admit that. If it were my wedding, I'd have a very large human guarding the door to make sure Coach Masterson couldn't come in.

She nodded, but she stared off into space, her face alive with doubt.

I tried to smile. "Look on the bright side. At least on Friday night you'll have all those naked guys to distract you."

She groaned. "God, I'm sorry Julie is being totally ridiculous with the strip club thing."

I was not at all upset about not being able to attend my sister's bachelorette party. Her other bridesmaids had decided the night would be incomplete without leather-clad men shaking their junk around, and luckily for me, no one was letting me into a strip club.

"Trust me, it's not a problem," I told her, getting up to put my shoes back on.

"Hey, maybe I can give Michael a call and he can come put on a private show for you." She waggled her eyebrows at me, and I tossed my shoe at her.

◦ ◦ ◦

After we got back to the apartment, Lily and I were discussing the validity of competitive cooking shows when I threw the door open, and we both stopped cold. My mother was crumpled on the entry room floor, crying.

Lily and I were on our knees on either side of her before the door had even fallen closed. For half a second, our mom didn't seem to notice we were there. She sobbed into her hands, dressed in a black pencil skirt and a white blouse, her high heels discarded on the floor beside her.

"Mom?" Lily asked because I couldn't. We looked at each other in horror.

"Oh God. I'm so sorry." My mother looked for a moment like she was going to paste on a smile and face us, but when she took in a deep breath, it seemed too much for her because she exhaled a sob and was crying again.

We helped her to her feet and led her to the kitchen table, where Lily sat patting her back while I put water for tea on to boil.

When my mother met my eye, she looked a little like a funhouse clown. Her makeup had run, her eyeliner trailing black marks down her cheeks and her bright-red lipstick smudged down her chin. "I'm okay, girls. Today was just a tough one. Turns out that no one wants to hire me, even with a master's degree. That's what I get for deciding I should be a stay-at-home mom for so long."

I knew she didn't mean her comment to be hurtful, but I still felt a twinge of guilt in my chest. If it weren't for me, if it weren't for Lily, she would have kept her old job, would have been perfectly successful, wouldn't be trying to start from the bottom.

My mother sighed, her momentary bravado gone and her shoulders sinking low. "I didn't mean it like that. I loved staying home with you girls."

———

I nodded, but turned to pull the teakettle off the stove so that I wouldn't have to look at her anymore. What was I supposed to do for my mother? How was I supposed to help her rebuild her life when I couldn't even figure out how to rebuild my own?

I dipped tea bags in three cups and turned back to face them. "Let's stay in tonight," I said, walking the few steps from the stove to the kitchen table and setting cups of hot tea in front of them. "I don't really want to go out. I can make spaghetti or something."

My mother smiled, obviously relieved. "That sounds nice."

I went to the pantry to take out pasta and sauce, pushing aside boxes still piled in front of the oven. Mom and Lily spoke quietly at the table while I started dinner, but I kept my eye on them as I worked. How had things fallen apart so fast? A month before, I was prepping for swim season—early-morning swims with Dad, late-night stretches to keep my muscles warm—and now I was listening to my mother cry.

I put water on to boil and tried not to look at Lily and my mom while I pried the box of pasta open. It felt like maybe if I didn't look, I could pretend it wasn't real. I'd never seen my mother break down like that, not even when my grandpa died.

"I'm just going to run to the restroom," my mother said, fanning her face and disappearing down the hall.

Lily got up from the table and leaned against the stove, her arms crossed. "Has she been doing this a lot?" she asked quietly.

I shook my head. "I haven't even seen her look particularly upset."

Lily sighed. "Maybe you guys *should* come stay at my place. I can help you look after her."

I waved her off. "She'll be fine. It's just been a rough week." After word had gotten out about what happened at the pool, my mother slept in the guest room in our old house while she found us a new place to live. She'd hidden in there for over a week, and when she'd emerged, it had been with a rock-solid plan for a new home and a new life. Maybe this wasn't her first breakdown.

"What about you?"

"I'm fine." I couldn't look at her while I said it. I wasn't so positive that I was fine. Or that I would ever be fine. But my mother was getting rid of evidence of a breakdown in the bathroom and my sister was getting married at the end of the week, so it was time for me to be fine.

She nodded, like she believed me. "Do you think we're going to be like that someday?" she asked.

I put a lid on the pot of water. "Who, me and you?"

"Me and Tom."

When I turned to look at her, her eyes were vacant. "What if hurting each other is inevitable?"

"Lily, Tom is not going to cheat on you. And he's not going to be Dad. They're nothing alike. Tom has a soul."

Lily smiled a little, but I could still see that wariness in her eyes, and I wanted to tell her that she and Tom would never end up like Mom and Dad, but what if that was a lie? What if it *was* inevitable that people who loved each other would eventually tear each other apart?

———

"You're getting married," I said to her, "and it's going to be great." And I tried to believe it.

∘ ∘ ∘

"Do you believe that you can really like someone after only meeting them once?" I asked Harris over the phone.

I couldn't see his face, but I could imagine him on the other end, scowling in thought. His voice came out loud from my phone's speaker while I unpacked books in my room, putting them on my bookshelf in alphabetical order.

"Sure, why not?" I heard him take a bite of something, and then he was speaking around the food in his mouth. "I don't think I believe in all that love-at-first-sight bullshit, but I *do* believe in lust at first sight."

I laughed. I supposed that made sense. What I was feeling for that cute boy across the hall wasn't love. It was definitely lust. Definitely, definitely.

"Are you asking me this because you have the hots for some guy you just met?"

"I might."

Harris snorted. "Damn. You've been gone three days, and you're already ready to give it up to the first guy you see?"

"Don't be an asshole. It's not like that. I just think he's cute. And he might be nice. But he smokes." I grimaced at the memory of cigarette smoke curling out of his mouth.

Harris chuckled. "Man, you really caught yourself a good one. So, what's the problem?"

"There's not really a problem. I'm just not good at boys."

He laughed. "It's really not that complicated. You smile a lot, you tell him how great he is, and *bam*, he wants to follow you around everywhere. April told me she liked my abs while she was wearing that bikini, the one with the cherries all over it. That's all it took. I was done for."

I snorted. "Oh, it's that easy, huh? I'll just walk up to him, tell him I really like his hair, and we'll live happily ever after? Well, thanks, Harris. Problem solved."

"What? It worked for me!" Harris said. "My relationship with April is totally simple. No drama, no games. It's the best."

"Yes, well, good for you, but *normal* relationships don't work that way, and I'm not just going to walk up to Michael, tell him I like his dimples, and assume he'll just fall all over me because of it."

"Your loss," he said with a sigh. "You seem to have a good list worked up. Hair, dimples."

"How was practice today?" I said over him, pulling the subject away from Michael's dimples.

I could practically hear him rolling his eyes. "You know how it is. Coach yelled way too loud and everyone ground their teeth until it felt like the world was going to split open. Cal hurled in the pool."

"Can you not call him Coach? It's weird."

Harris was silent for a moment. "That's the dumbest thing you've ever said to me. He's my coach. I've always called him Coach."

"I know, but everything's different now. It's like, you guys are there, and I'm here, and how can he be Coach when I'm not there?"

"That makes absolutely no sense."

———

I tossed the book in my hand onto my desk, where it landed with a loud *smack*. "I know it doesn't make sense." Nothing seemed to make sense in my brain these days.

"You could always come back."

I thought he meant it as a joke, but there was something about the silence that followed that told me he didn't. "Come on, Harris. You know that's not an option. I can't even look him in the eye without feeling like I'm going to be sick. Or claw his eyes out. Or both."

He sighed. "Yeah, I know. This all just feels so *wrong*, you know?"

It felt wrong to me, too. The whole world felt inverted, spinning in funny directions like a kaleidoscope. I thought going back to swim would make everything feel normal, but when I thought about it, my skin prickled and went hot in fear. But how could I be scared of swimming? "Okay, new topic."

"Yeah, um, there's actually something I wanted to talk to you about."

I didn't like the hesitation in his voice. It was like sirens going off seconds before a tornado hit. "What?"

"I'm not going to be able to make it to Lily's wedding. I'm sorry. I wanted to tell you earlier, but I didn't want to add to your stress."

"Oh." It was hard to explain why, but this news was a punch to the chest. Maybe because when my dad got caught, Harris was there every second afterward, and now, I hadn't seen him in almost a week, and that was somehow more painful than I thought it would be. "Oh. Okay. Other plans?"

"This stupid family thing. The parentals want me to look at

a college up in Seattle, and we have to visit my grandmother while we're there. We're driving up for the weekend. I really am sorry, Kate. I tried to get out of it."

"I'm not mad." It almost felt like the truth. It wasn't as much that I was mad as hurt, I supposed. "I was just looking forward to seeing you."

"Me, too. God. I didn't think I was going to miss you this much. Hey, now that you live closer, we should totally go to Hoochie's."

I laughed. "Yeah, you're right." Hoochie's was an ice-cream parlor in Hillsboro that Harris and I discovered after a meet freshman year. We used to drive out on special occasions to eat our weight in pistachio ice cream.

"Why don't we go out next week? Maybe things with your dad will have calmed down by then."

Things would never calm down with my father, but just this once, I thought I'd let Harris's optimism slide. "Yeah, maybe."

o o o

I couldn't sleep, thinking about meeting my new team the next day. I stared at the ceiling and tried to ignore the way the blood vibrated in my veins, the way anxiety started to roil in my stomach. I wasn't even sure what I was so afraid of. I knew that I could be the best here, just like I was the best back in Salem. But it felt like more than that. If I was the best, was the rest of the team going to resent me? If I came out of nowhere and outshone their hard work, was I going to be completely alone on the team, with only enemies and no friends?

I felt like a jackass, assuming I would be better than everyone when I walked in the door. But the research I'd done on my new school's swim team had told me they weren't ranked very high and hadn't made it very far last competition season.

The apartment was quiet, and I tiptoed past my mother's bedroom and into the kitchen, looking aimlessly for something to kill my nerves. Then I remembered the rooftop pool. I hadn't been up yet, but maybe it wasn't such a bad idea to go for a swim before practice tomorrow. I ignored the heavy pounding of my heart and went for the front door.

The door to the roof was unlocked, but when I stepped out into the cool Portland air, the smell of the pool's chlorine was tainted by the bitter aroma of cigarette smoke, and I immediately turned to leave. It was the middle of the night, and I wasn't interested in being stuck on the roof with a stranger. But when I saw the outline of the person perched on the edge of a bench against the roof's edge with a cigarette in one hand and a book in the other, I stopped.

I watched Michael for a moment in the light of a wall sconce, wondering if I should leave him alone, but before I could make up my mind, he'd lifted his head and spotted me. His eyebrows furrowed. "Kate?"

I lifted a hand in an awkward wave. Part of me still wanted to bolt, but I moved closer to him instead, until my toes were hanging over the edge of the pool beside the bench. He was reading *The Great Gatsby*.

"I guess your overachievement makes sense now." I nodded at the book.

He looked down at it, like he was surprised to find it in his hand. "Yeah. I don't sleep well."

I crossed my arms over myself, cold in my barely-there

pajamas out in the exposed air. I took a second to study the pool for the first time. It was generously sized and rectangular.

"You really shouldn't smoke," I told Michael. I might not have had the guts to make a comment like that normally, but I was caught off guard from my anxiety. Didn't they have health classes in Portland? I imagined the class I took at my old school. They'd shown us pictures of blackened smokers' lungs to discourage us.

"What, is it bad for me or something?"

I looked over my shoulder at him. He was smiling at me. He stubbed out the cigarette on the bench he sat on.

"That's the thing about addictions. They're hard to kick." He looked at me for a long moment, and the humor on his face seemed to fade. "You okay?"

I looked away from him, down at the water in front of me. I wasn't sure what I was, but I didn't think okay was it. How could I explain to someone that the girl who had set a state record in swimming was terrified to get back in the water?

When I didn't say anything, Michael hopped off the bench. "I'll give you some space," he said, and I was simultaneously relieved and disappointed that he was leaving.

I watched him as he went for the door, and then I was alone with the soft beating of the water against the walls of the pool. I stripped down to my bra and underwear and stared down into the water. I took a deep breath, trying to talk some sense into myself. This was my world. What did I have to be afraid of? I dove in.

The water was warm against my skin, peaceful for a moment before the world seemed to grow loud again. With the water pressing against my eardrums, it was almost like I could hear my father screaming from the sidelines.

———

"You're swimming like you aren't even trying! You can do better than this! I know it! Push harder! Where's your head at?"

Memories slammed into me. Harris in the lane next to me, pushing hard to beat me; Coach Judd on the sidelines; Jenny Carther and April tucking their hair into their swim caps; Chuck making obscene gestures; my hair still dripping when Jenny Carther threw open that door.

I broke the surface and pressed my head to the edge of the pool. My chest felt hot and tight, and I struggled to catch my breath. My hands shook, coming up to cover my face so that I could hear my panicked gasps against my open palms.

I pressed my back to the pool wall and looked out at the water I'd disturbed, splashing up against the sides of the pool in agitated waves. For as long as I could remember, the pool had been a safe space, an escape, a second home.

My stomach clenched, and I curled in on myself. I might not have been the most popular girl in school, and I might not have always gotten straight As or made honor roll or been voted class president. But I'd always had the water to come back to. If everything else fell apart, the pool was always waiting.

And now it felt like a trap, something that would pull me under until I suffocated beneath the weight of it. He'd already taken my home, and now he'd taken the only other place that had felt like mine.

Four

The next morning, Michael was waiting outside my door again. His dark hair was still wet from a shower, his denim button-down was rolled up past his elbows, and a cigarette was already between his fingers, prepared for the moment when we stepped outside.

As we stood on the curb, I tried not to be too obvious, but I couldn't seem to stop looking over at him, noticing every feature. I felt like I had to come up with something to say so that I didn't accidentally tell him that I liked the way his hair stuck up when it was drying in the wind.

"I'm not riding the bus home today," I told him. As soon as it came out, I felt like a complete idiot. Why did he care if I rode the bus home? He wasn't some puppy dog waiting with bated breath for me to re-enter his life.

"Why?" he asked, blowing smoke out into the air. The sky was painfully blue, the air crisp with oncoming autumn.

Well, except for the smell of the cigarette smoke.

"Meeting with my new swim coach after school." My stomach flipped and I took a deep breath, trying to forget whatever had happened the night before.

He shrugged. "Maybe you'll be done in time to ride the bus."

"I have to meet her at the pool. It's not on campus."

Like he did the day before, he put his cigarette out on the NO PARKING sign and tossed the butt in the street. "Yeah, they practice at the rec center, right? Why don't I walk over with you? We can take the TriMet back home."

The bus was approaching slowly. "The TriMet?"

He motioned for me to climb on ahead of him when the doors swung open, and then he clunked up the metal stairs behind me. "Yeah. The city bus. We ride free with our school IDs."

"You don't have plans or anything?" Didn't he have some beautiful girl waiting on him somewhere? Shouldn't he be walking her to things and not me, a virtual stranger he'd met the day before?

"No," he finally said. "No plans." So I agreed to let him walk me, and we fell into silence as the bus rolled its way past six more stops and then on to school.

When we got inside, he pointed me toward my first period class. It was different from the day before, since the school had an alternating A-day/B-day class schedule, and when I turned to leave, he stepped in front of me, successfully keeping me from Health Science.

"Hey, Kate?"

Michael stood only an inch or two taller than me, and I barely had to lift my eyes to see his dark-blue ones. His eyes flitted over my head for a second, scanning, and then he focused on me again. "I reserved the pool this Saturday night. Some people are coming over. It's not a party, really, just a few friends. But I thought maybe you'd want to stop by and meet some people."

"Yeah," I said without thinking. If my answer had come any faster, I would have steamrolled over his invitation entirely.

He smiled. "Great."

And then my brain kicked in. I put up a hand, like I could stop his expectations with it. "Oh crap, no. I can't. My sister's wedding is on Saturday."

His smile withered slightly. "Oh. Yeah, okay. You're in the wedding?"

"Maid of honor."

He nodded, his face serious, as if that was pertinent information. "Okay, well, that's great. I'll see you after school. Meet me at the bus stop, and we'll walk over to the rec center."

I opened my mouth to answer, but he'd already turned and hurried away from me.

o o o

I wasn't so lucky with my B-day schedule. I had zero classes with Michael, lunch period with absolutely nobody, and I felt like I was in one of those nightmares where you're wandering around school because you've forgotten where your class is. I was relieved when it was over and it was time to go to swim, even though my stomach was rocketing around inside me at the idea of it. Out of the frying pan and all that jazz.

The rec center was four blocks away from campus—not exactly a long walk, but all I could think about was what was waiting for me at the pool, and that made the walk go on forever.

"You're quiet," Michael said when we were almost halfway there.

I hadn't really noticed that we weren't talking, but as soon as he mentioned it, I became aware of the noise of the city around us: car horns, thumping music, the crunch of concrete beneath our shoes.

I hugged my arms around my waist. "Sorry. I'm just a little nervous."

"Makes sense," he said, pulling out a cigarette and lighting it without losing pace with me.

Luckily, the wind blew his smoke away from us, out into the air. "I've never done this without my dad with me."

When Michael looked over at me, it was with a completely blank expression. He was waiting for me to go on.

"My mom told you he was my coach, right?"

He nodded, even though I could see he wished he didn't have to. What was it about Michael that had made my mother think it was okay to give away all our secrets? And why did I feel like I needed to give him all the ones she hadn't, as well?

"He's always been my coach, and I've never had to do anything swim related without him right next to me. It feels . . ." I trailed off because I didn't really want to admit that I was scared. And really, it was more than fear. "Bizarre," I finally said. "Like none of this is real."

He watched me, his eyes fixed on me, until we were standing right in front of the rec center.

I smelled the chlorine as soon as we walked in the door, permeating the entire building like it had soaked into every surface. There was nothing like the sound of an indoor pool, loud with echoing voices and splashing water. The air was thick and moist, like the air before an oncoming storm, and it only took a second for it to stick to my skin.

———

The door slammed shut behind us, and all the movement in the room stopped. Spectators peppered the bleachers, and girls in full-body swimsuits hovered around the starting blocks. The only ones who didn't stop to rubberneck were the girls in the pool. They were running drills, and they had no idea that the universe outside of the pool had seemingly been thrown into suspension.

"Kate!" An Asian woman who I knew must be Coach Wu approached me with a smile, her face wrinkling around the edges. Her eyes went to Michael.

"I'll just wait over here," he said in lieu of an introduction. He pointed to the bleachers.

"Let's talk in here." Coach Wu gestured toward an open, generically decorated office. I turned to follow her, but at the last second, I looked behind me. Every single girl, even the ones in the pool, who had completed their drills and were floating with their arms draped over the side, was staring at me. Some of them just looked, some of them whispered to each other, and some of them watched me, their eyebrows furrowed or their faces twisted into rude expressions.

I stood there, taking it all in, and suddenly, everything turned villainous. The chlorine in the air burned my eyes, the moisture made me sweat, the eyes of the girls on me felt like pinpricks, stabbing into my skin. The room became a monster, ready to swallow me whole.

I'd been swimming for ten years. My whole life, from the moment I woke up to the moment I went to sleep, was nothing but the water, but standing in front of these people, knowing that I was an outsider, I felt the panic start in my stomach again and my head go fuzzy.

——

I pressed my back to the wall and bent over, trying to catch my breath, and I could feel everyone in the room looking at me. I covered my face with my hands and sucked in a breath. I couldn't believe this was happening to me here, in front of everyone.

"Kate?"

"Kate! Wake up! What was that first split? You call that pulling out ahead? You call that your best?"

He wasn't here. My father wasn't here. He couldn't make me get in that pool. I straightened up to see the look on Coach Wu's face, concern and horror.

My father's pride had turned into this woman's distress. The cheers of my former swim team had turned into the judgmental storm cloud of the girls by the pool. My satisfaction at being good at something had turned into this pain in my torso, this aching need to never do any of it again.

"I don't want to do this."

Coach Wu froze. Across the room, Michael watched us.

"I'm sorry, Coach. I know you probably had big plans for me, but I don't want to do this. I don't want to compete anymore."

"But—" Coach Wu started.

Behind me, I could hear the team talking, their whispers loud in the echoing room, some of them even giggling.

Coach Wu stepped to the side to see around me. "Girls! One-arm drills! Now! Switch off!" Her eyes were back on me then, her arms crossed tight. "Kate, your mother—"

"I know," I said. "I'll talk to her."

"I don't understand. You have so much potential. What about college?"

"I'm sorry," I muttered, and I turned and left. I heard Michael

---

follow me out of the building, and without speaking, he walked with me to the bus stop, where we sat on the bench under the awning.

We sat there for a long time before he spoke. "Are you okay?"

I stared down at the concrete, tires moving over it periodically with a gravelly crunch. "I don't know." The panic had started to subside, my body going back to normal. What was I doing?

"I never wanted this." It was the first time I'd ever really said it, to myself or to anyone else.

"You didn't want to swim?"

When I looked over at him, I saw the confusion written on his face, and it mirrored my own. Because of course I wanted to swim. But everything was different now, and how could I go back? "I've always loved swimming, but competing? That's always been hard for me."

"Then why did you do it?"

I looked at the cigarette dangling between his fingers, not even lit yet, and I reached over without thinking and plucked it from his hand, twirling it in my fingers before handing it back to him. "That's the thing about addictions. They're hard to kick." I wasn't sure if he knew that I wasn't talking about swimming. That the only thing I was really addicted to was making my father happy, making him proud, but I didn't say so, and he didn't ask.

o o o

I was grateful my mother wasn't home when I got there, and I went straight to my room to call Harris. He was the only one who I thought maybe could make sense of what I'd just done. I just quit swim. I just walked away from ten years of hard work,

_____

49

and why? I loved swimming. I loved being in the pool. But I could never just have the pool. With it came training and competitions and, of course, my father controlling my every move. Everything I did had to be for the next meet and the next goal and the next win.

And I kept doing it, even when I hated it or wanted it to be over. Because at the end of the day, there were two things I craved more than anything else—the feel of the water as it sucked me under and my father's affection. And those two things kept me going season after season.

And it all looked different now. The pool was a prison cell and my father a monster, and there was no going back.

When Harris finally answered the phone, he was laughing, and then his voice became clear, and he said, "Hey, Kate! Put me on video."

Without hesitating, I switched him over, and then it wasn't just him. There was Chuck behind him, giving me the finger, and Cal (200-yard free and Harris's closest friend on the boys' team) over his shoulder, waving at me enthusiastically. I could hear the sound of splashing water and laughter in the background.

"What's going on?" I asked as the other guys wandered off. "Are you at the pool? It isn't practice day."

Harris moved, and the noise got quieter until I saw the lobby of the aquatics center behind him. "We decided to meet to get some extra laps in without Coach on our backs."

I gasped. I'd been so distracted by the guys and his surroundings that I hadn't really looked at him. "You shaved your head," I said. Harris had always been opposed to male swimmers shaving their heads, saying it made them look like walking penises, but alas, there he was in front of me, completely bald.

He ran his hand over his scalp. "Coach thought it would help."

Coach. I felt that sizzle in my blood again. I took a deep breath. This wasn't about Coach Masterson. This was about me and my best friend.

"Did you change your workout regimen?" I asked him, squinting at the screen to see him as best I could.

"Uh, no. Why?"

The thing about swimmers is they're lean. Lean and toned, but there is very little muscle bulk compared to most other athletes. And Harris had always been the leanest of us all. But looking at him now, he looked bigger somehow. Bulkier.

"Well, for starters, your bicep is huge. Are you and Cal lifting? You hate lifting."

"Nah. Nothing like that. Just getting more protein." He sent me a half smile. "Anyway, why'd you call? You miss me?"

I stared at him for a moment, trying to gather the courage, trying to tell him what I'd done. But the words were buried in my chest under the weight of everything else. Looking at him practically glowing, I couldn't tell him. Seeing him in his jammers, his goggles hanging around his neck, I could almost pretend nothing had changed.

"Yep. Just needed a familiar face."

He scoffed. "I thought you'd be the star of the team by now. Slow going?"

"Something like that."

"Things haven't been so great here, either. It's tense, you know? Coach is on edge, and that's put everyone else on edge."

—

I stared at him. Why couldn't we go one minute without talking about *him*?

"He's been the biggest pain in the ass since you left. You thought he was bad before? Now he's a fucking tyrant. All he does is pace and scream and make us do drills until someone just gives up. He's fished more than one guy out of the pool this week."

I couldn't look at him. "Yeah, it must really put you in a bad mood to screw around on your wife and kick your family out of their house."

He was quiet for a second, watching me. I sighed.

"Sorry. Swimming is just, um, hard for me right now."

His eyebrows furrowed. "What do you mean?"

I meant having a panic attack in the pool the night before, I meant the way my heart pounded whenever I thought about getting near the water again, I meant having the stress of my parents' divorce without the comfort of the pool, I meant walking into that rec center this afternoon and feeling like I'd walked into a nightmare I couldn't escape.

Before I could answer him, he said, "I know this whole thing is really fucked up, but it won't be like this forever. You're the best swimmer I know, a hard-core athlete. You'll bounce back from this. Give it time."

"Yeah, I guess," I said, because everything else I needed to say felt stoppered up inside me.

"I should get back," he said. "They're calling for me."

And I was left staring at a blank screen. Harris was the only one who held my hand when I was trying not to pass out in the locker room; he was the one who snuck me my favorite foods when my father insisted I was taking in too many calories; he was the one who let me whine and complain to him when I didn't want to go to practice, and I wondered if all Harris and I had was swimming. If to him, like everyone else, all I'd ever been was the swimmer girl. And if so, where did that leave us now that I'd quit?

o o o

When we sat down to dinner that night with Lily, I was fully prepared to tell my mother about the swim team. I'd spent the afternoon preparing myself to explain to her what I'd just come to realize myself: I couldn't go back to swimming now that everything had changed. The pool was no longer a safe haven, and the sport had lost its appeal.

But my mother didn't ask about Coach Wu, not at first. Instead, she smiled over her plate at us. "Lily, I hope you don't mind, I invited someone to your wedding."

Lily grimaced. "Um, we don't really have room for anyone else." She darted a look at me, and I saw the panic in her eyes. "The catering company has the head count already."

"Oh, the number won't change. Didn't Kate tell you? Harris won't be there."

Lily scowled at me. "Harris isn't coming?"

I felt that familiar disappointment turn in my stomach. "No. He has a family thing."

My mother nodded sagely and then gestured to me. "And after you told me that, I ran into Michael in the elevator, and I invited him to take Harris's place."

I froze, thoughts of Harris vanquished. "You did what?"

Lily looked up at me, her eyes excited. "Michael, the cute boy at the bus stop?" She turned back to Mom. "How do you know Michael?"

My mother's eyes flew between us. "He lives across the hall."

Lily looked at me with wide eyes. "He lives across the hall? That's perfect!"

"Why is it perfect?" My mother seemed thoroughly confused, and so was I.

"Because Kate has a thing for him."

My mouth fell open. "I do not." I didn't think it was a lie. Or at least, I didn't think I could make a decision about that yet. I'd only know him for a day, and thinking someone was completely gorgeous wasn't the same as having a thing for them. Unless that thing was serious physical attraction. Then, sure, I had a thing for him.

"Oh, sweetie," my mother said like I was a little kid with her first valentine, "I didn't know you had a crush on Michael. Well, now I'm really glad I invited him."

"Mom, I don't have a crush on Michael, and besides, you can't go around inviting random people to Lily's wedding."

Lily smiled. "Oh, it's totally fine. I completely approve."

Great.

"I just thought you'd like the company," my mother went on. "Seeing as how you won't really have any friends there. And since Michael is really the only person you know—"

"Michael isn't the only person I know," I said, feeling a little defensive.

And then my mother gasped. "Oh, of course! The girls on the swim team! I can't believe I completely forgot. How was your meeting with your coach? When's your tryout? Not that you need one." She winked at Lily, like they were sharing some kind of inside joke.

My brain was so jumbled by the events of the last few minutes that I didn't have the courage to try to confess everything to her now. It was too much all at once.

So, stupidly, I said, "It was great," and hoped she wouldn't see that I was lying. "No tryout. They had a spot open. Practice starts next week."

"Oh, perfect," my mother said, already going back to her food. But when I glanced up at Lily, she was looking back at me, her eyes narrowed.

∘ ∘ ∘

"Before you say anything," I said to Michael when I stepped into the hallway the next morning, "I just want to say I'm sorry my mom tried to wrangle you into coming to my sister's wedding. It was totally uncalled for, and I don't even know why she thought that it would be okay. I mean, you barely know us, and you certainly don't want to spend your Saturday at a boring wedding, and I was thinking last night that you have that party going on, so you can totally use that as an excuse, and you won't have to hurt my mom's feelings. If you're worried about her feelings. Which you don't have to be. She'll totally be okay."

When I finally stopped talking, Michael was looking at me with an amused smile. He leaned against his doorjamb. "The wedding's at one, right? People aren't showing up at the pool until seven. Plenty of time for both. And you can come to the party after."

———

"Oh." *Oh.* He wanted to come to the wedding? "Don't feel like you have to come just because she invited you."

He raised an eyebrow. "I'd like to come. I mean, if you want me to."

I could feel my face heating up. If I wanted him to? If I wanted to spend my sister's entire wedding with him and then go to a party with him, almost like a *date*? "Yeah. I'd like that."

He did this thing with his mouth, a kind of half-cocked knowing smile that drew my eyes and also made me panic a little. Why was it easier to talk to boys when we were both in swimsuits?

"We're going to be late for the bus," I said, and bolted for the stairs.

o o o

"So, we were just wondering if you maybe wanted to go."

I didn't realize I wasn't listening to Marisol until she and Patrice were both watching me, apparently waiting for some kind of answer. I'd been thinking about a wedding and a party and a cute boy. "I'm sorry," I told them, "What is it, again?"

Patrice's eyebrows turned in slightly. "A party. Saturday."

I made a motion with my head like, *Oh, right, a party. Of course.* "Oh. Actually, my sister is getting married on Saturday."

Marisol grinned. "Oh, cool. Are you in the wedding?"

I nodded and picked at the Tater Tots on my plate. "Maid of honor."

"Here, in town?" Patrice asked, her eyebrows shooting up.

"At that Lutheran church right off the highway? Tom, my sister's fiancé—his family's been going there forever, so the whole thing is going to be there. Service and reception."

When I looked at them again, Marisol looked a little dreamy. She bit her lip and looked over at Patrice. "Do you think that'll ever be Jesse and me?"

Patrice's eyes widened a little, but I saw the moment that she took control of her expression. She smiled gracefully, the way she always managed to, and shrugged. "I don't know. Maybe."

"That's my boyfriend," Marisol said, her eyes shining. "He's so gorgeous. Right, Patrice?"

Patrice rolled her eyes. "Not my type."

Marisol snorted. "Right. Your type is scrawny white boys."

Patrice put her hand in Marisol's face. "I'm pretending I didn't hear that."

I watched the whole exchange with a smile on my face because I couldn't help but think that if it weren't for Marisol and Patrice, I'd be sitting alone in a corner right now, catching up on literature homework.

Patrice turned to me then. "Are you sure you can't come?"

"Sorry. After the wedding, I have this thing."

Marisol gasped. "Oh man. I've seen that look before. Are you going on a date or something?"

I was quick to shoot that idea down. I'd decided this was definitely not a date. How could it be, anyway, if we were going to be surrounded by people the whole time? My family would be at the wedding, and his friends would be at the party, or whatever it was, and there was no way it could be even remotely considered a date. Right?

"Nothing like that. Just a hangout thing after the wedding. Meeting people, you know."

Patrice nodded. "Good. You'll make a ton of friends, I'm sure.

———

But if something doesn't work out, you're more than welcome to come to our thing. I can absolutely hook you up with a cute boy. We have quite a few in our circle."

Marisol bit a Tater Tot off the end of her fork. "But you can't have either of ours." She smiled at Patrice, but Patrice looked weirdly uncomfortable. Marisol's smile vanished. She put her fork down. "Hey, is everything okay?"

Patrice shrugged, her whole body slumping. "I don't know. He's acting funny again. Probably nothing. You know how he gets."

Marisol pursed her lips and raised her eyebrows in my direction. "That, I do." She rubbed Patrice on the back, and Patrice sighed.

"Forget I said anything," she said, trying to smile again but failing miserably.

"I'm not going to forget you said anything."

Patrice seemed to wilt even further. "Boyfriends are hard work," she said, staring down at her plate.

I was starting to feel a little uncomfortable, partly because I didn't know anything about her boyfriend (and boyfriends, in general), so I couldn't exactly agree with her and partly because I was just terrible at consoling people. "I've never had a boyfriend," I said because I had no clue what else to say.

Marisol's eyes turned on me, wide. "Really? Never?" She said it like I was divulging this information at thirty-five instead of sixteen.

"Never. But my best friend is a guy, so I know how it is. Plus, I had to put up with a whole swim team of rowdy guys all the time, and I know what a pain it can be. It was like having fifteen older brothers all the time. And I know that's not really anything like having a boyfriend, much less fifteen of them, but I get the basic idea that guys are hard to deal with sometimes."

When I finally stopped blabbing, Marisol and Patrice both stared at me. Yes, I was terrible at consoling people.

"You know who would be perfect for her?" Marisol finally said just as the bell rang. She was looking at me, but she was obviously talking to Patrice.

"Who?" Patrice stood up, grabbing her tray.

"Ben."

Patrice's face split into a grin. "Oh God, you're right. It really sucks that you can't come to this party on Saturday. We could have totally introduced you to Ben. Maybe next time."

"Next time," I said to myself as I followed them to the trash cans.

Five

The morning of Lily's wedding, I woke to a notification on my phone. It was from Harris, and it was a picture of a calendar. His swim schedule. And next Friday was circled in thick red marker. Written in the little square were the words *Home Meet. Johnson Aquatics. 7 p.m.*

I stared at the picture for a long time. Harris wanted me to go to their first meet. And I guess I got that. I guess it made sense that he would want me there, since we'd never even been to a meet without each other. But the thought of being there, of seeing my father coaching the team, of watching them compete without me. It would be too weird.

I didn't answer him right away since I had to get up and start getting ready for the wedding, and by the time I remembered that the text was there, we were in the car on the way to the church. Lily sat in the front seat, completely silent, her hands clenched in her lap and her eyes on the passing streets as my mother drove.

I pulled out my phone to find that there was another text with a picture attached. This time, it was a picture of a picture, one that I recognized in its frame. I knew it hung on the wall of Harris's grandmother's house, as I'd seen it there half a dozen times. The picture was of Harris and me when we were in middle school, sitting by the pool, dripping, with our arms around each other.

Remember this? Harris's text read. *You were already a cocky brat.*

Maybe on any other day, his words would have made me laugh. I *had* been a cocky brat, just like my father taught me to be. But it didn't seem funny anymore. Looking at myself in that picture, all I saw was a girl who was completely confused about what she wanted. Swimming with Harris might have been fun, but my father was already running me hard, and it took a lot to keep that smile on my face.

I didn't answer him. I followed Lily and my mom into the church, ignoring the nerves in my stomach that I couldn't decide on the source of. Was I nervous about the wedding? Or was it because my mind kept flitting back to Harris's texts?

I waited patiently in the corner of the room while my mother set a string of pearls against my sister's neck and clasped it—my grandmother's pearls. I knew them well from the pictures from my parents' wedding, my mother and father smiling, so happy you'd never have suspected how it would end.

I pushed the thought away. Now wasn't the time for bitterness.

When Lily reached up to touch the necklace, her fingers trembled slightly. While I watched, she pressed her hand to her stomach and then clenched it into a fist by her side.

My mother turned to me. "You're all set, right?" The nervous energy that was rattling Lily seemed to be having the same effect on my mother. Her movements were jerky as she snapped the necklace case shut and stuffed it into her purse.

"I'm ready." Hair was done, dress was on, jewelry was firmly in place. I just needed to slip on my shoes.

My mother stepped back, holding Lily at arm's length. "You look absolutely stunning."

Lily smiled, but not in a way that said she believed it. Lily had always been the pretty one, but she'd also always been the first one to deny it. Her hair was pulled back into an elegant updo, her makeup perfectly understated, her dress flowing around her, dangling in waves around her legs. She fiddled with the capped sleeve of her dress and ran her hands down the length of her satin bodice, nitpicking at anything that might be misconstrued as an imperfection.

My mother searched through her bag, and I watched Lily fidget with her hair, her leg bobbing up and down as she waited for my mom to return to her.

In my bag on the floor, my phone beeped, and this time, I was ready for whatever Harris would throw at me. But there wasn't a picture. It was just a text.

> Been talking to Coach and my adviser about
> scholarship options. Think I'm good enough? Got my
> time down on the fly, and I think I can get it down even
> further by District. I might need some coaching from
> the best, aka you.

I tossed my phone back in my bag, the nerves dissolving into something like anger. Didn't we have anything to talk about but swimming? Did he have to bring up my dad in every single conversation?

There was a knock at the door, and before any of us had a chance to get to it, my father was stepping into the room, like Harris's text had somehow summoned him. It had been a month since the incident at that preseason practice, a month since my parents decided their marriage was over, a month since my mother started looking for a place for us to live. But somehow, with all of us standing in the same room, it felt like it had happened centuries before and we were together after being apart forever.

I noticed the careful way my parents tried not to look at each other. My father stepped up to the mirror, right beside Lily, and my mother stepped away, keeping her eyes trained on the floor.

"Wow," my dad said, and even though she was trying to hide it, I saw the way Lily glanced over at my mother, the way she tensed when my father reached out to hug her, the way she was the one to pull away first.

"Well, Tom certainly is the luckiest man, isn't he?" my father said, his hands still on my sister's shoulders. "You feeling okay? Feeling ready?"

Lily nodded, and she opened her mouth to say something, but my father spoke over her.

"Where are the earrings I gave you?"

Lily's mouth popped open in surprise, and my mother finally looked at my dad. "She decided that she didn't want to wear them."

I saw the moment the anger set in. My father's jaw clenched and his hands dropped away from Lily. His eyes fixed on my mother. "*She* didn't want to wear them, or *you* didn't want her to wear them?"

My mother made an exasperated sound in the back of her throat. "Oh please. You really think I would make a decision like that for my daughter on her wedding day?"

My father's eyes narrowed. "I wouldn't exactly be surprised, since you'll do anything to turn her against me."

Beside my father, Lily's eyes had gone wide, shooting from our mom to our dad and back again before finally securing themselves on her feet.

My mother barked out a laugh. "Oh, believe me, you did that all by yourself."

My father threw his hands up. "Look, I didn't come in here to endure the *We Hate Dad* show. I came to see my daughter. If that's a problem for you—"

"You're the one who turned this into a problem," my mother said through clenched teeth. "You always know how to be the most childish person in the room, don't you?"

My father looked like he was getting ready to snap, so before he could say anything, I reached out and yanked open the door.

"Why don't you guys talk outside?" I said as loudly as I could, covering up whatever he had been getting ready to spit at my mother.

Everyone looked at me, and I saw the moment my mother's anger dissolved into regret. Her eyes went to Lily, who looked ready to cry, her face flushing and her whole body shaking. My father stomped out of the room without another glance at anyone. I could tell my mother was thinking of staying behind, so I motioned for her to leave, and as soon as she was in the hallway, I closed the door behind her.

———

I turned back to Lily, but I could hear my parents moving down the hallway, bickering as they went. Their voices finally faded.

The air fell silent, and I felt like I was slipping underwater, the world going mute around me. Beside me, I could feel the tension coming off Lily, vibrating like a living thing. I could hear the unsteady tempo of her breathing. Her face had gone white. She backed up until she was against the dressing table, her hand on her stomach, breathing hard. "Oh my God," she whispered. "Oh my God."

"Lily." I reached for her, but she moved away from me.

"I can't do this." She plunged her hands into her hair, tugging with such force that strands of hair were coming undone to fall messily around her face. "I can't do this. I can't be like them, Kate. I can't do it."

"Lily." This time when I put my hands on her shoulders, she didn't move away. "It's not going to be like that for you."

She shook her head hard enough for pins to come lose. She'd spent almost two hours in a chair for that perfect hair, and it had only taken her thirty seconds to ruin it. "I can't do it. I can't. I thought I wanted this, but maybe . . ." She let out a heavy breath. "Maybe I'm not ready. Maybe this is wrong."

I had no clue what to do then. A good maid of honor was supposed to keep this very thing from happening, wasn't she? Wasn't I? Shouldn't I be telling her that she and Tom were different? That people don't always end up like Mom and Dad? God, but was that even true?

I should have found something to say. But I saw in her face the panic I'd felt at that rec center, that I'd felt looking down into the water.

———

I opened my mouth to tell her that she couldn't just leave, but hadn't that been what my father had done all this time, made my decisions for me until I didn't know what I wanted for myself? How could I do the same to Lily? How could I tell her she was wrong to run when I'd done the same thing?

"Get me out of here," she said, her eyes on the door.

My phone beeped in my bag again, and my attention was caught by it for just a second before my eyes found Lily again. Suddenly, I wanted to leave as much as she did. I surveyed the room and found what I was looking for: my mother's orange purse, lying in the corner next to my tote bag. Rushing over to it, I zipped open the front compartment, and there were the keys to her car.

Taking Lily's hand, I didn't look at her to try to comfort her. There was no time for a kind and sympathetic moment. If I wanted to get her out of there before people started to notice that she wasn't walking down the aisle on cue, we had to get moving.

I stepped out of the room first and looked both ways to make sure that no one was standing in the long hallway. One end led to the sanctuary, the foyer, and the other wing of the church, while the other end led to an exit. My parents were nowhere to be found, and when Julie, one of the bridesmaids, came around the corner at that moment, her heels clicking down the hallway, I shook my head at her, waved her away. Immediately, she stopped cold.

I threw the door open and made a run for it, my sister's hand grasped tightly in mine. I was glad I hadn't gotten around to putting my shoes on since I had no experience running in heels. Lily seemed to manage pretty well behind me, her heels clicking

66

on the laminate floors and her dress swishing loudly down the hallway.

The bright sunlight was disorienting when I threw open the back door. It took me a few seconds to locate Mom's car. By the time I spotted it, my heart was pounding so hard, I thought it would beat a hole through my satin dress.

I opened the passenger-side door and helped Lily in, scooping up the overflowing tulle of her dress and shoving it in behind her. I had just closed the door and started for the driver's side when I spotted Michael.

He was standing by the side of the church, not far at all from the exit where we'd just made our escape, a cigarette in his mouth and a surprised expression on his face. I stared at him for a second, so out of place in the middle of all my chaos. For just a moment, he bulldozed through the mayhem, a completely normal boy, and I forgot what I was doing, my hand wrapped around the car handle.

Then I yanked the door open, looking away from him. We had to get out of there before people realized Lily had just pulled a disappearing act.

"Thank you," Lily whispered as we peeled out of the parking lot. In the rearview mirror, I saw the church get smaller, like a bad dream fading away into reality.

Six

Hey, are you okay?

I stared at the words on my phone, the little cursor blinking as I tried to decide how to answer. Michael had sent the text almost as soon as we'd gotten home, hours ago. Why did he have to be there at that exact moment?

"You don't have to watch me," Lily whispered, her head on a pillow as she reclined on the couch. I sat on the floor at her feet, the TV on in front of us with the volume turned low.

"I'm not watching you," I lied, closing out the text just to be confronted with the fact that I never answered the texts Harris had sent me that morning. I hadn't even read the one that came in before we bolted. I could hear my mother at the dining room table, making phone calls to relatives to apologize for the events of the day, like she'd been doing for the last two hours.

The clock on my phone said it was after seven. The party on

the roof was probably in full swing, but there was no way I could go. I couldn't leave Lily after the day she'd had. I opened the text from Michael again to try to tell him why, but his words glared at me. No, I wasn't okay.

"You can go. It's okay."

I met Lily's eyes. She looked like she was about to fall asleep, her eyelids pink and drooping, and for the hundredth time today, I wondered if I'd done the right thing, helping her run from the wedding. I had to let her make her choices, and I knew that, but had it been the right one?

I'd told Lily about the pool party in passing after Michael had agreed to go to the wedding, and now I couldn't decide if I should regret it. I wanted to take care of my big sister, to be here in case she needed anything, but I also needed to get away. The events of the day seemed to hang over us, like humid air you can't blow away, and when I thought about going upstairs, meeting Michael's friends, it seemed like the perfect escape.

"Are you sure?" I asked her. "I don't want to leave if you need me."

Her eyes fell closed, and she yawned. "I think you've done enough for today." She was quiet after that, and I couldn't tell if she'd fallen asleep or not, but I decided not to question it anymore. I got up quietly and went to the dining room.

I waited for my mother to get off the phone. She sighed and pressed her face into her hands.

"Are you okay?"

She dropped her hands to the table and looked up at me, her eyes flitting quickly over my shoulder to the living room. She nodded. "I'll be fine. Just doing a little cleanup."

"Anything I can do?"

She made a dismissive gesture. "Of course not. You don't need to worry about all this. You've got enough to worry about."

I was thinking the same thing about her, but I didn't say so. Someone had to worry about Lily.

"I was thinking about going up to the pool," I said. "Unless you need me to stay."

She looked up from her cell phone, where she'd been texting away while I spoke. "Getting some practice in?" she asked, but then her eyes focused on me. "You're not even in your suit."

"Michael is having some friends over. I told him I would go up and meet them. Is that okay?" I'd never really asked my mother for permission to do anything. My social life before had consisted mostly of hanging out with Harris and going to the occasional after-meet party during the season. I almost never had anyone else to hang out with. The people on the swim team were my only friends.

"Sure. Don't take your keys. I'll leave the door unlocked for you."

◦ ◦ ◦

Light music reached me as the roof's door fell closed. There were about fifteen people milling around the pool, most of them girls, their voices escaping out into the open air. I didn't linger long on their faces. Most of them huddled together in a corner of the pool, almost all of them wearing bikinis, even though it was September and a little too cold for so little clothing. It was a good thing the pool was heated. I was distracted by all their tan skin and their obvious confidence, and I suddenly felt stupid for not wearing a suit. I didn't want to swim, but standing there in a sweater and jeans, I felt like an idiot.

Then I recognized Michael, his back to me, hanging out at the edge of the pool with his feet dangling in the water. He was talking to an Asian boy I didn't recognize whose wet Mohawk was spiked up playfully. The boy, facing the doors and bobbing in the water, met my eye and said something to Michael, who twisted around to look. I saw the moment he processed my face, his mouth pulling into a smile. He pushed himself up to come over to the door, leaving wet footprints behind him.

He didn't seem to care that I wasn't appropriately dressed for a pool party. I had tried to block out the fact that he was shirtless before, but now that he was standing in front of me, it was completely unavoidable. I held his eyes so I wouldn't be tempted to look at his chest.

"Hey. I didn't think you'd come." He had a strange look in his eyes, and I tried not to picture him standing next to the church, watching me pack my sister into the getaway car. "Just because . . ." He trailed off, and we both looked around, as if anyone would be interested in our conversation, as if they would know what we were discussing to begin with.

"Oh, um. No, it's fine. I mean, it's not fine, but it's just—" I bit my lip, and he waited. "I'm here," I said, and then immediately wanted to smack myself.

"Oh. Okay. Great," he said, but his eyebrows were still pulled together.

I took a deep breath. "I just mean, we're okay. We're going to be okay. So I'm happy to be here."

He smiled. "Okay."

Someone came up beside us, and when I recognized Marisol, I couldn't believe my own stupidity. We'd been talking about the same party at lunch yesterday. At a school with so many more students than my school in Salem, it had never occurred to me that Michael would know Marisol and Patrice, or that we might be going to the same party on a Saturday night.

Her eyes brightened as she took both of us in. "Hey, Kate!" She smiled so big I could see all her teeth. They were a little crooked, but she still had the prettiest smile I'd ever seen. "Oh my gosh! Was our party and your *thing* the same thing? What are the chances? We had no clue that you knew Michael. How awesome!" She was beaming like this was greatest thing to happen to her all year, but when I glanced over at Michael, he had a strange look on his face, and it made me uneasy.

"Uh, yeah. I know Michael."

Like she'd been shocked, Marisol jolted. "Oh, I forgot why I came over here." She smacked Michael on the arm playfully. "Your girlfriend needs you."

Once, when we were younger, a boy from Lily's class told her that if she unscrewed a hot light bulb and then spit on it, it would change colors. But the light bulb didn't change colors. It exploded.

This is what I imagined my heart did when Marisol said the word *girlfriend*.

"Oh. Okay." Michael turned to me, and I saw it in his eyes that he was being cautious. "I'll be back." I watched him go, and suddenly I felt so out of place. Of course Michael had a girlfriend. Had I really expected to just walk into this life, instant friends, instant boyfriend? Had I really expected it to be that easy?

"You're wearing your hair down," Marisol said. "You look great."

"Thanks." I instinctively reached up to touch my hair.

She smiled. "I still can't believe that you know Michael. And that we didn't even know we were going to the same party. And here I thought you were going on a date." She laughed, but my heart stopped.

I bit my lip. "Uh, yeah. I didn't know you knew Michael, or I would have—"

She reached out and touched my arm. "Hey, no problem. I don't expect you to invite me everywhere." If she suspected that I liked Michael as anything more than a friend, she didn't let on.

My eyes traveled over to where Michael had floated off to, one of the round poolside tables. And there they were, he and his girlfriend. It was Patrice, shapely and tan in her one-piece bathing suit. Patrice had the kind of figure that made guys drool, all curves and softness. Exactly the kind of girl a guy like Michael would be into.

When my sister spit on the light bulb, she was pierced by three large shards, one on both arms and one on her leg.

This is what it felt like to discover that I already knew Michael's girlfriend. That the boyfriend she'd been talking about at lunch all week was the same boy I'd been developing a crush on. That the overly sweet person I'd been hoping to become good friends with had what I wanted.

"Marisol, my love, can you please bring me a soda?" The question came from the guy in the pool that Michael had been chatting with.

Marisol rolled her eyes. "Get it yourself."

"But, Marisol, beautiful creature, why should I get out of the pool when you're *already* out?"

Marisol, in a tiny navy-blue bikini, didn't have a drop of water on her, so I assumed she hadn't been *in* to begin with. Her long, black hair was piled in a knot on top of her head. The heat of the setting sun still hung in the air, but I saw goose bumps on her arms. She sighed. "Want anything?" she asked me.

I shook my head, and she walked away to go to a large cooler standing open by the door, leaving me standing alone by the pool. I felt droplets splatter on my bare feet.

"Oh," I heard the guy in the water say and found that he was staring directly at me. "Hi."

I opened my mouth to respond, but my attention was caught by Patrice standing on her tiptoes to kiss Michael on the cheek. Michael wasn't particularly tall, but Patrice was particularly tiny. I had never been one for *jealousy*, but that was the only word to describe the twist of my stomach at watching them.

"Do I know you?" the guy in the pool asked.

I ripped my eyes away from Michael. "Um, no. I'm Kate."

His expression, which moments before had been nothing short of perplexed, sparked with recognition. "You're the new girl!"

"Something like that."

He smiled up at me, and I got a full view of just how attractive he was, with wide cheeks and dark eyes. Having the full force of his attention made my pulse stutter.

"I've heard quite a bit about you."

"You have?" I might have been the new girl, but I was a new girl in a 6A school. I wasn't exactly a popular topic of discussion.

———

He slung his arms over the side of the pool. "Sure. Michael's my best friend. He mentioned you moved in across the hall. Also something about a state record? Pretty impressive."

I stared down at the boy for too long without saying anything. In my head, I imagined Michael telling this boy about my swimming achievements only to also tell him that I had a panic attack instead of actually joining the swim team. I glanced over at him and Patrice, still talking cheerily. If he'd mentioned me to his best friend, why hadn't he bothered to mention me to his girlfriend?

The guy's smile seemed frozen on his face. "Everything okay?"

"What'd I miss?" Marisol asked, tossing a soda into the pool in front of the boy. It splashed beneath the surface and then floated back up.

"Lovely." He pulled the can out of the water and popped it open, fizzy soda pop exploding over his hands into the pool. The carbonation didn't even faze him. He held the can to his lips and licked up the foam. He took a long sip and then sent Marisol a close-lipped smile. "Just the way I like it."

Marisol shoved his shoulder with her foot. "I'll be back." She winked at me. "Come find me if you get lonely." She walked around the pool to meet up with a very muscular guy with buzzed hair and tattoos who looked more like he was in college than high school.

"I mean, I have my doubts," the boy in the pool said, sweeping a hand up in my direction and splashing water on my jeans. "What kind of swimmer doesn't even wear a suit to the pool? For all I know, that championship thing is all hogwash."

———

He kept a straight face, but I smiled down at him. "Didn't feel much like swimming tonight."

He pointed a slightly crooked index finger at me. "You know, Michael said you were pretty, but he didn't say you were *this* pretty."

My smile fell then. Michael had told him I was pretty?

"And really," the guy, whose name I didn't even know, went on, "I feel like I should be offended that no one's bothered to introduce us yet."

"You go to Lincoln?" I asked him.

"Yeah. I'm finally a senior, and I'm still hanging out with the lowly juniors."

"I'm a lowly junior."

His charming smile was back. "Kate, you are anything but lowly."

Michael and Patrice appeared at my elbow. Michael was already groaning when he approached. "Let her breathe, Ben." He smiled over at me. "Sorry. If I'd known he was going to pounce so quick, I would have warned you first."

Ben splashed Michael from the pool, getting most of us wet in the process.

Michael smiled big, and I thought maybe I was seeing him in his element without really knowing he was out of it anywhere else. And it made me see how wrong I'd been. Of course he hadn't been flirting with me. He was just a nice guy. "Kate, this is my girlfriend, Patrice."

"We've met, sweetie," Patrice said up at him. "Kate and I have Chemistry together."

Michael's mouth popped open. "Oh, cool."

"No one's ever accused Michael of being the brains of the

outfit," Ben, still bobbing in the water, said. It didn't seem to bother him that he had to crane his neck just to be part of the conversation.

Michael sighed. "And that's Ben."

I smiled down at Ben, who smiled back up at me. "You should join me."

"No suit, remember?"

He shrugged. "So?"

"Hot tub, anyone?" Patrice asked, her smile so bright it made the darkening sky even darker. "I'm getting a little chilled." She tugged on Michael's hand, and he followed her to the hot tub.

I watched them go, completely unable to resist admiring the curve of Michael's back even as I knew I shouldn't. They settled into the hot tub, the water sloshing around them.

I rolled my pants up to my knees before taking a seat next to where Ben was floating in the pool. Against the other side, Marisol and Tattoo Boy were making out.

"That's Jesse," Ben whispered to me. I leaned over and put my elbows on my knees to get closer to him. I could see below the waterline Ben's slim waist, his trim body, his board shorts. I tried not to be distracted from what he was telling me. "He's twenty-two and the love of Marisol's life."

"What about you?" I asked. "Do you have a love of your life?"

I could have sworn that I felt his hand brush against my calf. "Not yet."

I felt myself blush, and when I snuck a peek at Michael, he was watching us over his shoulder until Patrice said something that caught his attention.

"Are you adjusting to Portland okay?"

I tore my eyes away from Michael and Patrice to look down at Ben, who'd pressed his head against the wall of the pool. "Um, yeah. I guess so. I mean, I just came from Salem, so it's not like I moved across the country."

He shrugged. "New places are hard. I moved here from New Mexico two years ago. I was feeling pretty lame about the whole thing, but these guys kind of adopted me."

I watched Marisol happily splashing around with her boyfriend. "They've been really nice to me." It was completely true, and I suddenly felt awful for being even the slightest bit jealous of Patrice, who had been nothing but kind to me. "I guess I'm not really used to that. I hung out with a lot of male athletes back in Salem. They spent their free time playing pranks on each other. They wouldn't know how to be nice to a stranger." I laughed, remembering an infamous prank from when I was a freshman. "One time, the guys put a possum in the trunk of my best friend's car. My friend was so mad, and all the guys got in so much trouble, but it was pretty great." I smiled, thinking about it, even though it wasn't funny at the time, especially not to Harris.

"You have a nice smile," Ben said quietly, like he almost didn't mean to be heard at all. Up until that moment, Ben's personality had seemed a little like a performance, but for a second, I felt like he might actually be trying to flirt with me, and it made my stomach warm.

I looked away to hide that I was blushing. "Anyway, no, I'm not really used to people being nice to me. At least not so soon. On our swim team, you had to earn that kind of thing. Rivalry was high."

Ben pursed his lips. "I see."

"Hey, let's play Marco Polo!" Marisol shouted from the deep end.

"Are we in third grade?" Michael asked from the hot tub.

"I love Marco Polo," Patrice said, and climbed out of the hot tub. Michael watched her go and then glanced over at me.

I made myself focus on what was going on in the pool. It was impossible to say if I would have made a move on Michael at all, but the knowledge that I was no longer allowed to made the fact that he had never mentioned a girlfriend that much more uncomfortable.

I watched from the edge of the pool as everyone got into place and Marisol closed her eyes to be the first Marco.

"You playing?" Ben whispered to me, but I shook my head. What was I supposed to do, walk around the edge of the pool, yelling *Polo*?

Marisol shouted out to the rest of them, everyone shouted back, and I had visions of seventh-grade pool parties, the boys suggesting Marco Polo because they could fake ignorance when they collided open-palmed into a girls' chest. Marisol giggled as she moved around with her eyes squeezed tight until she finally cornered Jesse against the side of the pool. He tried to dodge her, but she lunged for him.

The radio sitting beside the cooler blared out a song with thick, thumping bass while Jesse moved around aimlessly in the sloshing pool, his fingertips coming close to grazing the arms and shoulders and necks of several people before finally coming into contact with Michael's back.

I watched Michael take a step into the middle of the pool, his arms out in front of him like a zombie. I didn't want to keep my

———

eyes on him for too long in fear that I would get caught noticing how adorable he was with water dripping off the ends of his hair.

Nevertheless, my eyes were stuck to him when a wet hand wrapped around my wrist. The hand was attached to a grinning Ben, and I tried to shake him off.

"Ben, no," I whispered. I didn't want to catch Michael's attention, but he seemed to hear us anyway.

He froze and turned slowly in our direction. He was standing devastatingly close to us, as he hadn't ventured far from the shallow end, and I clamped my lips inside my teeth and shook my head at Ben, who was tugging on me slightly.

My eyes went back to Michael, still tiptoeing through the pool as everyone moved away from him as quietly as they could. His eyes were closed tight and his hands skimmed the surface of the water as he drifted through it. *Marco Polo, Marco Polo, Marco Polo.*

I looked back at Ben, who was still smiling at me, but he'd stopped tugging on me, and when our eyes met, he gently let go of my hand. The party was moving closer to our side of the pool, Marisol's boyfriend moving so close to me on one lunge that he bumped my foot.

I felt the warm water sloshing around my feet, heard the joyous laughter of someone almost being caught, smelled the chlorine scent wafting up out of the water.

I took my phone out of my pocket and tossed it onto a nearby bench piled high with towels. I took a deep breath, closed my eyes, and slipped into the pool.

The water closed over my head. It shouldn't have been so disorienting, but the heavy sweater I'd forgotten to take off was wrapped awkwardly around me, and for a second, I couldn't tell what was up and what was down. As I pushed up toward the surface, I felt the panic start to settle against my chest, felt the way I did when I wasn't sure I was going to make it to oxygen before my lungs burst.

I got my feet under me, and right at that moment, two hands found me, holding on to me clumsily as I rose through the water.

When I broke the surface, I was face-to-face with Michael. His fingers were tangled in my wet sweater, and his eyes traveled over my face, like he was confused.

"Hi," he said, not letting me go. I felt his fingertips through the material of my sweater.

"Hey." I breathed hard, out of excitement and nerves.

"Kate's playing!" Marisol shouted, breaking through my silent brain and bringing the rest of the noise from the pool in with it. I heard the music and the splashing and Ben's laughter.

Everyone was looking at us, and when I noticed Patrice's eyes, her smiling mouth, her wet hair, I backed away from Michael. He let his hands drop, and I swiped the water off my face before taking a deep breath.

Ben raised his eyebrows at me. "You're playing?"

"I'm playing." I ducked down until I was up to my shoulders in the pool. "This is a little heavy." I struggled to get my wet sweater off and tossed it over the edge of the pool. I was glad I'd worn a black camisole underneath.

"Good," Ben said, floating along the surface on his back like a piece of seaweed. "Because it's your turn."

As I stood there with the water sloshing against me, I became aware of my calm breaths, the normal pump of blood in my veins.

I wasn't panicking. I didn't feel like I was going to die. In fact, with the warm water pushing against every inch of my skin, I felt good, relieved.

I closed my eyes.

"Marco."

∘ ∘ ∘

I lay on a bench by the pool and stared up at the stars. The clouds were moving across them, making it seem like the stars were swaying back and forth across the sky. My skin was slowly starting to go cold as the warm water dried away, but I wasn't ready to go back to the apartment, back to the stifling world we'd created for ourselves.

Something brushed my arm and then Michael appeared in my line of vision, blocking half the stars from view. He held something out to me, and it took me a second to realize it was my sweater. He'd already put his own shirt back on.

"It's still a little damp, but I figured you were cold."

I sat up and took my sweater from him, looking around at the empty roof. "Everyone's gone?" When I'd collapsed on the bench, Ben and Marisol had still been buzzing around, but the roof was quiet now.

"Yeah. It's pretty late."

He sat down to perch at the edge of the pool, his legs dangling in the water, his back to me. I smelled cigarette smoke, and he turned his head to blow smoke into the air. "How's your sister doing?"

"As well as can be expected, I guess." I looked away from him, pulling my legs up to my chest, still embarrassed that he'd been there this afternoon. I couldn't imagine how that scene looked from his point of view.

"What happened?" he asked, his voice slight.

"My dad happened," I said, feeling it start to rise in my chest again. I squeezed my eyes shut, determined not to let it consume me. "I can't stand that smell." I didn't mean for it to come out angry, but I was so angry about so many things.

I opened my eyes to see him pull the cigarette away from his mouth and roll it between his fingers. "Patrice hates it, too."

"I can understand why."

He was silent for a long time, and then he stubbed out his cigarette and looked at me closely. He had been looking at me like that since we met, but it seemed to mean something different now, so I looked away from him.

"Patrice is really sweet," I said, and he flinched.

He opened his mouth to say something but then closed it again. "Yeah. Yeah, she's sweet." He looked away from me, down at his hands, and then back up at me. "I should probably get home. Are you okay out here by yourself?"

I just nodded and watched him go, looking away so that I wouldn't give away just how disappointed I really was.

Boys with girlfriends flirted with other girls all the time, and I was pretty certain he hadn't even been flirting at all. He didn't owe me anything, and I knew that, but the knowledge that he'd never mentioned her was still a twinge in my chest.

Once he was gone, I stood up, wrapping my cold arms around myself to look down at the pool. It was the same pool it had been earlier, when we'd been playing around and Michael had put his hands on me. But looking down at it now, it seemed bigger, more alive. The ripples along the surface were barely perceptible, but I watched them, willing myself to dive in.

I held my foot over the surface, watching the light bend around my toes. It would have been so easy to just jump, barely any movement, and I would have been shoulders-deep. But I pulled my leg back and grabbed fistfuls of my sweater to hold in the pain in my chest. Because I couldn't do it. Why couldn't I? Why was it so much easier when it was full of people, when Michael was there? When the distractions were loud enough to cloud my mind?

I sat back on the bench and put my face in my hands, crying hot tears that dripped from my palms and down my arms to mingle with the water still clinging to my sweater.

And then my phone rang. When I snatched it off the bench, I saw that it was Harris and answered immediately.

"Hi," I said, forcing down any emotions that had started to arise. It had been such a strange day, full of upsetting and confusing things. I just wanted this one thing, this conversation with my best friend, without the rest of the world interfering.

But that wasn't going to happen.

"Hey, guess what. Coach just told me that he wants me on the relay. Can you believe that?"

I actually couldn't. Harris had never been on the relay before. His times had never been good enough. "Really?" I tried to sound invested. I tried to sound like every tiny mention of the team or the pool today hadn't been killing me. I tried to pretend I was surprised that my father, Coach Masterson, had called Harris while Harris was away for the weekend, on his daughter's wedding day—no, on the day his daughter *ditched her own wedding*.

Of course the first thing on his mind would be who was swimming the relay. "That's great."

"I know! You're coming to the meet, right? I can't wait for you to see me in action. It's going to be—"

"Harris." I wrapped my arms around myself. "Can we just . . . not talk about swimming right now?" I felt his confusion in the silence that fell then, and I sighed. "I just don't want to talk about *him*, okay?"

"He's still my coach, Kate." I could hear the control in his voice, like he was trying to be gentle with me. "I'm sorry he acted like a jackass, but I still have to answer to him. I still have to practice with him every week."

"I get that." I could feel the tears rising again. It wasn't supposed to be like this. What had happened between my parents wasn't supposed to screw with Harris and me, too. "It just feels like you're taking his side."

"I'm not taking his side. He's an asshole. I get it. But what am I supposed to do, not talk to my best friend about this? Am I supposed to quit?"

"No, of course not, but . . ." I couldn't stop the tears. I sniffled and covered my mouth to hide the sobs, but Harris heard anyway.

"Shit. I'm sorry," he said softly in my ear. "I'm sorry. Damn it, I don't want to fight with you."

But I wasn't mad at Harris, not really. This wasn't his fault any more than it was mine. "I hate him," I said. "I really, really hate him." I wiped my face and my lips tasted like chlorine and salty tears. "I did everything for him, Harris. I did everything to make him proud of me, and he screwed it all up."

———

"You didn't do it all for him," Harris said, gentle as ever. "You did it for you, too."

I shook my head but didn't say anything. He was wrong. I'd never done it for myself. The water was for me, but the race had always been for him.

"It's all tainted," I told Harris. "I look at the pool, and it's all ruined for me now. I think about him, and he's like a stranger to me." I hadn't even realized it was true until I'd said it out loud.

"It's going to be okay, Kate. It is."

But he didn't sound like he believed it. I didn't believe it, either. We were quiet for a long time, until my tears had stopped and the only sounds were the traffic on the street below and the gentle lapping of the pool in the wind. I thought about telling him about the wedding, but this didn't feel like the time. I was tired of talking about every disastrous thing in my life. It was all beginning to pile so high that it was exhausting.

"I'm going to see you Tuesday, right? Hoochie's?"

"Yeah." After everything, I'd almost forgotten about Hoochie's.

"I'll see you then. Get some sleep."

I stared at the sky until my legs started to go numb, and then I went back downstairs to take a hot shower. I walked through the quiet, dark apartment, stopping in the living room to check on Lily.

But Lily wasn't on the couch like I'd expected her to be. A blanket was draped across the cushions where I'd left her before Michael's party, but she wasn't beneath it. I cracked open my mother's door and peeked in. She was asleep under the light of her bedside lamp with a book open on the mattress beside her, but Lily wasn't there, either.

I peeked into my bedroom. Sure enough, Lily was curled up beneath my comforter with the light still on.

I went to take a shower, holding my face under the water until my swollen eyes returned to normal and my skin felt a little less puffy. I changed into pajamas before crawling in beside Lily and turning off the light.

When I settled in next to her, she startled awake. "Kate?"

I turned onto my side to look at her. "Yeah?"

"I'm scared," she whispered, the words muttered low and almost inaudibly. Her hair, still in curls from the wedding, bracketed her face, her makeup smudged around her eyes.

"Me, too." I set my head beside hers on the pillow and wrapped my arm around her. "But everything's going to be okay," I said, mimicking Harris's words. This time, I tried to believe it.

Seven

$\mathcal{L}$ily was still asleep when I got up the next morning, but my mother was gone. I made coffee and toast and sat down in the tiny space between Lily's feet and the end of my bed.

"Lily?" I held out a mug to her with both my hands.

She groaned and opened one eye. "Is it next year yet?"

"Not quite. But I made you coffee."

"Good enough." She sat up, the comforter bunching around her waist as she leaned over to take the coffee from me. She looked a mess.

I felt something hard under my hip and reached beneath me to pull out whatever it was. Lily's cell phone. And there was a text on the screen. Tom had sent it at three in the morning.

Lily. Please call me.

I handed the phone to her, and she read the display. And then

---

she started crying. Between the two of us, I was surprised the Willamette River hadn't flooded already. I took her coffee cup from her and put it on the nightstand. I moved in close and wrapped my arms around her. I just held her as she cried into her hands.

When she'd finished, I pulled away.

"I can't believe Mom and Dad went at each other like that yesterday," she said. She wiped her face and ran a hand through her messy hair. "All I could think was how could I be getting married when Mom and Dad are going through a divorce?"

"But you love Tom."

She pulled her legs up to her chest and wrapped her arms around them, and I was reminded of us as kids, sitting in her room, talking about the boys we had crushes on. Lily went to college when I started high school, and it had been lonely without her around to complain to all the time about boys and Dad and swimming. To have her back now, when my whole world was falling apart, felt glorious, even though I knew it was selfish.

"Of course, I love Tom. But it just feels like bad timing."

Bad timing, in my opinion, was realizing you don't want to get married ten minutes before the ceremony starts. "You don't want to get married?"

She closed her eyes and leaned back against the headboard. "I thought I did, but I don't know anymore. What if we're not as compatible as I thought? What if we were just staying together because it was easy? I mean, I thought Mom and Dad would be together until they died. I thought they had this perfect marriage. Maybe no couple lasts forever."

"Maybe you should talk to Tom about all this."

"I tried. A week ago."

———

"You did?" She hadn't mentioned it to me, and neither one of them had acted as if anything was going wrong.

"Yeah. I thought it might be insensitive to plan the wedding right under Mom's nose after all that stuff with Dad, but Tom didn't think so. He thought the planning might help take her mind off things. Now, I know that wasn't true. It just gave them something else to argue about. I certainly didn't think he was going to start a fight at the wedding, like *he* wasn't the one plowing a woman in his office."

"Okay. *Ew.*"

"Sorry. I'm upset."

"So, what now?"

"I don't know."

"You don't want to call him?"

She shook her head. "Not yet. Can we watch *SpongeBob* instead?"

"Sure. Hey, you know what would be even better than *SpongeBob*?" I hopped off the bed and went for the closet. A lot of my stuff was still in boxes, and I had to dig through more than one before I found what I was looking for: a stack of DVDs in blank cases.

"What are those?" Lily asked when I sat down in front of the DVD player and put one of them in. It was times like these that I was glad I'd begged my mother for a TV for my room last year. Then, it was so I could watch the World Swimming Championships in bed, but now, I mostly just watched talk shows while I got ready for school.

"Last season's dance competitions. I burned them off Dad's DVR before we moved out."

Lily clapped excitedly. "No way. Oh, that would totally un-bum me out."

I hit PLAY and curled up on the bed next to her, pressing my head back into the pillows and watching the couple on the screen, fully decked out in ball gown and black suit, twirling expertly around the dance floor. Watching ballroom dancing competitions was akin to therapy.

I turned to say something about a fumbled step on-screen, but I noticed that Lily's eyes had gone shiny with tears. I couldn't tell if it was because of nostalgia or because her mind was on Tom again, but I knew I needed to snap her out of it.

I muted the TV, letting the couple dance in silence. "I quit swim."

She gasped loudly, and her eyes went wide. "What? You quit swim?"

I nodded.

Her eyebrows furrowed. "Why? I thought you loved swimming."

I pressed my head against the bed frame and looked over at her. "I don't know. I guess the same reason you left your wedding: I freaked out. I wasn't sure if it was what I wanted or what everyone else wanted."

"Have you told Mom?"

"No. She's been so distracted that I didn't know how to do it. I don't even know how she's going to react, and now with the wedding and everything . . ."

"You think she's going to be mad?"

"I don't know. Swimming is what I've always done, and she was so confident that I'd always want to." I paused. "I just want to start over, you know? I want to pretend like the other Kate, the one everyone knew as a swimmer and a record holder, and the best freaking freestyle swimmer in Oregon, doesn't even exist. And I thought maybe I'd get that chance when I met Michael, but . . ."

Her mouth fell open. "Wait. Are you serious? I was right about something for once? You *do* have a crush on him?"

I rolled my eyes. "I don't know if it's a crush, exactly. But he's so cute, and he was being so nice to me, and I thought we were hitting it off, and then he showed up with his girlfriend."

She grimaced. "Ouch."

I glanced for a second at the TV so I wouldn't have to see the pity written all over her face. The couple on-screen was dancing a samba in bright-red costumes. "Yeah, he has a girlfriend. And she's the nicest person I've ever met."

"Things really aren't working out for you, are they?"

I blinked at her. "Says the girl whose ex-fiancé was texting her at three in the morning."

"Says the girl who quit swimming and hasn't told anyone."

"Says the girl who slept in her little sister's bed last night."

She rolled her eyes but smiled at me nonetheless. "Okay, fine, you win." She stretched out on the bed and put her head in my lap with a pillow between us. She still had stains on her cheeks from the tears. "Man, we're really messed up."

o o o

Michael was in the living room chatting with Lily when I made it out there on Monday morning.

"We're going to be late," he said, his backpack slung over one arm. He said it so gently, as if I could dally for another hour, and he still wouldn't have the heart to pin the blame on me. Lily was stretched out on the couch, and surprisingly, she almost looked happy. Michael had a way of putting everyone in a good mood.

Everyone but my mother, it would appear. She was rushing back and forth in an arc around the dining room table, scooping up papers and shoving things into her purse.

"Kate!" she bellowed.

"I'm right here." I went into the dining room and tried to stay out of her way as she spun around the room like a Tasmanian devil.

"Do you have practice today? You have practice today, right? What time does it start? Do you need me to take you to the pool?"

I put a hand on her shoulder, and she sighed and finally stopped moving for a second. "Mom."

Her eyes were pits of panic. I knew I should tell her about the team because I'd been presented with an opening, but I couldn't do that to her. Not when she looked like this. Like Lily said—bad timing.

"Practice is tomorrow," I told her. "Nothing to worry about."

"Right. Practice tomorrow. Okay. Great. You should go. Michael's been waiting for you for a little while now. Wouldn't want you to miss the bus."

Over my mother's shoulder, I saw Michael watching us. He wouldn't have time to smoke his cigarette. "Okay, we're going."

I avoided looking at Michael and Lily as I made my way out the front door. I was not about to have them send me their knowing looks. I knew I was a filthy liar. I didn't need them to reinforce it.

Michael and I rushed silently down the stairs, and I was

———

thankful that we were in a hurry. No small talk. About his girl-friend or my mom. By the time we made it out to the curb, how-ever, the bus was pulling away.

"Hey!" Michael shouted, rushing after it, and I took off after him. Michael caught up to it, seeing as how it wasn't moving very fast in the Portland traffic, and banged on the accordion door.

"Bus doesn't wait for anyone," the driver said when he opened the door, and Michael rolled his eyes as we sat down.

"Sorry," I told him as we started moving again.

"It's okay."

We'd taken a seat in the back, and I did what I thought was a pretty good job of pretending it wasn't painful to sit so close to him. He didn't even smell like cigarettes. For once, I wanted him to smell like cigarettes so I could be less attracted to him.

"Hey, Kate?" He used his thumbnail to scrape at the back of the seat in front of us. Brown vinyl.

I continued to look out the window as the city passed by. "Yeah?"

"Why'd you tell your mom that you have practice tomorrow when you didn't join the team?"

I pressed my forehead to the window. "Because I'm the worst daughter in the history of all reproduction."

"Somehow I doubt that."

He was watching me with those eyes again when I finally gathered the courage to look at him. "I don't know how she's going to react. I haven't told anyone else. You and Lily are pretty much the only ones who know." I scrubbed my hand over my face. It was too early in the day for this conversation. "Could we maybe talk about something else?"

"Okay. What do you want to talk about instead?"

I groaned. "Oh my God. I don't know. What do normal sixteen-year-olds talk about?"

He shrugged. "The usual. Sex, drugs, alcohol. Self-annihilation."

It hit me then—what it was about Michael that made my stomach clench in that way it did even though I'd only know him for a week: Michael didn't expect anything from me. My father, my mother, even Lily, they all expected something from me, whether I was ready to give it or not.

But Michael just looked at me like he was waiting. He was waiting to see what I would do next, what I would say next, who I would be in the next ten minutes.

I looked away from him. Sitting next to each other on this tiny seat was too close. I felt like I was sitting on his lap. I pulled my backpack around in between us, a welcome barrier, and then remembered what I had inside it. I'd bought a bag of peppermints while grocery shopping on Friday with the intention of giving them to him today, but now I wondered if the gesture was too intimate. I bit my lip and looked at Michael, but he was doing something on his phone.

Not too intimate, I decided, reaching into my backpack. They were just peppermints, right?

"I got you something," I told him, pulling out the bag and shoving it at him.

Michael picked the peppermints up from his lap like I'd just handed him a bag of gold nuggets. "Hey, thank you. This is really nice."

I shrugged, trying to play it off. "I thought it might help if you had something to distract you. You know, all that oral-fixation stuff."

His smile faded just a little, and I bit the inside of my cheek. Thankfully, the bus pulled up to the school then, and we could awkwardly ignore each other as we separated.

o o o

I waited for Michael that afternoon, but when the bus pulled up behind the school, he hadn't shown up yet. I lingered, tying my shoes and fiddling with the straps on my backpack until everyone was on the bus and the driver yelled at me to get on.

And the next morning, there was no Michael in my living room, or waiting outside my front door, or standing on the curb, or chasing after the bus.

Eight

"All I'm saying is, they should have gotten a higher score." Lily stuck a forkful of rice in her mouth and gestured at the TV.

Our mother, accustomed to our obsession with ballroom gowns and boys doing the cha-cha, drank her tea before replying. "They definitely had more chemistry than the other couple. And their footwork was truly impressive."

I was watching the door. I might have only known Michael for a week, but I thought I knew him well enough to know that he didn't just abandon people without a word unless something was wrong. But maybe I'd freaked him out with the peppermints. Maybe I'd given myself away. Maybe he knew I liked him, and he was avoiding me so as not to give me any ideas.

"Kate?" Lily was looking at me, concerned.

My whole body buzzed. I wanted to stay here with Lily. I

didn't want her to get lonely and fall into a pit of despair if she started to dwell on Tom and the wedding, but I couldn't sit still when I knew something might be wrong.

"I'm just going to get some air," I told them.

My mother's eyebrows crinkled. "Okay. Be careful."

But standing in the hallway, I had no clue what to do next. Michael had been in my living room, but I had never so much as stepped on his doormat. It said *welcome* in a curly font.

I lifted my hand to knock, but just as I did, the door swung open, and I found myself face-to-face with Patrice. Or rather, I found myself face-to-hair.

"Kate?" She looked at me like I had just appeared before her wearing a tutu and a horse mask.

I took a step back, and she came into the hall and closed the door behind her. "I was just coming to check on Michael. Since he, um, wasn't at school. I guess I was just a little worried. Not that I have anything to be worried about, but I just feel like it's not like him, you know, based on previous experience." God, I was babbling.

She crossed her arms and leaned against Michael's doorjamb. "I guess he didn't tell you?"

"Tell me what?

Her face, usually covered in a wide smile, was downcast. "His mother had an episode. Michael got called out of school yesterday to go to the hospital with her. She had to get an oxygen tank, and he's been monitoring her all day. She isn't great, but as far as I can tell, she's doing much better."

I wasn't sure what to say. Obviously, I knew Michael's mother was sick. I'd known that since my first night in Portland. But

I didn't know that she was so sick that she had to be on oxygen or that she apparently had to go to the hospital on a regular basis.

"I'm sure he'd love the company if you want to go in." Patrice pointed a thumb over her shoulder.

"Oh. No. That's okay. I don't want to bother them. I just wanted to make sure he was okay."

She smiled then, that blinding smile that I knew well. "You're a good friend, Kate. He told me about the peppermints."

I waved it away. "Not a big deal."

"I mean, I wouldn't get your hopes up. He's been trying to quit for a few months and hasn't had any luck. But every little bit helps, and having one more person pestering him about it is always great. Anyway, I should get home."

She left me standing there, and I still wanted to knock. Yes, I'd heard it directly from her mouth what Michael was dealing with, but part of me wanted to see him with my own eyes, see if he was really okay, not physically but emotionally.

I backed away from the door and went back inside my apartment. I slid back into my chair and tried to act normal.

"Kate, is something wrong?"

Mom and Lily were watching me. I had done a good job at keeping a happy face on in front of my mother. I couldn't let her worry about me. I couldn't give her something else to stress about. I hadn't missed the fact that a stack of divorce papers had graced our kitchen table this afternoon or that my mother had taken more time than usual to get ready for dinner, probably fixing her makeup after another crying jag.

So even though she'd given me yet another perfect opportunity

———

to spill my guts about the swim team and Dad and Michael, I shut her down by plastering on a smile.

"Yeah, everything's fine."

o o o

The next morning, I waited outside in the hallway. And then I waited at the bus stop. And then I rode to school alone, rain splattering against the bus windows.

"So how bad was it?" Marisol was asking Patrice when I sat down at lunch.

Patrice bit her lip and then put down the plastic fork she'd been using to scoop up her peas. "She didn't look great. Real pale. I don't think it was anything worse than the usual."

"The usual?" I asked, feeling a little shocked.

Marisol nodded. "Yeah. Michael's mom kind of has episodes pretty often. Sometimes they're not a big deal and Michael just hangs around at home for a day and everything is fine. But sometimes she ends up in the hospital."

"One time she was in the ICU. Fluid in her lungs. It was awful," Patrice added.

I should have gone to his apartment the night before. I should have been there in case he needed someone.

Patrice sent me a sad little smile. "How was he after I left?"

"Oh, um." I didn't want to admit that I hadn't knocked because I was too chicken. "Actually, I didn't end up seeing him. Something came up with my sister, and I had to go back home." I was a terrible liar.

"Oh. Okay." She looked down at her tray, her eyes sad, and I understood why Michael was with her. She was so caring and kind, and I felt guilt curdle in my stomach at even thinking about Michael in a romantic capacity.

"Hey, not to change the subject, but do you guys have any idea what we should do for our chem project?" Marisol asked. She went back to her salad, and I stared down at my tray. I'd gotten nachos and soda, things my father wouldn't let me have when I was training. No soda for the whole season and no junk food. I couldn't remember the last time I'd had junk food in September.

"Not really," I said. "You'll soon discover that I'm not exactly creative." As a group, we were supposed to make a periodic table of elements using a unique medium. "I couldn't even decide what color to paint my bedroom. It's currently white."

Patrice snickered a little, and there was something about the sound that was encouraging.

"We could make the periodic table out of food," Marisol suggested. "Fruit and veggies and stuff. And we could eat it after."

"What about a giant cookie? We'd be Dr. Stewart's favorite table," Patrice said. "Maybe he'll finally forgive Marisol for being a pain." Marisol snorted. "It would take a whole truck of giant cookies for that to happen."

Patrice grimaced. "Maybe food isn't a good idea. First of all, the food would be covered in glue. Second of all, it would be gross by the time we got it to class."

Marisol pointed at Patrice with her plastic fork. "You're one smart cookie. Pun completely intended."

◦ ◦ ◦

After school, I waited for Harris on the roof. I wasn't positive when my mom would be getting home from job-hunting, and if

I was home when she got there, she would ask me questions about swim, and I wasn't in the mood to answer them.

I stared down at the pool and thought about how to tell Harris that I'd quit the team. I figured that it was going to be easier to tell him than it would be to tell my mom, and telling him at Hoochie's, our place, felt right, a comforting mixture of my old life and my new one. Also, he would have ice cream to console him.

I tried to rehearse how I would tell him. I would start by saying that it had nothing to do with him, because I could imagine him taking it personally. To a certain extent, a less severe extent, swimming belonged to Harris and me almost as much as it did to my father. We'd started at the same time, we'd gone through all of it together, we'd pushed each other all these years.

My phone rang, and excitement mixed with nervousness rocketed through my stomach as I grabbed my bag and headed for the door, my phone already pressed to my ear.

"Did you cut class to get here this early?" I asked.

"Not quite," Harris said, and I paused halfway out the door, staring down into the dark stairwell.

"But you're here, right? Or on your way?"

He sighed, and that's when I heard it. A splash in the background.

And my father's voice.

"You're still in Salem?"

"Your dad called a last-minute practice. I can't skip."

"Yes, you can." It came out much more forcefully than I'd meant it to. I lowered my voice. "Harris, he can't make you go to that. Tell him you already have something to do."

He was quiet long enough that I heard my father yelling for

Cal to start drills. "This is really important to me. I have to stay, okay?"

I pulled my phone away from my ear, completely ready to just hang up without another word. I watched the seconds tick by on the screen, my jaw set in frustration and anger and just plain disappointment.

I put the phone back to my ear. "Okay. I guess I'll see you later." I hoped he didn't hear the quiver in my voice.

"Don't forget the meet on Friday. Please come."

"Yeah. Maybe." I hung up.

I dropped my backpack in the doorway to the stairs and sank down next to it. For a second, I was afraid I might cry. But I took a deep breath. I couldn't blame him. I couldn't tell him to give up just because I had. If things were reversed and I *had* joined the team, I would have bailed on him for a practice any day of the week. If he felt like he owed my father another practice, then who was I to stand in the way?

I scrubbed my hands over my face and pressed my head to the doorjamb. And then I heard footsteps on the stairs below. I started to push myself up, but then Michael's face appeared around the corner, and I felt the fight go out of me.

He froze when he saw me and then took the last few steps hesitantly. "Kate?"

I closed my eyes. I was glad to see him because I'd been worried, but I didn't want him to see me like this. I thought maybe if I closed my eyes, I could make him disappear.

"Are you okay?" No such luck.

I sucked in a shaky breath and prayed that my voice wouldn't tremble when I spoke. "I'm fine."

When I opened my eyes, I saw he had an unlit cigarette in his hand, but when he leaned against the wall beside me, he tucked it into the pocket of his jeans.

"You don't look fine."

I forced a smile. "It's so stupid. Trust me, it's not worth your time. Please don't even worry about me. How's your mom?"

He was quiet. He had a strange expression on his face. Maybe I wasn't supposed to know that she had gotten sick, or at the least, I wasn't supposed to say anything.

"Patrice told me. Please don't be mad."

His expression didn't change. "Not mad." He pressed his back to the doorway. "My uncle is here to help out. I just needed to get away for a second." He let out a shaky breath and then leaned his head back against the wall. "Tell me what's going on."

I shook my head, insistent. "You don't need my problems—"

He spoke over me. "I could use the distraction. Please." One of his hands gripped the doorway by his side, and I saw sadness flash in his eyes, just momentarily, before it was gone. "Is it your dad?"

When I started to say it, it sounded like the stupidest thing I'd ever said to anyone, especially Michael. "I was supposed to hang out with my best friend tonight, but he got called in for a last-minute swim practice, so now I'm all by myself. I'm just upset because we've barely seen each other since I moved, and I realize that it hasn't been that long, but we got into kind of an argument after Lily's wedding, so everything is a little tense, and he doesn't know that I quit swim and now I guess I feel like he's getting close with my dad, which kind of makes me sick because I'm still mad at my dad for being a huge asshole to my mom. And none of this even matters compared to the fact that your mom was in the hospital. I'm ridiculous. You really shouldn't have offered to ride the bus with me last week. Then you would be free of my complete insanity."

He smiled a half-hearted shadow of a smile, and it highlighted the exhaustion on the rest of his face. He had bags under his eyes and a slight pallor to his skin. "Are you okay?" I asked him. I got that he wanted a distraction, but I was worried, and I needed to know he was okay more than he needed to know about Harris.

He put up his hands. "Okay. One thing at a time. First of all, I'm really sorry about your friend, but if it makes you feel any better, you can hang out with me. I might not be as cool as him, but I'm really not that bad."

I wasn't really sure I was the best person to act as the deciding factor on that front. I was completely biased in favor of the cute boy in front of me.

"Second, anything that goes on in your life matters. Don't think it doesn't just because someone else's problems seem bigger. My mom is fine. This isn't the first time this has happened, and I'm fairly certain it won't be the last. Third, I'm really glad I offered to ride with you last week, because I don't think you're insane. I really like you."

I was pretty sure I stopped breathing when he said that, but he kept going before I had a chance to react.

"And fourth, yes, I'm okay. I'm a little tired. But I'll be okay."

"We were going to go to an ice-cream shop."

His eyebrows furrowed. "What?"

"Me and Harris. We were supposed to go to this ice-cream

shop that we used to go to all the time. It's a really long drive for him, so I shouldn't be surprised that he flaked on me, but we used to skip school to go all the time, you know?"

"I have ice cream in my apartment."

"That's really sweet, but it's not triple-chocolate brownie ice cream from Hoochie's."

"Hoochie's?"

I nodded.

"Do you think maybe my ice cream will do, for now?"

I bit my lip. It wasn't like I could go home. Not while my mom thought I was at practice. "Okay."

He smiled and clapped his hands together once. "Great. I'm actually really hungry. I'll run down and get it." He was gone like a shot, and I closed my eyes, letting myself forget everything for just a moment. I could pretend that Harris hadn't ditched me and that Michael didn't have a girlfriend, and maybe I could be happy for just a second. I went to take a seat by the pool, on one of the plastic benches there, and watched the water sway slightly under the pressure of the wind.

The door opened with a creak and Michael came out onto the roof, a bowl in each hand. "So, we had rocky road and chocolate chip. I didn't know which one you'd want, so I got a bowl of each. You pick."

I picked the chocolate chip. He sat on the arm of the bench, hunched over his bowl. We ate in silence, and I couldn't keep myself from looking over at him. He did that thing with his spoon where he flipped it over before sticking it in his mouth, so that the ice cream hit his tongue instead of the roof of his mouth.

Finally, he looked at me. "So, tell me something that your

mother doesn't know. Something she's not likely to let slip to a stranger in the lobby of an apartment building." He crunched at the nuts in his rocky road ice cream.

I shrugged. "Other than swimming, there's not a whole lot to know about me."

"I don't believe that for one second."

He watched me for a long moment until I had to break the eye contact, my face a little flushed. I placed my empty bowl on the bench next to his black sneakers. "Here's something you don't know: If I keep eating like a swimmer when I'm not swimming, I'm going to gain a lot of weight." That much was true. I already felt bloated from eating seconds at every meal but not burning off the calories like I used to.

Michael rolled his eyes. "No more swimming-related subjects. Tell me something else. There's more to you. I know it."

I ran the tip of my spoon through the melted ice cream at the bottom of the bowl. "Okay. Promise you won't laugh?"

His eyes went wide for a second. "I mean, I can't *promise*. Not if you're going to tell me that you dress up as a rhino and run through the streets every weekend."

I smiled. "It's nothing like that."

He pursed his lips. "Okay, then I'm fairly certain I'm not going to laugh."

"Okay, so, since I was a kid, I've always been into ballroom dancing. Like, really, dancing of any kind, but I used to tape the ballroom dancing that they showed on cable, and me and my sister would watch it in the middle of the night while my parents were asleep."

"Why just when they were asleep?"

I shrugged. "My dad didn't really like me to be into anything that girly, you know? We watched football on the weekends and stuff like that, and sure, I like football, but I love watching dancing competitions. The costumes and the footwork. It's so beautiful."

He was staring at me. But the upside was, he wasn't laughing. He set his empty bowl in mine, the porcelain clanking against my spoon. "Why would I laugh at that?"

I shrugged. "I don't know."

I watched him, his nervous fidgeting. He probably wanted a cigarette, but he wasn't reaching for the one in his pocket.

"Why would your friend be getting close to your dad?" he asked after it felt like we were going to sit there all night in silence, listening to the traffic noises below.

I hadn't been prepared for the question, and my heart thudded in my ears while I considered it. "I guess he's probably not. Not really. My dad is his coach, so he's just trying to keep the peace. And I get that. We've just never really been apart. It's harder than I thought it was going to be."

He chewed on his lip, sucking it into his mouth in a way that distracted me a little. "Salem's not that far."

I threw my hands up. "I know. That's the worst part. It's not like he lives on the other side of the world or something."

"Are you, uh, into him? I mean, is he, like, your boyfriend or something?" He stumbled so hard over his words, and when I looked up at him, towering over me just enough to make me feel small beside him, I saw the downward curve of his mouth.

I found myself stumbling as much as he had. "No. He's not

my . . . He's not anything. I mean, he's my best friend, but we're not into each other in any . . . romantic . . . way . . . at all."

And then we sat there for a long time, staring at each other. I felt like my heart was going to explode out of my chest and take a dive into the pool.

He picked up the bowls before hopping off the bench. "I should probably get back. They might need help down there."

I just nodded, and he left me there, feeling like I'd done something wrong.

Nine

When I got back to the apartment, Lily was making dinner. I could make out the smell of garlic, and the area around the kitchen was degrees hotter than the rest of the apartment.

"Since when do you cook?" I asked her, opening a cabinet and pulling out a glass. I got a pitcher of filtered water out of the fridge and poured myself some, leaning against the fridge to drink it as I watched Lily drain a vat of pasta and then stir a curious sauce on the stove. It was an orange-red color.

"Tom taught me a little here and there," she replied without looking at me. She moved with sure limbs, and I remembered the Lily that lived with us when I was in middle school, completely unable to even make grilled cheese without ruining it.

"Didn't you set the microwave on fire trying to make mac and cheese once?"

She dumped the sauce into the pasta and then stirred it in.

Once the pasta was orange, she dipped the wooden spoon into the pot and pulled out a few orangey noodles, which she presented to me. "Try it, smart-ass." She pushed the spoon in my direction.

I leaned forward and pulled the pasta off the spoon with my teeth, tilting my head back to keep it in as I opened my mouth to let the steam out. The pasta was hot. When it cooled enough to really let me taste it, I found that the sauce was like a creamy marinara. It was delicious. "Wow. Okay. Point made."

Lily grinned just as the front door flew open. My mother swept into the apartment, a huge smile on her face. "Girls! I got a job!"

"That's great!" I swooped over to give her a hug while Lily shoveled pasta onto plates.

My mom's eyes went wide. "Lily, how sweet. You didn't have to cook dinner."

Lily turned her back to get drinks from the fridge, and my mother snuck me a devastated expression. I laughed, and Lily slammed the fridge shut. "You two just calm down and have a seat."

My mother admitted defeat after she'd taken a bite of the pasta, and Lily boasted mercilessly.

"So this job?" Lily asked. "What is it?"

"I took an activities director position at a nursing home on Washington. It might be long hours starting out, but I really think it could go somewhere." My mother was sitting straighter. She'd gotten her color back since that meltdown, and maybe some of her confidence. She waved a hand at both of us. "But let's not get too excited about it until I know for certain it's a good fit. Lily, Kate, how were your days? Class? Practice?"

Lily and I exchanged glances. Lily hadn't gone to class, a fact that she apparently hadn't told my mother about, which I found comforting. It was nice to know I wasn't the only one keeping secrets.

Neither of us said anything. Lily munched away on her food, avoiding my mother's eyes, and I tried not to panic when she turned to me. "Kate? Practice? What's your new team like?"

"Practice was great," I said, trying not to be too annoyed that Lily had avoided her drama so easily. "The team is really great, and Coach Wu is nice."

When I chanced a look up at my mother, her face was bright, and if I wasn't mistaken, her eyes were a little teary. "I was so worried that you weren't going to be able to get your stride back, but that's just great." She sniffled. "Oh God, I'm a mess." She laughed and wiped her face, and I felt like the scum on the bottom of someone's shoe. Why couldn't I just tell her that I wasn't swimming?

"Did you get a schedule? I need to know when your meets are so I can make sure I'm there."

"Oh. Um. I'll have to get a schedule from Coach Wu next week. I forgot."

"Okay. Sounds great." She munched away, and the happiness in her eyes made guilt gnaw at me until I had to look away.

o o o

"So I was thinking," Michael said as soon as we got out into the hallway the next morning.

"Okay."

"Maybe we could strike a bargain."

We made our way down the stairs. "Strike a bargain? What are you, a 1920s oil tycoon?"

"I'm serious," he said, but I could hear the smile in his voice. "Look, I'm going to tell you something that not many people know about me. A few things, actually."

My stomach tilted. He'd barely told me anything about his personal life since we met, and I was ready for the secret sharing to be a little less one-sided, even if I was a little nervous about what those secrets might be.

"Number one, I can't swim." He paused on the stairs, and I knew that he was giving me room to react.

"You can't swim?" I wasn't sure what I'd been expecting, but it wasn't that.

"No. I mean, I can dog-paddle, but sometimes I have dreams of driving into a river or going down in a plane crash, and I imagine myself trying to dog-paddle to safety. I always die."

I tried not to laugh. "Your dream self should really have more faith in your real self. Dog-paddling *could* save your life." I scowled at him. "Why did you throw a pool party if you can't swim?" I thought of him floating at the shallow end during Marco Polo. I suddenly realized I couldn't remember him straying past halfway, even when he was *it*. When he'd gotten to me, we'd been standing in water up to our chests. Looking at him now, I pushed the memory of his hands pulling me up from the water out of my mind.

"No one expects you to do the butterfly at a pool party, okay? You stand by the edge or you sit in the hot tub, and no one really knows the difference." He kept walking. "So anyway, then I thought, well, I have the swimming state champion living in my building. Why not ask her to teach me?"

———

"Michael . . ." All the joy that had slowly been soaking into my bloodstream at his excitement seemed to seep out again. He wanted me to teach him to swim? I wasn't even sure I could get in the water. Would I be able to handle it if only Michael was there? Or would I have another panic attack?

He stood on the landing below and craned his neck to meet my eye. "I know what you're thinking, but I'm not asking you to do this for free. I have something to offer you in return."

"I'm listening."

"Well, how would you like to learn to dance?"

I started down the steps toward him slowly. "Wait. What?"

The smile was starting to take over his face again, and he glanced sideways at me. "That's the second thing about me. I might know how to salsa. Would you like to learn?"

I sputtered.

His smile lost some of its luster. "I just mean because you told me you and your sister liked ballroom dancing. I thought it would be fun."

"How in the world do you even know how to salsa?"

"Okay, first of all, don't sound so shocked. Second of all, my father was a Spaniard, and he taught my mother to dance, and she taught me." He smiled and threw open the lobby door.

I hesitated for a moment on the fact that he'd mentioned his father in the past tense, but he kept talking before I had a chance to ask him about it.

"Don't feel pressured," he said, his hands up. "It was just an idea."

Swim lessons in exchange for salsa lessons? That could be . . . interesting. "Okay."

"Okay?" he sounded eager, like a little boy being told he was about to get his first bike. He rushed to follow me outside. "Really?"

"Sure. How about tomorrow after school?"

"Yeah. That's good."

We stood by the traffic light, and he smiled a little as he rocked back on his heels, and I felt the same way, holding in my smile until he reached into his pocket and pulled out his pack of cigarettes. My eyes fell to the pack and then I looked up at him, and my distaste for those cigarettes went beyond plain disgust. If he kept smoking, would he end up like his mother someday?

His fingers froze on the pack, and he stared back at me for a long second. And then he reached into his pocket again, shoving the cigarettes back in and retrieving something else instead. It wasn't until he'd unwrapped it that I realized it was a peppermint.

He popped it into his mouth, and I smiled as I climbed onto the bus.

o o o

"So, Ben has been asking about you." Marisol wiggled her eyebrows at me over the lunch table. "He wants to know when we're all going to hang out again."

I froze with my soda halfway to my mouth. "What? Why?"

Marisol chuckled. "What do you mean, why? You guys were totally flirting like crazy at Michael's party. He said he really liked you."

I tried to think of what to say that would make me sound like I was more interested in Ben than I was in Patrice's boyfriend. "Why don't I ever see him around campus?"

Patrice shrugged. "He's a senior. A lot of his classes are off campus. He does, like, community service projects and internships. He's getting ready to apply for early admission at Stanford."

"Wow." Stanford was a pretty big deal. "I don't even know if I'm into him. I mean, I barely know him."

"Well, sure." Marisol's face lit up. "You don't know him now. But you'll get to know him, and you'll love him, just like we do. When I first met Jesse, he was *so* annoying, and now he's my favorite person on the planet." She grinned at me and then Patrice, and I saw the way Patrice focused on her food like she was trying not to say something.

"Hey, do you guys want to get together tomorrow night to work on our project?" Patrice asked, reaching across her tray to peel open her chocolate milk.

Marisol frowned. "I thought you were hanging out with Michael tomorrow."

Patrice shrugged. "I was, but he canceled on me second period. He said he and Ben had something they wanted to do."

I felt my skin go hot. Michael had told Patrice that he was going to be hanging out with Ben when he was actually going to be hanging out with me? He'd lied to her?

"It's not like we've been spending much time together lately anyway."

Marisol made a pouty face at her. "What about last night?"

Patrice shrugged. "Okay, fine. We don't hang out unless his mother is really sick. But isn't that just as bad as not hanging out at all? Like, it feels like he really only calls me when he's lonely."

I focused on chewing my broccoli. I didn't want to be the cause of any problems between Michael and Patrice. If I had

———

known they had plans, I never would have suggested we meet in the first place.

"Um, I actually have plans tomorrow," I said. If I was being honest, I didn't want to cancel my plans with Michael, even if he did lie to Patrice, but I still felt guilty, like I was the one who'd lied, even though I wasn't.

Patrice slumped a little but Marisol nodded. "That's okay. We have no clue what to do for the project anyway. Maybe we should ask Roger, the world's worst lab partner."

She and Patrice laughed, but I stayed frozen, completely unable to find humor in the situation.

o o o

When I took my seat in American Lit, I was feeling jittery. I tapped my fingers on my desk and waited for Michael to show up.

"Am I not supposed to tell Patrice about the salsa and the swim lessons?" I asked as soon as he sat down. "Because she said you told her you were hanging out with Ben tomorrow night." I didn't want to come right out and accuse him of lying to his girlfriend, but, well, it was pretty clear that was exactly what he'd done.

The casual happiness on Michael's face melted away. "Oh. Well, I thought I might surprise her. You know, it could be fun, learning how to swim without telling her. Thought maybe I could drive her out to the beach when I can do more than dog-paddle. She'll be impressed."

His smile returned, but I could tell it was forced, and something in my chest was beginning to ache.

"Okay," Mrs. Hure said, her face glowing. "Did everyone finish the book?"

The response this time was a little more encouraging, but there was still a fair amount of lazy grumbling. "You were supposed to be done by today so that we could discuss," she said, though her voice wasn't particularly stern. "Your quiz is next class, and I expect perfect As from everyone."

More grumbling.

"What did we think about the end result for Daisy and Gatsby?"

My mind still buzzing from the Michael situation, I spoke without thinking. "I thought it was kind of stupid."

Mrs. Hure turned to me, and she was already making her way down our aisle, beautiful and intimidating. She looked surprised to hear me talking. Maybe I was a little surprised, too. "Why's that?"

I shrugged. I'd finished the book three days before, after yet another night of insomnia. "Gatsby did everything for this completely self-obsessed woman. It's all fake. He completely changes his life and who he is just to get her, and in the end . . ."

I was babbling again, but this time, everyone was looking at me.

". . . in the end, he loses everything."

Mrs. Hure nodded at me. "I think that's a fine observation, but I think there's a lesson to be learned there. Gatsby built Daisy up in his head. He created an entire life, perhaps one that wasn't true to himself, just to make Daisy happy, but the dream wasn't real. Nothing could have made her happy enough." She took a deep breath, her curly golden-highlighted hair rising and falling with her shoulders. "Michael? Care to weigh in?"

Michael looked straight ahead at the dry-erase board for a long moment and then shook his head.

———

Mrs. Hure made a thoughtful noise in the back of her throat. "Well, thank you for your input, Kate." She spun around quickly, her long skirt swaying around her ankles. "That was actually an excellent segue into our first topic, the ever-elusive green light."

I looked over at Michael. He was rigid in his seat, his hands folded together and his gaze straight forward, like he had no intention of meeting my eye.

Ten

$\mathcal{I}$'d spent a large portion of my life hanging around guys who were wearing nothing but jammers without so much as blushing, but when Michael walked onto the roof for our first swim lesson wearing nothing but a pair of shorts, I thought I felt my heart stop. Even though I'd seen him shirtless at the party, I still felt a little flustered at the sight of his bare chest.

I had a million swimsuits: bodysuits, one-piece suits, some more utilitarian than others, and I also had a vast array of bikinis. Harris and I had spent a lot of recreational time throwing each other in the pool back at my house in Salem, and wearing a suit that went to your knees wasn't ideal for pool parties. The bikini I'd chosen for today was red with orange polka dots, and I wasn't so blind that I didn't notice that Michael was also trying not to let his gaze stray any farther south than my chin.

He grinned. He was bouncing on the balls of his feet. "I've always wanted to learn how to swim, but my parents weren't interested in teaching me. I mean, what kid knows how to rumba but doesn't know how to swim?"

I let out a huff of a breath. "You know how to rumba?"

He shrugged. "Not great, but passably."

His eyes roved over the roof then, because we weren't the only ones there. On the other side of the pool, a woman watched her young daughter, probably four or five, float in the shallow end of the pool. She waved at us, and I waved back.

"Uh-oh," Michael whispered, leaning into me slightly.

"What?" I whispered back.

"I didn't think about the possibility of people. They're going to see you teaching me and they're going to know that I can't swim." There was humor in his voice, and a hint of a smile on his mouth.

I rolled my eyes and patted him on the shoulder. It was warm and soft, and I tried to be subtle as I ripped my hand back. "Your pride is just going to have to take a hit tonight, sir. I think you'll survive."

He smiled, and then we stood there awkwardly.

"So do we just . . . ?" Michael motioned toward the pool.

"Go for it," I said.

He went to the far side of the pool, close to where the little girl was standing in the shallow end, and descended the stairs slowly, his hand gripping the metal of the rail tightly. It shouldn't have been as surprising as it was, but I'd seen him floating around the shallow end at the pool party and I thought he would, at the least, gently hop over the edge where the water was only four feet deep.

When he was finally all the way in, he looked up at me, grasping the edge of the pool. "What?" he said.

I bit back my laughter. He was doing his best. "Nothing."

He narrowed his eyes at me playfully, but my amusement died when I looked down at the pool. I wasn't sure what to expect anymore. Would Michael's presence be enough to keep me from tipping over the edge, or would my father's voice in my head keep ticking away until I couldn't even look at the water without feeling like it was drowning me?

Only one way to know. I took a deep breath and hopped over the edge. I let myself drift under the surface for just a second to get my skin wet, waiting for the moment when it would be too much while I let the water move through my fingers. I could see Michael's legs, his feet pointed in my direction.

The moment never came, and when I finally went back up for air, I felt steady. In the daylight, with Michael watching me, and that little girl and her mother close by, it didn't feel as scary. I could forget everything but right now.

"Okay, are you ready?" I asked.

"I am." But he didn't seem very confident.

"Really quick," I said when Michael had waded over to me. "Do you need nose plugs?"

"Nose plugs?"

"Yeah. Do you need to plug your nose to go under?"

He shook his head, and I tossed the nose plugs that I'd been holding over the edge of the pool. Michael watched them go. "Wow. That would have been embarrassing."

"It's not embarrassing. A lot of people have to plug their nose, even professionals. Okay, so the first thing I'm going to teach you is the streamline position. It's the most important thing you're going to learn because all forms of swimming come back to it. It's where you start and it's where you end."

Michael cocked an eyebrow at me. "You just went into a whole different mode, didn't you?"

I rolled my eyes. "Okay, on your stomach. You can grab onto the wall." He held the lip of the pool with both hands and kicked back so that he was sticking out straight into the pool.

The little girl, bouncing around in the shallow end with orange floaties wrapped around each bicep, watched us.

Michael started to sink.

"Kick your legs," I told him, and he did, his body floating back up to the surface. "Okay. Back straight, arms and legs stretched straight out in front and behind you, tuck your arms close to your head, keep it tight. Okay, overlap your hands on the wall. Hold your breath and go under to straighten your spine."

He was so focused on holding his breath and getting his body right that he stopped kicking and his legs began to sink.

"Don't stop kicking." Without thinking, I moved forward and put a hand on his stomach to keep him from sinking. He stopped moving altogether, and I pulled my hand away quickly. "Keep kicking."

He kicked so hard that he splashed the little girl, and she laughed. When he was able to keep himself up in the water, I told him to let go of the wall.

"What?" he demanded, his voice a little shaky. "If I do that, I'll drown."

I crossed my arms and watched him kick his legs while holding on to the edge of the pool for dear life. "You're not going to drown. Come on. I'll take care of you."

He stopped kicking for a moment, and then, his face down in the water, he let go of the wall. Michael didn't really need to know

—

the streamline position. He wasn't trying to learn how to swim competitively. He didn't need to know proper form. He just needed to know how to not drown. But when he tucked his chin and arms, doing it exactly as I'd told him to, it made my skin tingle with the thrill of teaching him.

Even though the previous experience had been a little daunting, I put my hands beneath his chest and stomach to stabilize him while he floated, belly down. "Okay, kick your feet and keep your arms at your sides."

We glided like that, me holding him up and him propelling us from one side of the pool to the other. It was almost an hour before I thought we could call it quits. But when I let him go, the feel of his skin on my hands was branded on me. We leaned against the side of the pool, the water sloshing up under our armpits as we draped our arms over the edge.

"I'm exhausted." He leaned his head back and closed his eyes. "That's a lot of work."

"Ha! Believe me, I know."

"Can I ask you something without you thinking I'm just using you because you're a crazy good swimmer?"

I snorted. "I guess."

"Can I see you swim?"

His words made everything inside me dim a little, like I was no longer in on some big joke. The water started to feel like a nightmare again, pushing in on all sides. I took a deep breath. "Why?"

Across the pool, the little girl splashed loudly and screamed joyously at her mother.

"I want to see what it's supposed to look like. I want to see the way you move." He held my gaze, and just like that, the power had shifted from me back to him. When he looked at me like that, I felt like I'd do anything to keep his attention.

"Okay."

He drifted over to the other side of the pool slowly, standing by the girl, who was now watching with interest as I positioned myself opposite them in the shallow end. I stood with my back against the side, looking out at the straight line of water in front of me, unobstructed by anything. Michael, the girl, and her mother all watched me closely.

I thought about that last practice with my father, about floating at the side of the pool as that door flew open. Just the day before, we'd been practicing at the house, and my father had run me so hard, I'd climbed out of the pool and vomited on the concrete at his feet.

What the hell are you waiting for? Get your ass in the pool already.

I closed my eyes for a second. My father wasn't here. I wasn't racing a clock, I wasn't racing another person. I was doing this for Michael, Michael who'd, in the last hour, pulled his arms so tight against his head to please me that he couldn't hear any of the instructions I was giving him. Michael, who had slowly sunk to the bottom of the pool like a sack of potatoes while trying to get into position.

I pushed off the wall, going under the surface as I pulled my body into a long, tight streamline. I started in butterfly, the hardest stroke and probably my weakest. I never swam the fly, and it wasn't as effortless and fluid as it might have been for someone else. I didn't have goggles, so I was swimming blind, counting on my years of practice to tell me when the end of the pool was approaching. I counted the strokes in my head, letting my fingertips graze the wall before executing an open turn and heading back toward the start, this time getting into position for a backstroke.

Even though I wasn't a backstroke swimmer, I'd always loved it. I loved watching the ceiling roll by as I swam, instead of staring down at the bottom of the pool or looking to the sides to see the other swimmers. The backstroke was almost relaxing. I pulled it slow, giving myself time to look up at the sky. I could see the building beside us, could almost count the windows.

I touched the wall, pushed through a flip turn, and came up into breaststroke. I pulled myself in tight, pulling my body under me in the modified streamline and staying under as long as I could before pushing my arms out and breaking the surface. Open turn and then finally, finally up into freestyle.

Freestyle was my stroke. I loved the feel of propelling myself forward, attempting as little drag and splash as possible. I loved seeing how long I could stay under before having to finally come up for air. I loved plunging my arms down below me and being able to feel how much water there was in the depths. It felt like the entire weight of an ocean under me as I plunged my arm down and then speared it forward.

I hit the wall and came up with an uncharacteristic gasp. Swimming was such a high, that feeling of being powerful and fast and strong. For just a second, I pressed my forehead to the side of the pool and breathed it in. This was what I loved, the feeling of being able to do anything in the water, the sheen of it on my skin.

But my father was still in the back of my head, waiting to resurface. *Push harder, push harder, push harder.*

I heard clapping, and I turned to see the girl and her mother standing at the edge of the pool, smiling in my direction. The little girl was clapping so enthusiastically, water was splashing off her hands.

"Again! Again!" she screamed, and her mother leaned down to whisper something in her ear.

Michael had a strange look on his face when I swam over to him. "So, am I going to be able to do all that?"

I laughed. "Let's just start with keeping you afloat, okay?"

We toweled off, and then I leaned over the side of the pool. I took out my ponytail and rinsed my hair with the bottle of water I brought with me.

"What are you doing?" Michael asked from behind me.

By now, the woman and her daughter had left, and we were alone by the pool. "The chlorine breaks my hair down," I explained to him, scrubbing my hair lightly. "This'll keep it from getting brittle."

I set the bottle at my feet and wrung my hair out. I glanced over my shoulder as I did it and caught Michael running his fingers through his own messy, wet hair. He brought his fingers away and inspected them, like that one hour in the pool would send him into early balding.

I straightened and tried to flatten my wet hair. After a moment of finger combing, I realized he was watching me. I let my arms fall to my sides. "Why are you looking at me like that?"

His mouth was a strange shape, somewhere between a smile and not, unsure. "You're amazing," he said, and my own sense of feeling light and carefree fell to the ground with a *splat*.

"What?" I sputtered.

Michael shook his head, and this time, the shape of his mouth was a complete smile. "Your mom told me you were amazing, but

I didn't think it was going to be anything like that. You are completely and totally incredible."

I crossed my arms. I felt exposed somehow, with my towel wrapped around me, even more than I'd been when I was half naked in front of him. I felt like I'd shown him a part of my soul, and I didn't know how I felt about it.

"Are you ready to go downstairs?" he asked, leaving me to catch my breath again as he went for the door.

I followed him down, his words from the pool replaying themselves again and again in my head, and feeling guilty when I compared them to the look on Patrice's face when she'd told me Michael had canceled on her. He'd said he wanted to surprise her. It really didn't have anything to do with me. I'd had tons of guy friends before. What I had with Michael was no different. We were just friends.

Michael's apartment was a cookie-cutter version of ours. It was dark inside, the only light coming from the kitchen and a very small lamp next to an armchair, where Michael's mother was reading a book. She looked up, an oxygen tube tucked into her nostrils and a pair of reading glasses on the end of her nose.

I knew immediately where Michael got his kind face and always-smiling eyes. I wondered if she recognized me from that first night in the parking garage, but her expression didn't give anything away.

"Mom, this is Kate." Michael led me into the living room with a hand on my lower back. It was warm against the cold, mostly wet towel.

She set her book on the table beside her and reached out to

shake my hand, bending just slightly at the waist. "I'm Harriet," she said and then wheezed out a little cough.

"You feeling okay, Mom?" Michael asked, taking a cautious step toward her.

She waved him off. "I'm fine."

"I'm going to change," he told me, already walking in the direction of the hallway. It was strange to think that he slept in a room that was just like mine but completely different, that our surroundings perfectly mirrored each other but had nothing in common.

"So you're the swimmer girl," his mother said, and I whipped around to look at her. She tugged a little at her long hair. "I've been hearing about you a lot lately. We're both very excited about having someone from Michael's school right across the hall."

"Really?" I went to sit on the sofa and was already on the clean tan fabric when I remembered that I was wet and jumped back up. "Oh my God. I'm wet! I am so sorry! I completely forgot!" There was a water spot on the fabric in the shape of my butt.

From the hallway, I heard Michael laugh. "Hey, don't worry about it, Little Mermaid. That sofa was secondhand. You're not ruining anything special."

From the armchair, Harriet sighed. "I miss salsa." She smiled dreamily up at me. "Michael's father was an extraordinary dancer."

There it was again, the past tense. Again, I wanted to ask about Michael's dad, but I definitely didn't want to do so in front of Harriet.

"My lungs don't really allow me to dance these days. Not to mention the oxygen tank." Harriet laughed, but I couldn't bring myself to respond. I'd seen her unable to catch her breath that night, and I'd known she had an oxygen tank, but there was something about having it there before me, physical evidence that his mother might be more than just a little sick, that made it hard for me to even look directly at her.

"I should change," I said quietly, snatching up the change of clothes I'd brought with me. "Um, where's the bathroom?"

In unison, Harriet and Michael said, "Door at the end of the hallway."

I smiled and slipped away to change. It was pretty typical. Beach themed. The clear shower curtain featured tropical fish and bright pink and orange coral. The soap dish was shaped like a seashell. There were rainbow fish on the toilet seat. I got undressed, standing naked for a few minutes to let my skin air-dry, and then changed into my warm clothes.

When I got back, Michael was standing by a stereo in the corner of the room. There was an iPod sitting on the dock on top, and he scrolled and clicked around on the screen. Salsa music exploded into the room, and Harriet winced.

"Sorry," Michael muttered, and turned it down to a more manageable volume. He came over to me, and I tried to look confident when I faced him. I didn't miss the way his gaze slid down my body. "Okay, come here."

I met his eye. I expected him to have that jokey smile on his face that he always did, but his face was full of quiet seriousness, like this salsa lesson was of utmost importance. He held out his hand to me, and I was suddenly very aware that his mother was watching us. I put my hand in his, and I felt it all the way down to my toes. He curled his fingers around mine and then he tugged me toward him, taking my other hand.

———

I looked down at my feet, seeing his bare toes inches from my own, and when I looked back up, his eyes were so close, settled on me.

"Don't follow the music. I just want to show you the basic step. Okay, so on one, you go back with your right foot. On two, you pivot onto your left foot, and then on three, you step back to starting position. You don't move on four. On five, you do it again, but step forward instead of back. Does that make sense?"

I'd been staring at his lips. This close to him, I could see every tiny detail in them, the ridges and lines. I nodded.

And then he started counting. I stepped on his toes more than once, every time Harriet chuckling a little, but not in a condescending way. She laughed like this was the greatest day of her life. Michael's hips twisted gracefully as we moved forward and back and forward and back, and mine stayed firmly in place. He tried to coax me into movement, demonstrating how to twist my body.

"You just, you can use your whole body if you need to," he said, demonstrating a hip movement that started from his chest, all the way down to his feet, and I stood there, frozen. There was no way I was going to attempt a full-body maneuver like that, not in front of him, and certainly not in front of his mother.

"It's no use," I said instead of duplicating the movement. "I'm a robot."

Harriet laughed. "Awfully lifelike characteristics for a robot. Don't let Michael fool you. When he started learning to salsa, you would have thought all his joints were glued together. He couldn't move his hips, either."

I smiled at Michael. "You talk a big game for someone who started out stiff like me."

———

He rolled his eyes. "It wasn't that bad. You expected me to be able to do all those things in the pool. I bet you weren't so great at first, either."

"Actually, I was a natural."

Michael snorted and took up his place in front of me again, and I was happy that I'd managed to get out of attempting to roll my whole body in front of them, even though I was still completely unable to keep up with Michael's hip movements.

"Okay, Miss Robot, now do the exact same thing but out to the side instead." He nodded at me as if that should make perfect sense, and when he stepped out to his side, I went forward, and we slammed against each other.

"Sorry." I was blushing all the way down to my ankles. Maybe the dancing hadn't been such a great idea after all. There was a reason some people did it on TV and others didn't do it at all.

Michael smiled at me. "You're doing great. Here, let me show you."

Both of his hands dropped to my waist, his fingers digging wonderfully against my bones, and I shivered.

"Cold?" he asked, and even though he was still gripping my waist, he was doing an excellent job of avoiding my eyes.

"Just a little," I whispered. A lie.

He pressed into my hips on either side to show me which way to go, and once I had the step mostly down, he took my hands again, back into our earlier formation.

"You're doing so well," Harriet said from her chair, and I glanced over my shoulder at her. Her book was still open on her lap, but her eyes were fixed on us.

After we'd danced through a few songs, he stepped back from me. "Are you ready for a spin?"

My stomach jittered, and I let him lead me, showing me how to step under his arm, our hands twisting over each other as I spun around back to him.

"Okay, again."

I spun again, but this time, he spun, too, maneuvering under my arm so smoothly that I almost missed it.

Beside us, Harriet clapped her hands. "You're doing so good, Kate. You two work well together."

There was something about the way she said it, *you two,* that made me pull away from Michael. The music kept going, but I turned away from him, my stomach feeling all hot and churny as I looked over at the clock on the wall, out of show as opposed to actual concern about the time. "I should probably get home. It's getting late." I couldn't look at Harriet as I made my way to the door.

I was out the door before either of them could say anything, trying not to slam it behind me in my haste. I rushed into my apartment and shut the door as if the double layer of doors between us could fix whatever I'd broken.

When I lay in bed that night, all I could hear in my head was the sound of his voice counting, over and over.

One, two, three, four, five, six, seven, eight. Almost like counting swim strokes.

Eleven

$\mathcal{I}$t was an hour and a half drive from our spot in the parking garage to the aquatics center where my old high school held their swim meets. I took a spot in the stands as soon as the first race began, finding a place where I could let the people in front of me, a very enthusiastic group of adults, hide me from the room. I didn't want my father to accidentally catch a glimpse of me, even though he wasn't much one for scanning the stands.

My eyes traveled the room, the huge pool and the swimmers from the other team crowded around it, people in bodysuits waiting to warm up and their parents whispering in their ears. I scanned all the way to the end of the stands. I hadn't seen Harris when I came in, even though a handful of swimmers from the girls' and boys' teams were lounging by the starting blocks. For just a second, my eyes froze on them. They smiled and joked and some of them stretched, and it felt strange to be up here instead of down there. I'd never known life in the stands, and now I'd never be down there again.

I snapped myself out of it when I realized Harris was already on the block. They were starting with the relay, and I'd completely forgotten that he'd said he was swimming the event. Harris was a strong swimmer when he set his mind to it, but he'd never been able to outswim the other guys for a spot on the relay. They called the shot, and Harris dove into the pool.

I watched in shock as Harris pulled out in front, giving the team a significant lead that had them finishing far ahead of everyone else. Cal, always the last man on the medley, came out in an easy win, and while everyone else cheered, I watched as the other guys on the team patted Cal and Harris on the back and high-fived them.

I just stared at Harris. Way past six feet tall, he'd always been my giant best friend who could swing me over his shoulder with one arm, but this was different. His biceps bulged, his chest was solid, and I could see every muscle in his abdomen. He'd said he wasn't lifting, but he looked bigger to me.

My father approached him. I knew neither one of them was paying attention to the stands, but I still hunkered down behind the group in front of me until I was certain they wouldn't see me. I recognized their serious expressions, had experienced those small talks on many occasions. My father would take me aside and tell me quietly what weaknesses he'd spotted in the other team, what was wrong with my form, how I could pull ahead. Fixing, always fixing, to make sure I had the best time. I watched them now and felt something unpleasant collect behind my chest bone.

Harris put his sweatpants back on, leaving a damp mark around his middle. He watched the girls' medley without wavering, his eyes glued to the pool. I'd never seen him that interested in results. We were usually on the sidelines making fools of ourselves until my father got angry.

And then Harris glanced up at the stands.

I couldn't even bring myself to hide because I'd missed him so much. I saw the moment he recognized me. His eyes swept the stands, springing right by me until they came back with a double take, landing on me. Without worrying how it would look to anyone else, he raised a hand and waved. I waved back excitedly, but my joy was short-lived. My father caught Harris waving and searched the stands. When his eyes found me, I half expected him to smile, to actually be happy to see me.

But his face was blank as his eyes centered on me for just a moment and then turned away, yelling something to Coach Judd. Three more events took place, alternating between the girls' and boys' teams, before the teams lined up for the butterfly. Harris had always swum this event, so I moved down in the stands. I wanted to see how the new Harris moved up close. No point in hiding anymore.

I'd seen Harris swim a butterfly for the last ten years, but nothing like this. He plunged off the block and stayed under longer than everyone else, pushing himself immediately into first place. When he came back up, he was a like a cannon out of the water. He wasn't graceful. He was willful. He pushed himself hard, coming up on every other stroke for a breath, and I could see it there, in his face. He was concentrated. He wasn't blowing this off. He wasn't looking beside him to see his competition. He was pushing it, moving faster than I'd ever seen him move before.

When he hit the wall first on his last lap, I jumped up,

screaming loudly, even as everyone around me stared at me. When it was over, and I was still cheering, my father came up behind Harris. He put a hand on Harris's shoulder, turning him toward the hallway and the locker room. Even though I knew it would be a while before Harris had gotten his muscles back into shape, I followed them, only turning into the hallway after they'd vanished. I took a seat on the floor outside the boys' locker room.

"Hey, All-Star!"

Cal came down the hallway toward me. He was extremely cute, and I'd always effectively avoided him so as not to get him into trouble with my dad. He wore gauges in his ears when he wasn't swimming and had the longest hair of anyone on the team, his mane and eyebrows gold like straw. But how he was right now, coming down the hallway, was how I'd always known him: in jammers, a cap on his head, his earlobes empty, and a pair of goggles dangling from his hand.

"Hey, Cal." I pushed myself up the wall and leaned against it. Cal came close, the way he always did, standing just inside what I would normally designate my personal bubble.

"How's it going up there in Portland?" he asked, pressing one wet, open palm against the painted brick beside my head. "Not much competition, huh?"

I shook my head. "Are you calling yourself competition? Because I'm pretty sure that Harris just kicked your ass out there in the pool."

He snorted and pushed away from me. "Oh, give me a break. Harris has been your dad's little pet since you left. Those two are Frankenstein and his monster."

"Better be careful. Your jealousy is showing." He could say

anything he wanted behind Harris's back, but Harris was the one out there working hard enough to put himself in first after always getting lost in the middle.

"All right, Cal, keep it moving," a voice called from just outside the locker room. Coach Masterson was headed in our direction, his face stern.

Cal scrambled away from me and into the locker room.

"Come to see your old man?" my father asked. He was actually smiling. I guess he had reason to smile. He had a new accomplished swimmer, a new girlfriend, no sullen teenager to take care of. Maybe he was living the life he'd always wanted.

"I came to see Harris," I said coldly, staring down the hallway at bulletin boards and pictures of children playing in the pool plastered along the walls.

"Well, you can talk to me while you wait for him."

"I don't want to talk to you." I decided that I would just go back to the pool and see Harris later. We could go out for dinner or something, just the two of us. He could miss the after-meet party this one time. I made for the exit.

"Kate, come on," my father called.

I spun around. "I said, I don't want to talk to you." I'd been angry with my father before. He'd cheated on my mother, he'd kicked us out of our house, he'd tortured me in the pool for ten years only to throw it all away, but all that felt like nothing compared to the fact that he scared Lily into ditching her wedding. That was unforgivable.

My father stared at me, every single line on his face visible, until the door of the locker room swung open. Harris stepped into the hallway.

"Coach," he said, stepping up to my dad, his face focused and concerned. He didn't even see me, standing at the end of the hallway, trying to split just moments before. "Look, I know Cal's a great swimmer, but he's not focused enough on his last split. If he could keep his head in the game for the entire last leg, we'd be able to widen the gap. We could—" His eyes finally found me, and his sentence came to a halt. His entire expression changed, the stern curve of his mouth melting into a smile. "Kate!"

He stepped around my father and swept me up into a hug.

"God, work out much?" I said as he crushed me against him with arms of steel. He set me back down, and I tried to ignore the fact that my father was still standing close by, watching us.

"Yeah, well, when I'm not spending all my time entertaining my tiny little best friend, I have more time to spend in the gym."

I rolled my eyes. "Oh, please. Like April isn't taking up all that extra time?"

He opened his mouth to say something, but my father broke in. "Harris, we weren't finished talking."

Harris's eyes went wide and he spun around, like he'd completely forgotten that my father was even there. "Oh. Sorry, Coach. Um, I was just saying that I think Cal could use some work on his concentration."

My father's eyes swept to me quickly before focusing on Harris again. "I think we could all use a little work on our concentration. Maybe you shouldn't invite Kate to our meets if you're going to get distracted."

Harris looked like he wanted to respond but couldn't find the right words. I could.

———

"I'm not allowed to come to the meets anymore? I'm pretty sure you don't get to decide that."

"You're not part of this team anymore, Katherine. You shouldn't be here."

I tried not to let his words sting. He was right, after all. I *wasn't* part of the team anymore, but hearing him say it somehow made it more real. Why had it felt like they might not be able to go on without me, when they were obviously doing just fine? When my father had found my replacement so easily?

I didn't let him see that his comment hurt. "Shouldn't you be busy coaching other swimmers or something?" I said more confidently than I felt.

"That's what I have assistant coaches for." He focused on Harris again. "Get an early night. I want you ready for practice tomorrow."

I narrowed my eyes at him. "Don't you think he deserves a night off?"

"That was always your problem, Kate," my father snapped. "You weren't willing to work for it."

I could feel my body vibrating from my hairline to my knees. How dare he say that I didn't work for it? All I ever did when he was my coach was work my ass off. Day and night I was in the pool at home or at school, always eating what he told me to, always spending my time how he thought I should. No real social life. No boyfriend. Nothing but him and the water, all the time.

I wanted to snap back at him, find something that would hurt him as much as he'd just hurt me, but my brain was so muddled by his words that nothing would come out. My father had won. He'd successfully torn me apart, and he knew it.

———

Instead, I threw open the double doors at the end of the hall and went for the front door of the aquatics center, people staring as I rushed past them. When I finally made it outside, where cars were cruising past and people were coming into the center with their children in tiny swim trunks in tow, I felt like I was going to throw up.

"Kate!" Harris caught up with me. He put a hand on my shoulder and turned me to face him. "Hey, I'm so sorry."

I shrugged him off. "Go ahead. Go spend all your time with your new coach. I'm so glad to see that you're not the disappointment that I always was."

Harris shook his head. "You're not a disappointment. He's just lashing out. He's hurt."

"Oh, and I'm not?"

"I'm not saying that you're not. I'm just saying—" He broke off, running one of his large palms over his bald head. Then his eyes found mine, fierce and determined. "If you're so pissed at him, then show him. Swim your fucking heart out the next time we're all in the pool, and show him that you're still swimming your hardest. Show him that your power came from you and not from him."

"I'm not going to show him anything because I quit." I wanted to take it back as soon as I said it. That wasn't how I wanted to do it. I wanted to tell him out of confidence, not out of anger.

Harris went still, his eyes narrowing. "What do you mean?"

I threw my hands up. People were starting to file out of the center now, the meet finished. "I quit the team."

Harris shook his head aggressively. "You're the best. You can't quit."

"I can do whatever I want!" I sucked in a breath, and it felt like the whole world had gone quiet.

I could see his jaw moving beneath his skin. "You love the pool."

"Maybe I did, but . . ." I couldn't even bring myself to say it out loud. It felt like a bullet. "It's not enough anymore. All the bad has just covered up all the good."

His eyebrows creased in, and he looked like he was in pain.

"Do you hate me?" I asked carefully.

"Of course I don't hate you. But I think you're making a big mistake."

Behind him, I saw my father walk out of the center. His eyes found us standing on the curb, and his face went stiff.

"It's like I never even existed," I said without thinking. "You're his new favorite toy. All my work meant nothing."

Harris's eyes went hard. "You know this isn't about what he did to you. This is my future. I have parents to please, too."

He was right. I wasn't being fair. My father's personal life had nothing to do with Harris, but I couldn't seem to separate the two when everything hurt this much.

I just nodded. I couldn't be here anymore. I couldn't look at this life that I'd chosen to leave behind and be happy that Harris was still in it. "Call me later," I said. "You did really great." And then I turned and left.

◦ ◦ ◦

"Go! Go! Go! Come on, Kate! Come on!"

I could see the girl in the lane next to me every time I came up for a breath. She was almost a whole stroke ahead of me.

My arms burned and my lungs screamed, but I could hear my father on the sidelines, screaming my name so loudly that he drowned out everything else in the room. It echoed off the walls and around in my brain.

I knew the wall was approaching. I took one last breath to see that the girl next to me was pulling even farther ahead, and then I tucked under for my turn and kicked off the wall as hard as I could. When I came up, we were stroke for stroke. I had pulled ahead in my turn, and I could feel it, the energy pushing me forward, my legs kicking, kicking, kicking.

"Go, Kate! Go!"

I couldn't go any faster, didn't have anywhere else to pull speed from, but I kept pumping. I kept pushing, holding my breath for almost the entire last split, until my fingers hit the wall and I came up for air.

I didn't even see the scoreboard. I knew I'd won because my father was screaming, standing over me at the end of the lane. He reached down into the pool and pulled me out under my arms.

He held me to him, crushing me against him so hard that it was only a second before he was soaked, both of us dripping as the crowd cheered around us. "That was amazing. That was amazing," he was saying in my ear, over and over. I could hear the crack in his voice, and I thought he might cry, right there in front of everyone.

"Did I win?" I asked because I still hadn't seen the scoreboard.

My father threw back his head and laughed, finally letting me go. He grabbed me by my shoulders and spun me around to face the board, to see my time. Not only had I won first place, but I'd also set the state record in my event. I clapped my hand over my mouth at the same time that my father lifted me off my feet.

———

I wrapped my arms around him and closed my eyes, letting the moment soak into my skin.

"You're amazing," my father said in my ear. "So amazing. You were incredible. I can't believe you."

○ ○ ○

"Kate?"

I wiped the tears off my cheeks as fast I could before turning around to face Michael. He was barefoot and had a wrapped peppermint in his hand. I'd been on the roof since the moment I got home from Salem almost an hour before.

"Hey," I said, thinking maybe I could play it off like I hadn't been sobbing. Or at least maybe he would be nice enough to pretend he hadn't seen.

His eyebrows wrinkled, and it was like there was some direct connection between those eyebrows and my tears because I started crying again.

I groaned, pressing the heels of my hands into my eyes. "Just leave me here. I'm such a mess."

"Messes aren't so bad. People who have it all put together are overrated."

I opened my eyes, and he was standing with his knees pressed against the bench where I was sitting. I laughed a wet, snotty laugh.

"So, what happened? You went out to see your friend, right?"

I nodded and wiped my face with my hands. "Yeah." He was probably expecting more, perhaps expecting a monologue about how awful my life was. But I was too tired to give him that.

His eyebrows shot up. "Does that usually make you cry?"

I sniffled, embarrassed that he had to hear it. "No, but my dad kind of ruined everything." My dad *always* kind of ruined everything.

He finally sat beside me, the still-unwrapped peppermint crinkling in his fingers. "He's good at that, huh?"

I watched him open the peppermint and then pop it in his mouth. The minty smell was almost immediate. "Pretty much."

He stuck the wrapper in his pocket. "I know I might not be the best swimmer, and I know you disapprove of my smoking," he said, meeting my eye, "but I promise you can talk to me. If you need someone, I mean."

I sighed. "It's not a secret or anything. I just feel like I complain about my dad too much."

He shrugged and leaned back on the bench. "So? Is there a limit to how much you're allowed to complain about something? I don't remember them passing that law. I have a feeling people wouldn't stand for it."

I smiled down at my feet. "You never complain." It was true. He never so much as complained about getting behind on his homework. No matter what, he always seemed to have a smile on his face. And what did that say about me, the girl who was always crying and bitching about her parents?

"It's just not my style. Doesn't mean you don't have a right to."

I pulled my feet up onto the bench and rested my head on my knees. "You'll get tired of listening to it." *You'll get tired of* me.

"No, I won't."

He was so sincere, so completely confident in that fact. It was comforting. I looked at him for a second, at his lips pursed adorably as he sucked on his peppermint, at the messiness of his hair, at his bare feet, at the darkness of his eyes looking right back at me.

"My dad said that I didn't work hard enough. And then Harris and I kind of got in a fight, and I told him I quit the team, and I don't know where we even are right now."

Michael grimaced. "Sorry your dad is kind of an asshole."

I laughed. It was refreshing to hear him say that. To everyone else, my father was passionate. He was strong-willed, levelheaded, and a hard worker, and if I ever complained about him, I was just a spoiled teenager. Hearing Michael say something like that without even a hint of hesitation or even the smallest consideration of how things might look from my dad's point of view was such a relief that some of my tension melted.

"We ordered pizza. Why don't you come down to the apartment?" He gestured in the direction of the door.

"Who is *we*?"

"Oh, ya know, Ben, Marisol, Patrice, Jesse, and Mom."

"Oh. Okay." It wasn't like I felt like going home. If I'd wanted to go home, I wouldn't be on the roof right now. "I just need a second to not look so emotional." I wiped harder at my face, getting rid of the tear tracks and trying to let the cold air dry out my swollen eyes. "Did you come up to the roof just to eat a peppermint?"

He laughed and pulled out another peppermint as he crunched the other one between his teeth. "Got used to the fresh air. I might be able to give up the cigarettes, but I don't really want to give up the quiet time, you know?"

"Sure." I had no idea what he meant. Compared to the noise of my life before, the swim meets, the after-parties, the constant chaos of my own and my father's schedules, my life now felt like it was moving in slow motion. I wasn't looking for peace and quiet on the roof. I was looking for a distraction.

I could feel him looking at me, could feel his eyes burning into my skin, but I knew he didn't mean anything by it and that when he looked at me, he just saw a girl he could be friends with, maybe a girl he could trust. And I wanted him to see me that way. He made me feel so safe and so warm and so . . . normal.

We went down to his apartment in silence, and I stood aside as he opened the door. At first, no one seemed to notice us coming in, but then Ben, standing in Michael's tiny kitchen, said, "Hey, it's Kate!" and Patrice and Marisol smiled over at me. They were both on the couch, leaning in close to each other. Patrice spun around to face me as the door closed.

"Kate! I'm glad you're here! We were actually just talking about the chem project. Please tell us you have a brilliant idea."

Jesse was sitting on the end of the couch, doing something on his phone, and I didn't even see Harriet around. I could only assume she'd chosen to go to bed early. But a glance at the clock told me it wasn't really that early at all.

I took the seat by the reading lamp, the chair that Michael's mom had been sitting in when we'd met the day before, while Ben clattered around in Michael's kitchen.

"Actually, I had this kind of ridiculous idea," I said, "but I wouldn't even know how to make it."

Marisol made a face. "M'kay. What is it?"

"What if we made a blanket?"

They both sat in silence for a minute, and I thought I would die. They thought the idea was stupid. It was something that

—

came to me between the parking garage and the aquatics center that afternoon, and it seemed like a good idea at the time, but obviously I was completely and totally out of my mind because Marisol and Patrice still hadn't said anything when Ben finally came and took a seat at my feet on the blue carpet.

"What are we making a blanket for?" he asked, sipping on a glass of water.

Patrice and Marisol looked at each other, and then, as if they were communicating telepathically, they both wiggled their brows, frowned exaggeratedly, and then nodded their heads, all without speaking.

"That's not a bad idea," Marisol finally said to me. "My mom's been keeping my big brother's old jerseys in the garage since he went off to college. It would be totally cool to rip those up and use the letters and stuff."

"Yeah, we could use the numbers from them. That would be perfect," Patrice added. She looked excited now, like their hesitancy had never happened. In the dimness of the living room, her eyes shone like stars.

"You know, Michael's mom is really good with her hands." Ben ran a quick hand through his hair. "Remember I had that wardrobe malfunction before homecoming sophomore year, and she sewed it right up for me."

"What a touching story," Marisol said, "but I'm not asking Michael's mother to help us with our chem project."

"Why not?" Michael had grabbed a slice of pizza on his way into the room and was dipping his head back to take a bite. He spoke with his mouth full of stringy cheese. "She needs something to distract her. Give her something to do, please." I watched him scoot in close to Patrice, his arm going around her shoulders easily. He gobbled down the rest of his slice of pizza. "Kate, there's pizza in the kitchen. Want me to get you some?"

I shook my head. "No, it's okay. I can get it myself."

Patrice and Marisol went back to discussing the details of our project while Jesse watched with zero interest, and I went into the kitchen to scout out the pizza. There was still some cheese left, and I snatched up a slice.

"Want to help me ice the cupcakes?"

I jumped and spun around to find Ben leaning against the stove, his glass in his hand. I hadn't even heard him come into the kitchen, and I hadn't noticed the cupcakes that sat in the pan on top of the stove burners. "You made those?"

He nodded. "Baking is kind of my thing. They should be cool by now if you want to ice them with me."

"Sure."

He set his glass down, and I put my slice of pizza down. He handed me a knife and a container of icing. He took out another knife for himself as I popped open the lid. He handed me a chocolate cupcake. There was something about his proximity that I found unnerving. But I didn't move away. I dipped my knife into the icing and spread it in swirls on top of one cupcake.

"So baking, huh?" I asked him.

He narrowed his eyes at me. "Please do *not* tell me you believe in adherence to gender roles. That's just uncool. Coming from a female athlete, I would find that very disappointing."

I laughed. "I didn't say anything about gender roles." I swirled frosting onto a cupcake with my knife, not nearly as gracefully as he did.

He finished with one cupcake, set it back in the pan, and pulled out another one. "Some of the most famous pastry chefs in the world are men. Maybe those old gender roles were mixed up to begin with. Maybe the guys were meant to bake the pies while the girls went down into the coal mines."

I nodded. "I'd be much more successful as a coal miner than as a baker."

"Now that's what I'm talking about. You'd be hot covered in coal soot."

He smiled at me, and I felt myself blush. Ben was just the kind of guy who could make anyone blush, even if they were currently much more interested in the very *not* single guy one room over.

"I just didn't really see you as the baking type, that's all." I wasn't exactly sure what the baking type *was*. Martha Stewart, I guess. "How did you get into it?"

He shrugged. "I have seven aunts, and all of them make pies good enough to make your toes curl. I grew up watching them bake, and it's a little addictive. It's like free therapy." He smiled and licked icing off his finger.

"My mom was never really into baking, and I'm not much of a cook. Spent all my extra time in the pool." The sugary icing and the chocolate in the cupcake in my hand smelled so good. "Guess that doesn't really matter now."

A crease appeared between his eyebrows, but he only glanced at me for a second before focusing again on his cupcake. "What do you mean?"

I shrugged. "Nothing. I just, uh, decided not to join the swim team."

He pursed his lips. "Oh. Well, now you'll definitely have time for me to teach you how to bake."

He smiled, and I focused on the cupcake in my hand so that he wouldn't see my face flush. It was so strange to have someone show no reaction to me not being on the swim team. To him, it wasn't some grand revelation.

"Speaking of swimming, Michael told me you were teaching him."

I almost dropped my knife. I managed to hide my fumble. "He did?" To be honest, I was pretty surprised that he'd told Ben and hadn't told Patrice, but I guess guys tell each other things they don't tell their girlfriends.

"Yeah, and he also told me he was teaching you how to dance. To be honest, I'm a little offended you didn't ask me. I'm almost as good a dancer as I am a baker."

And before I even had a chance to put down my frosting-covered knife, Ben had spun me into his arms and we were slow dancing across the small kitchen, Ben holding me and me still holding the knife. We slid past the stove and Ben stopped long enough to take the knife out of my hand and set it on the cupcake pan.

When he looked down at me, his face had lost its flirtatiousness. His brown eyes traveled over my face, and I felt that look in my stomach. He smelled like sugar and expensive cologne. His eyes flitted into the living room, and I knew before I looked that Michael was watching us. I could feel it the whole time, the heat of that acute gaze that was always impossible to ignore.

We stopped moving abruptly, and I could hear the voices of

everyone chattering on as Ben reached over to pick up an iced cupcake. "Your cupcake, madam," he said, and I pried my eyes away from the couch. He smiled, so I took the cupcake as his arm fell away from my waist. I took a bite and licked the icing from my lips.

When I turned back to the living room, it was just in time to see Michael lean forward and kiss Patrice quickly and softly on the mouth.

o o o

At two in the morning, I was still staring up at my ceiling. I could hear Lily snoring softly in the living room through my open door, but I wasn't even close to falling asleep.

I got out of bed and walked silently into the living room. In the light from the TV, I could see Lily on the couch, her blanket halfway to the floor and her mouth hanging open.

I wasn't even sure what I was doing. I couldn't go up on the roof, like I normally would have in the middle of the night. I wasn't sure what was going on between the pool and me anymore, and I definitely couldn't see Michael. If anything, I needed to put some distance between us. It was getting too easy to let him be the person I went to when I was lonely, when I needed someone to lean on, and that wasn't fair to him or to Patrice.

I went to the door and pressed my head to it. This was about the time that he would get up for a cigarette. Would he get up in the middle of the night for fresh air and a peppermint? The door was cold, and I pressed my cheek to it to cool my burning skin.

Then I heard the door across the hall open. Without hesitation, I pressed my eye to the peephole and watched Michael step into the hallway. It was hard to tell through the distortion of the peephole, but I didn't see a cigarette in his hand.

He closed his door behind him, and then he just stood there. He looked one way down the hall and then the other way, and then he looked right at my door. It took all my effort not to flinch from the peephole. He couldn't see me, and I knew it, but with his gaze turned on me like that, it was hard not to react.

He ran his hand over his face and leaned back against his door, like we were about to start a conversation.

"Kate?"

I spun around at the sound of Lily's voice. She was sitting up, looking at me over the back of the couch.

"What are you doing?"

"Nothing." I walked back to the living room. "Nothing. You can go back to sleep."

She stretched out against the cushions, but she didn't go back to sleep. Her eyes were wide open. "Are you okay?"

I nodded, sent her a hopefully convincing smile. "Yeah," I lied. "I'm doing great." I knew I didn't have to lie to Lily, but it was two in the morning and I'd just been spying on the boy across the hall, so I didn't want to tell her the truth.

She watched me for a second, and when her eyes fell closed, I went back to bed.

Twelve

"You look tired."

I did my best not to glare at my mother for her comment. "I didn't get much sleep last night." After I'd gotten back in bed, I'd stared at my ceiling for another hour and a half before falling asleep.

Lily watched me over the rim of her coffee cup. She didn't know what I'd been doing the night before, but she'd obviously been aware enough to remember our exchange. She stayed quiet.

"How was practice on Thursday?" my mother asked, entwining her fingers under her chin and looking at me, waiting for an answer.

I opened my mouth, preparing a lie, but a knock at the door kept me from having to answer.

"I'll get it." I scrambled out of my chair and rushed to the door. Because he was the only person to ever knock on our door, I expected it to be Michael, but when I opened it, Patrice and Marisol were on the other side.

"Hi, Kate!" Marisol's smile was so bright, I felt a little blinded.

"Hey, guys." It was an odd thing to have people to whom you'd never given your address show up on your doorstep. Of course, you didn't have to give people your address when you lived one door from their boyfriend/friend.

"We're going to O'Dell's," Patrice said. "We thought you might want to come."

I was already reaching for my jacket. "Mom, I'm going out." I closed the door behind me and waited, expecting Michael to join us any second, but Patrice and Marisol went for the stairs. Apparently, it was girls only.

"Hope you don't mind," Marisol said to me over her shoulder as she headed down the hall. "We're trying to get more exercise."

"Not at all," I said, relieved. "What's O'Dell's?"

"O'Dell's is the best coffee shop in Portland," Patrice informed me. "It's completely necessary if you live here. Cozy and delicious."

"Including Leo, the gorgeous barista." Marisol nudged Patrice, who rolled her eyes.

We walked seven blocks to O'Dell's, a tiny coffeehouse with red walls and twinkle lights, and Marisol bought me a cappuccino despite my insistence that I could pay for it myself.

"So, do you want to work on the project this week?" Marisol asked once we were settled around a tall table on stools that Patrice had struggled to get onto. She was kind enough not to complain about our table choice. "You guys could come to my house and we could go through my brother's jerseys."

"This week works," I said, and as we sat there, I wished more than ever that everything else in my world would disappear. I wished I hadn't lied to my mom about quitting the team, I wished things weren't weird between Harris and me, and I wished that I didn't have a crush on someone else's boyfriend. Because if everything else in my life wasn't so screwed up, this moment would have been perfect: a chilly Sunday morning at a beautiful coffee shop with two people who'd been so kind to me and whom I really liked.

It could have almost been perfect, but then I saw a familiar face over Marisol's shoulder.

"Oh my God."

Patrice's eyes went wide. "What is it?" She and Marisol whipped around in their chairs.

It took Tom a second to notice the three teenage girls staring at him. He was ordering his coffee, and the three of us watched as he handed the cashier his credit card. He finally spotted us. His face went from relaxed to surprised to tense in a single moment, and then he raised one hand and waved in our direction.

I slid off my stool and went to him without excusing myself. "Hi," I said when I was close enough.

"Hey, Kate. You're here with your friends?" He nodded in the direction of Marisol and Patrice. They were watching us with rapt attention.

"Uh. Yeah." *Friends*. I liked the sound of that, but when I glanced back at them, I thought maybe I didn't deserve the title.

He smiled, but there was something sad in his eyes. "Glad to see you're doing well." He had no idea the mess I'd gotten myself into. "So, um . . ."

I blurted it out. "Lily isn't doing so great." Maybe on another day, I would have had more discretion. But I'd just ditched a conversation with my mother, I was having coffee with a girl whose boyfriend I had a huge crush on, and Lily's face moments before she asked me to get her out of that church was burned on my brain.

His eyebrows furrowed in a sad expression. He looked like a puppy after it had been smacked on the nose. "She's not?"

I shook my head. Lily might not have said it out loud, but I could tell that she wasn't okay. And maybe that meant she regretted what she did, or maybe it just meant she was lonely, but either way, she wasn't happy. "She misses you. She doesn't say so, but she's been skipping classes and sleeping a lot when she's home. She seems really sad. I shouldn't even be telling you this." I wasn't so sure Lily would approve.

He watched me fiddle with a cup full of sugar packets. "Then why are you?"

I shrugged. Because Lily was always looking out for me, and just for once, I wanted to be able to look out for her. Because I felt terrible about helping her ditch her wedding instead of talking her into staying. Because I was screwing up my own relationships so royally that the least I could do was try to fix someone else's. "Because I don't think you should give up on her."

His mouth turned down thoughtfully, but he didn't say anything, and I wondered if I'd overstepped my boundaries. It wasn't really my place to convince Tom to fight for Lily. I didn't even know for certain that Lily *wanted* Tom to fight for her. But I wanted her to know what it felt like for someone to care enough not to give up.

"Anyway, I should get back to my friends."

Tom nodded silently, but I saw something in his eyes, maybe something hopeful.

"Who's that?" Marisol asked when I made it back to the table. We watched Tom walk out the door with his coffee in his hand.

I settled back into my seat and found that my cappuccino had gone cold. "That's Tom, my sister's ex."

I saw Marisol bite her lip and glance at the door where Tom had disappeared. "He seems sad."

Patrice nodded and took a sip of her coffee before saying, "Was it a bad breakup?"

I hesitated, tapping my fingers on the table. Hadn't I passed Lily's business around enough? I looked up at them, their eyes focused on me.

"You don't have to tell us," Patrice said quickly, pressing her palm flat to the table between us. "It's okay. We just want you to know it's okay to talk to us about stuff. You know, if you need to."

I looked at her, and she didn't look away. The corners of her mouth curved up slightly, almost a smile. She had such an affectionate face, the kind of face that made you feel safe, the kind that made you feel like she'd never judge you.

"She kind of left him at the altar, and I kind of helped her."

Their eyes went wide.

"Wow," Patrice whispered. "That's, um . . ."

"It's been kind of awful," I said when she didn't seem able to finish her sentence. Once I started talking, it wasn't so easy to stop. "She's been sleeping on our couch, and I can tell she misses him, but she's scared that they'll end up like my parents, who are getting a divorce and are at each other's throats any time they're in the same room."

Their eyes got wider.

"We had no idea." Marisol was looking at me like I was a child who'd lost her favorite toy. "Are you okay?"

"I'm fine." It was the first time that I thought maybe it was true, that maybe I could be okay here as long as I had friends like Patrice and Marisol and Michael, people I could open up to without feeling guilty. Maybe here, with them, I didn't have to hide. But even as I opened up to them about these things, I bit back my secrets.

* * *

"I'll walk you up," Patrice said when we got back to my building. Marisol had gone home, but Patrice had walked with me back to my place. "I think I'll see if Michael wants to hang out. Do you think your sister is going to be okay?" she asked as we went back up the stairs.

"I honestly don't know," I told her. "She's always been so put together, you know? And now, she's just falling apart."

We stopped in the hallway outside my door. "People need to fall apart sometimes." She lifted her hand to knock on Michael's door, and I tried to make myself turn around and go inside, but I was desperate, desperate for these people who seemed to care about me even though they had no real reason to.

When Michael opened the door, his eyes went to me first, probably because I was at his eye level while Patrice, almost a foot shorter, stood between us. Then he noticed her.

"Hey," he said to both of us. "What's up?"

Patrice motioned over her shoulder at me. "Me and Marisol took Kate to O'Dell's."

"Oh. O'Dell's. Sounds like a great time." He smiled from her to me, and it seemed like his face was frozen like that.

Patrice glanced at me and smiled. "It was good." She turned back to Michael and pushed up on her toes to kiss him.

I turned around and unlocked my door.

"We'll see you tomorrow?" Patrice asked, and I gave them an awkward wave over my shoulder.

"Yeah, I'll see you guys tomorrow."

They disappeared into Michael's apartment, and I was left staring at the number on his door.

o o o

"Your friends are nice," I told Michael at our next swim lesson as we sat on the edge of the pool. "So different from everyone I knew at my old school." I didn't mention that that was because I mostly only hung out with Harris unless there was something swim related going on.

Michael laughed. "By different, do you mean boring?"

I dipped my feet into the pool and splashed just a little. Michael splashed back. "What are you talking about? They're not boring."

"Pizza and project talk?"

"If it weren't for you guys, I'd be spending all my time watching *America's Next Top Model* with my sister, so this week has been an upgrade."

"What would you be doing if you were in Salem?"

I made a humming noise, like I even had to think about it.

"On a Friday night after a meet? If my dad let me, I would have been at the after-meet party."

He held up a hand. "See? Exciting."

I swatted his hand away. "*Or* if my dad hadn't let me, I would have gone home, sat with my dad while he verbally perfected my technique for our next meet, gone to bed early, and then gotten up early for a jog before a nice early-morning swim practice."

He whistled. "Fun weekend."

We were silent for a moment, and just when I was wondering if I was a buzzkill, Michael said, "It looks like you and Ben really hit it off."

I was getting cold, now that my feet were in the warm water and the rest of me wasn't. "Yeah. He's sweet." I didn't look at him.

Maybe I really *did* like Ben. He made me smile, and it was nice to be noticed. Not many of the guys at school had really noticed me. I'd caught a few looking as I walked past, but other than Ben and Michael, not many of them even talked to me.

When Michael didn't respond, I said, "Patrice is really sweet, too. How long have you two been dating?"

He looked away from me, down at the water, running his fingers through his hair. "Four months."

Four months felt like a long time. "Ben said you and Patrice have been friends since you were kids."

"We met in kindergarten. Grew up together. We met Marisol in middle school and then we met Ben two years ago, when he moved here."

"Is he really going to Stanford?" I wasn't sure why I found the concept so surprising. Ben was obviously smart and talented. I supposed it was because he seemed so relaxed, as if I could judge someone's work ethic by the way they acted while icing cup-cakes.

Michael nodded. "That's the plan at least, but nobody's doubt-ing that he'll get in. Ben's a pretty smart guy." He pushed himself up abruptly and stood over me. "We should probably get started."

The sound of his wet feet smacking against the concrete gave me goose bumps. We were the only ones at the pool. People rarely came up at night and during the week, which was perfectly fine by me. I liked not having an audience for once.

"Okay, get in streamline," I told him, slipping into the water from the edge instead of walking around to the stairs like Mi-chael had. It was still as cute this time as it was the last time he did it, but I pretended not to notice.

Like before, the water was almost peaceful, but there was some-thing tentative about it, like it was a living thing that could turn on me at any moment. As long as I kept my mind focused, kept out thoughts of everything else, the water was almost my friend again.

I showed him how to do a freestyle stroke, but like every other casual swimmer, he had trouble keeping his head down. Coming up to breathe on the side wasn't a normal movement, and he didn't like it. And since he wasn't exactly training for the Olym-pics, I let him bring his head straight up to breathe, even though it negatively affected the rest of his stroke, pushing him out of form to make his shoulders hunch forward as he did it.

"Okay, I'm going under. I want you to do it one more time. Don't forget that you're trying to move the water back. You're not trying to propel yourself forward."

"Wait," he said before I'd even really gotten the end of my sentence out. "You're going under? What do you mean?"

I pointed at the bottom of the pool, even though his view of my arms would have been distorted past the waterline. "I'm going to lie on the bottom so I can see your stroke from underneath."

His eyes flitted straight down and then back at me. "You can do that?"

I didn't tell Michael that I could hold my breath for just over two minutes, even though I knew he would probably find it impressive. Michael had a really hard time holding his breath, seeing as how he had the lung capacity of a mouse, thanks to smoking. I didn't want him to feel any worse than he already did.

"Yeah, I can do that," I told him. "Once I'm on the bottom, push off from the side. Don't leave me hanging too long. I'm not David Blaine or anything." I pulled in a lungful of air before blowing it out and letting my body sink to the bottom of the pool.

Before chaos had disrupted my life, being under the surface was my favorite thing in the whole world. I loved how quiet everything got. How you could hear everything going on in your head, the sound of your heart beating. I loved letting the water plug my ears and the muted groaning it made all around me, like whale noises. I loved letting my limbs float up like they weren't attached to me at all, my hair coming out of its ponytail to swim like seaweed around me. This, beneath everything, where nobody could touch me, had once been the safest place on earth.

But now I could feel myself teetering on the edge. My heart beat faster than it should, and I was almost desperate to shoot back to the surface for air. But I held myself down, letting out tiny breaths to kill the quiver in my stomach.

And before something terrible could take hold, Michael pushed off the wall, catching my attention. I watched as he swam freestyle from one side of the pool to the other. It was a sloppy lap, but he made it the whole way.

When he touched the wall, I pushed away from the bottom, coming up to take the kind of breath that was cold and relieving and somehow disappointing. I wiped a hand over my face, and when I opened my eyes, Michael was smiling.

"Hey, I did it."

I laughed. "Well, you would move much faster if you actually kicked your feet, you know."

His smile faded. "I wasn't kicking my feet?"

I laughed again. "Not really. You may have flapped once or twice."

He was contemplative, like if he thought hard enough, his mistake would become a success.

"So this is where you've been spending your time," I heard someone say, and both of us splashed around to see that my sister had walked out onto the roof, her towel wrapped around her shoulders like a blanket to protect against the cold air until she could get into the heated pool.

"I've been teaching Michael to swim." I catapulted myself out of the pool as Michael took the stairs, and then we were both shivering and wet in front of my sister. Her eyes went back and forth between us, and I felt like the principal had just caught us skipping classes.

"Is this what you've been doing when you tell Mom you're

at practice?" she asked, and I saw Michael fidget uncomfortably.

I turned to him. "Hey, why don't you head to your place? I'll meet you there in a minute."

He took off for the door. It closed behind him with a slam.

"I'm going to tell her," I said once he was gone. "I will."

Lily shook her head and tossed her dry towel onto a nearby bench. Michael's own towel was draped over the table beside it. He'd left it in his hurry to get away. I went to grab it, along with the stuff I'd brought with me, but Lily put her hand on my arm before I could snatch it all up.

"Kate, are you sure this is a good idea?"

I sighed and moved around her to get my towel. I wrapped it around me and turned to face her. "I'm going to figure out a way to tell Mom soon."

"I'm not talking about Mom." Her jaw had gone tense, and in a strange way, she reminded me of Dad, but her eyes were infinitely softer.

I looked at the door, which had firmly shut behind Michael.

Lily put her hand on my arm again. I sighed, clenching my towel around me tighter. "How do you make yourself stop wanting someone?" I asked her.

She didn't bother to answer. We both knew she didn't have the answer.

I headed for the door. "We're just friends," I finally said. "I want to be his friend."

With a hand on the doorknob, I glanced back at her standing by the pool with that look on her face that said we were both drowning.

———

"I'll figure it out," I told her. "Don't tell Mom, okay?"

She nodded, and I left her there.

*   *   *

Before I'd even shut the door to Michael's apartment behind me, he had a finger to his lips to tell me to be quiet. He'd already changed into dry clothes.

"My mom's asleep," he whispered, coming close to me. "Is it okay if we do it in my bedroom?" He blushed. "I mean . . . I just meant the lesson. Is it okay if we do the lesson in my bedroom?"

I tried not to smile. Michael was supremely adorable when he was flustered. I just nodded as I felt myself relaxing. It was always somehow relieving not to be the most nervous one in the room.

I lifted my clothes between us. "Could I change first?"

When I came out of the bathroom a few minutes later, Michael wasn't in the living room anymore. I knew that his mom's room was the one by the kitchen, the master bedroom, just like my mom's was. So I went back down the hall and tapped on the closed door next to the bathroom.

He opened the door, and I stepped in and froze. Behind his bed was a huge mural of a beach. The sky was blue and the waves were rolling in, and I walked up to it.

"This is amazing." I went around the side of his bed to see it better. Up close, the sand was pixelated, everything a little less perfect, a blown-up image instead of a painting. It was beautiful, and I reached out and touched it before I even realized what I was doing. I snatched my hand back and turned around. Michael had closed the door. "Sorry," I told him. "I didn't mean to barge in here."

He put his hands in his pockets. He had changed into a gray T-shirt and blue jeans, and I was suddenly very aware of him in this room with me. We'd never been alone in an enclosed space. The bed was between us, and he looked so amazing standing there with his wet hair pulled in all directions, and I realized I shouldn't have agreed to come to his bedroom because I wanted to launch myself across the space between us and kiss him.

I needed to distract myself. "Can I ask you a question?"

His smile stayed intact. "Sure."

"How long has your mom been sick?"

He frowned, but not like he was sorry I'd asked. We never talked about him, and the longer I knew him, the more I thought that was the way he liked it, like he could erase all the bad things if he never spoke about them.

He sat down at the end of his bed, and I moved to stand in front of him. I hadn't noticed anything else in his room until that moment. It felt the way normal rooms feel lived in, with clothes in random places and water glasses by the bed. His bed was made, his bookshelf messy. A framed picture of Michael and his mother sat on one shelf.

"She got really sick when I was eleven. My dad was already gone by then. He died when I was a baby." He placed his hands on his knees, his shoulders slumped. "She started smoking when she was just a kid. She was in almost perfect health until one day she just couldn't breathe. She went to the hospital and they thought she'd just had an asthma attack even though she'd never had asthma before. They said sometimes people develop it as adults. Then she had a horrible case of bronchitis. And then that turned into pneumonia, and then they told her to stop smoking. She didn't. She smoked for two more years before she quit, but the damage was done. Her lungs never really healed the way they were supposed to, and it's hard for her to do things. She has these episodes where just sitting up in bed makes her wheeze. And sometimes we go to the hospital so they can pump her full of steroids."

I sat down on the bed next to him. "I'm so sorry."

He shrugged. "People make stupid decisions that come back to bite them. It's nothing new."

I nudged him a little with my elbow, felt how cold his skin was from being not quite dry. "How long have you been smoking?"

"It used to be a game Patrice and I played. We'd put my mom's cigarettes in our mouths to look cool when we were hanging out alone here. We went to this party one night, and I had my mom's cigarettes in my pocket. I was fourteen. That was the first night we lit them. A month later, I was hooked. Patrice hated them." He shrugged again. "I've been trying to quit. It's only been three years, I should be able to, you know? But things have been hard with my mom, and I keep coming up with reasons why I need to sneak out at two in the morning to have one." He scrubbed his hands over his face. "I'm such a loser."

I put a hand on his arm, feeling the tiny fine hairs across it. "You are not. Being addicted to something doesn't make you a bad person."

"Right. It just makes you weak."

His eyes met mine, and there was a sort of desperation in them.

I wasn't supposed to be the person who comforted him, who helped him through bad times. He had Patrice. He had Ben. But then why did it feel like he was confiding in me?

"You're anything but weak," I whispered. I so desperately wanted him to believe it. I wanted him to see himself the way I saw him: brave and beautiful and kind.

His eyes found mine, scanning my face with a sadness that I couldn't quite decipher. I hated to see him lose even a little bit of his light.

"Hey, do you want to dance?" I asked him.

"Yeah." His voice was still a little weak, his face drooping.

I took both of his hands in mine and pulled him up off the bed, up against me. Some of the life sparked in his eyes when we stood close, and even though we didn't turn on any music, we started to move.

During our last lesson, there'd been enough space between us to fit an ocean, barely any contact, and quick movements to keep us occupied. But there in Michael's bedroom, he held me just a little too close, gripped me just a little too tight as he taught me how to do different turns. Every time I went under his arm and he spun me back against him, it was with such force that we bumped together, until eventually, we weren't even trying to salsa anymore, and I had my head on his shoulder as we swayed.

"I don't want anything to happen to you," I said against his shoulder. It was sharp and digging into my cheekbone, but I didn't care.

I felt his fingertips in my back. "Yeah?"

I pressed my forehead into the skin of his neck, knowing we shouldn't be dancing like this, closer than I'd danced with Ben the night before, closer than I'd ever been with anyone in my life.

I knew that he wasn't mine, that he belonged to someone else who he cared about enough to hold on to. And I knew that we could hurt her—Patrice and her kind smile.

But she was hard to focus on when I felt his breath on my ear. "Okay."

Thirteen

The next night, Lily brought a guy to dinner. It really shouldn't have been that shocking. Lily was beautiful and smart and successful. She was the kind of girl guys wrote poems for and followed around like puppy dogs when she was in high school. Guys would show up on our doorstep, asking with desperate eyes if she was home.

This guy didn't look desperate. He looked like he knew he belonged with her. He had dark hair and bright eyes and came to dinner wearing a suit, which told me he was probably someone she met through one of her business major friends. He sat at the head of the table and smiled every time someone glanced at him for even a second. He knew he was handsome.

We were all quiet, unsure what to say with a stranger at the table.

"Any news on your first meet?" my mother asked as we all cut into our steaks. I wasn't a big fan of steak, but it had become a staple when we lived with my father. He was always waxing poetic about how an athlete like me needed the correct amount of protein, and I could only ingest so much chicken.

I knew I wasn't going to be able to lie much longer. I'd just gone to Harris's first meet. The districts weren't all that different. I had to have a meet at some point, right?

"Soon. But you totally don't have to come. It's not even that big of a deal, and you probably need to work." How much bullshit could I throw out before my mother got suspicious?

My mother shook her head. "Absolutely not. I'm not going to miss your first meet."

"Well, I haven't been paying as much attention as I should at practice. I'll find out on Tuesday." That bought me a whole four days.

"What sport do you play?" the hunk asked me. He stopped eating for a moment to look at me, waiting for an answer and not putting food in his mouth so that he could respond.

"Kate is a swimmer," my mother answered proudly, saving me the trouble. "She came in first in her event at the State Championships last year. She's absolutely incredible. She could even go to the Olympics someday." My mother was glowing, and I felt my stomach twist. I was never going to the Olympics, and the longer I held on to this secret, the more it was going to hurt, and I knew it. But I couldn't make myself say anything in front of Lily's date. Lily was staring down at her dinner plate.

When dinner was over, my mom and I sat on the couch, sharing a handmade blanket we'd gotten on a trip to Idaho. Her eyes were glued to the TV, watching a home remodeling show that I found particularly boring, and I watched her closely. She'd barely given any sign since her breakdown before the wedding that anything was wrong, but I could see it in the lines around her mouth, the bags under her eyes, the too-much enthusiasm anytime she smiled.

"Mom, are you okay?"

She glanced at me quickly. "Yeah. I'm not cold. Do you need more blanket?"

"No, I just meant . . ."

She looked at me more fully then, her eyes understanding. "Sweetie, I don't want you to worry about me. You have a lot to think about, okay?"

But I wanted to worry about her. My father and I had always worried about each other because we were together so much, but maybe it was my mother I should have been looking out for. She was the one who always got left behind, the figure in the doorway waving good-bye as we sped off someplace.

"I won't lie and say it's been easy," she finally said. "Nothing makes much sense right now. I don't know that I . . ." She trailed off, tucking the blanket around her toes. "I don't know that I would have been able to do this without the two of you here. I just want you to be happy. You've got the team, and Lily has—" She cut off, her eyebrows furrowing. "Lily has school, of course, and this new guy." I could tell by the downward curve of her mouth that she couldn't remember his name. "I'm not so sure about him. It's great that she's moved on, but I think I just miss Tom."

It was the first time I'd heard her mention Tom since the wedding. In fact, we hadn't discussed the wedding at all.

"I think she still loves him." It was much easier to talk about it when I wasn't talking about it with Lily.

———

Her eyes flitted to the closed door. Lily and her date had gone out for "fresh air" half an hour ago. "You think so?"

I shrugged. "I definitely don't think she's done with him yet. And I think maybe he's not, either." I didn't really want to tell her that I'd spoken to Tom. I still wasn't positive I had done the right thing by butting into their business.

She eyed me for a long time, and I could see the doubt on her face. "It doesn't always end like this," she said. "People don't always give up on each other. Your grandparents were married for sixty-five years before Grandpa died."

"Right." But when I tried to imagine my grandparents, happily married for as long as I knew them, I imagined instead Michael's parents, dancing and laughing.

I turned to face my mom and put my knees up against my chest. "Why do you think it is that some people can be happy even when their lives are falling apart? And some people can't seem to be happy even if they have everything they thought they wanted?"

She blinked at me. "That's a very serious question."

Across the hall, Michael was taking care of his extremely sick mother who had been sick for so long, and he still smiled at me. He still wanted to teach me to salsa and had a mural of a beach on his wall and brought me ice cream on the roof. How did he do that? How could he be such a comfort to me when his life was so hard?

And here I was. I'd been given the chance to start over, to quit the swim team, to get out from under my father's thumb, and I just felt . . . numb.

She pondered for a moment. "Being happy is a choice. It's not a destination as much as it is a state of mind. No one can be happy all the time, but you can let yourself be happy in certain moments. Hold on to what's good in your life and try to let go of what's not. I know it sounds easier than it actually is, but you can always find something to smile about. Even if it's something small."

I had things to smile about. Michael and Patrice and Marisol and Ben had all been so kind to me when they didn't have to be. I'd lain at the bottom of the pool and watched Michael swim for the first time in his life. I'd watched Harris swim in a way he had never been able to before. He'd worked hard and motivated himself enough to push ahead of everyone else who'd told him he wasn't good enough, and I'd been happy when he'd crossed the finish line.

None of these things was perfect, but they were good enough.

"Do you have things to smile about?" I asked.

She reached over and pressed her hand to my knee. "I've got you."

○ ○ ○

Mom went to bed, and Lily was still off with the hunk, so I went to my room. I was supposed to read a book for Lit, *The Crucible*, but my eyes kept drifting closed.

Then the sound of my door creaking open woke me up. Lily was just a shadow in the room that was only partially lit by my bedside lamp. She was still wearing the clothes she'd worn to class, her pants rustling in the silence as she came in and shut the door. She stopped for a second, and I didn't think she knew I was still awake. She walked over to my window and put her hand against the glass.

——

She turned and saw me watching her, and she came over to get into bed with me. I scooted over to let her in, and she curled her hands up under her chin the way she had when we were kids and we'd shared a bed because she'd been watching scary movies.

"I don't know what I'm doing," she whispered to me.

"Me neither," I whispered back. It was probably the most honest thing I'd said all week.

"I miss him."

I had a lot of things I wanted to say, but I let her fall asleep without saying any of them.

o o o

When my phone rang loudly on the bed between us, it made us both jerk awake. It was still dark out, and I didn't know if it was late at night or really early in the morning. My bedside lamp was still shining down on me. Michael's name flashed across the screen.

"Who is it?" Lily mumbled, her eyes already halfway closed.

"No one," I told her, and put the phone to my ear. I turned over so my back was to her. "Hey," I said quietly.

He didn't say anything at first, and I thought maybe he'd pocket-dialed me. "I really want a cigarette," he said finally, and I was surprised by how intimate it felt to have his voice in my ear.

I tucked my arm around myself, like I could hold my emotions inside my skin. "Michael, you've been doing so well. Why don't you have ice cream instead?"

He chuckled. "Not quite a nicotine kick."

"You're right. Ice cream is way better."

After a long silence, he said, "Meet me in the hallway."

He hung up before I could answer, and the screen blinked his name at me to let me know the call had been disconnected. I sat up in bed, feeling jittery even through my sleepiness.

"Where are you going?" Lily asked, her hand coming up to rest on my arm.

"I'll be right back. Go back to sleep." I was glad I'd never changed into pajamas so I didn't have to worry about Michael seeing me in another pair of superhero boxers. I turned off the lamp and hoped that Lily wouldn't remember a thing in the morning.

I walked as silently as I could through the apartment, praying that my mother had been able to sleep and wouldn't be sitting up in her bed listening for sounds the way I sometimes did when I woke up too early in the morning.

Out in the hallway, there was a bowl of chocolate-chip ice cream on the floor waiting for me. Michael sat with his legs stretched out and his back against his front door, a bowl in his lap. I sat opposite him, next to my apartment door, my legs straight out beside his.

"Thanks for distracting me."

"Thanks for the ice cream." I ate a large spoonful. I was taken by how quiet it was in the hallway. It felt like the whole world was in a snow globe, water pressing in on our lives until everything was artificially peaceful.

"Wasn't sure what flavor you wanted."

"This is great." Something about the air between us was strange. He didn't say anything, and I didn't say anything, but it wasn't because we didn't have anything to say. His blue eyes refused to meet mine.

"Michael."

He looked up.

"Talk to me." Other than that one conversation in his bedroom, he almost never talked about himself. But I could see the need behind his eyes. I could see the way things were building up inside him.

He sighed and dropped his spoon into his bowl. He shook his head, as if what he was about to say was the dumbest thing he could imagine. "I have this fear that in the middle of the night, Mom is just going to stop breathing, and I'll be sleeping and I won't have any clue, and she'll be gone by the time I wake up."

I gripped my spoon tightly. "You can't torture yourself like that."

"And yet, I do." He sent me a weird close-lipped smile. "Tell me I'm not crazy."

"You're not crazy."

The corners of his mouth tipped up. "Tell me something you're afraid of."

I let my head fall back against the wall behind me. "Sometimes I'm afraid I'm going to wake up and everything's going to go back to the way it was, that my father will be waiting outside my room, ready to go on our morning jog."

He was already done with his ice cream, and he set the bowl aside. "Was it really that bad?"

I shrugged. "I didn't really think so at the time. It just felt normal. But when I got here and I realized I didn't have to do it anymore, it was a relief. Like I could breathe. I miss the pool, but I don't miss him."

He didn't say anything for a long time, but he had that look in his eyes that he got when he was waiting to see what I would do next, like he was trying to figure me out, all the way down to my DNA. "Tell me something good about him. Your favorite thing."

I stared at him, watching the way his fingers moved absently over the ridges in his spoon. My own bowl sat half-empty on the floor beside me. I set my head in my hand and watched him, taking in, just for a second, how beautiful he was. "When I was a kid, we would take these road trips every summer out to California and spend, like, two weeks at the beach. And every time we went, Dad and I would be at the beach from sunup to sundown, riding the waves and letting them pull us back to the shore. It was always so much fun, and I just remember loving it because it was the only time he ever really got in the water with me. He was always just a spectator, not a swimmer. It was nice to have him beside me instead of yelling at me from the sidelines."

"You're a beautiful swimmer," Michael said, his voice transparent, like it wasn't quite whole.

"You're not so bad yourself." I meant it completely. Michael had learned really quickly for someone who'd only known how to dog-paddle.

"Tell me something about your mom."

His face lost a little of its ease, but he spoke anyway. "She has this obsession with the aquarium downtown. We used to go all the time to visit the fish. She was always so fascinated by this idea that we could be so different from them and that they could breathe underwater, like it was some secret to the beauty of the universe."

"What fish is her favorite?"

This time, he smiled all the way. "Jellyfish. She likes that

———

they light up." His eyes lost their focus, and I let him wander off without me.

We were quiet together, and it felt nice to have someone I could just be silent with.

"You should go back to bed," he said when my eyes started to fall closed. There was still ice cream melting in my bowl, but I had had a few too many sleepless nights and couldn't seem to stay awake this time.

"I don't want you to smoke."

He laughed. "I won't. Now go get some sleep."

I nodded, not really in a position to fight him. He helped me to my feet, and I gave him the white porcelain bowl before opening my front door.

"Hey, Kate?"

"Yeah?"

"Thanks."

I looked at him standing behind me, bowls stacked and mouth pulled down solemnly. I didn't say anything else; I just went inside and crawled back in bed beside Lily.

∘ ∘ ∘

Patrice, Marisol, and I spent almost an hour in her parents' two-car garage, locating boxes of her brother's old jerseys. At first, I thought for sure that nobody owned enough sports jerseys to make an entire table of elements from, but when we started opening the boxes in the middle of Marisol's living room, I found that I was wrong.

Every jersey that I pulled out had the last name of an athlete with their number on the back. The boxes seemed never ending, and when Marisol's mother came into the living room, her long, dark hair in a low ponytail on the side of her head and a bottle of water in her hand, she just shook her head, sighed, and left the room again.

"I think your mom needs to let go of her golden boy," Patrice muttered.

Marisol scoffed. "Yeah, like that'll ever happen. Speaking of golden boys, what's going on with Michael? He went over to your place last night, right?"

My mind shot to last night, sitting in the hallway with Michael, eating ice cream.

"Yeah, he came over. It was nice. We had a good time. Watched TV. I don't know. You know how Michael's been lately. I feel like he can't concentrate on anything."

It felt like she was talking about some stranger and not Michael, whose eyes were always so focused, so intense.

I separated jerseys into two piles, one that I could use and one that didn't have anything that I needed. A printout with the table of elements sat in the middle of our circle.

Marisol rolled her eyes. "What I really want to know is, has that boy divested you of your virtue yet?"

I felt sick to my stomach, and I kept my eyes glued to the jersey in my hand, pretending that I was paying attention to it when my hands were frozen. Perhaps I'd just died and this was rigor mortis.

Patrice smacked Marisol on the shoulder. "Michael has been a perfect gentleman."

"Sure, but after four months, even a gentleman tries to get him some."

They both giggled, but I couldn't see what was so funny. I

could feel my face getting hot, and tried to remember that Patrice was my friend and not some rival to be jealous of. I decided to start cutting out letters with a pair of sewing scissors we'd found in Marisol's junk drawer.

Patrice kept talking. She must not have noticed that I was dying. "To be honest, I'm not really sure what he's waiting for. I'm sending him all the signals. I've been waving him home for almost a month now."

As if the hands of fate would prefer I didn't hear such a scarring conversation, I ripped through a patch of fabric too quickly and cut myself with the scissors.

"Ouch! Shit! Son of a—!"

Both the girls gasped and reached out for me, but Patrice got to me first. She stared down at my hand, which was stinging and throbbing at the same time. And bleeding.

"How deep is it?" Marisol asked as she scrambled up off the floor.

Patrice examined my hand. "Not too deep. Not stitches deep."

"Okay, good," Marisol said, rushing down the hallway. When she reappeared, she had a first-aid kit with her, and to my relief, Patrice passed me over to her. Marisol used an alcohol swab to clean away the blood, applied Neosporin, and covered it with a bandage.

The doorbell rang.

Marisol sent me a devious grin. "I'll get it."

I narrowed my eyes at her and watched her disappear around the corner.

"Did she invite Roger?" I asked with a laugh, but Patrice just smiled at me as we listened to Marisol open the front door. And then Marisol was back, and Ben was trailing behind her.

"Hi," Ben said.

"Hey." My stomach rioted with nerves, and it only took one glance in Marisol's direction to tell me that she had invited Ben over because I was here.

"I was out for a walk," Ben said, pushing his hands into his pockets. "I live just down the street. I don't know if Marisol told you."

"Nope." I sent Marisol a wide-eyed look, but she pretended not to notice.

"I was just stopping by to see what Marisol was up to, but maybe if you wanted to finish my walk with me?" Ben smiled, and there was so much confidence in it. He knew I knew that this was all a setup, and he was clearly fine with the fact that I knew. And he was certain of success.

I stumbled over my words. "Actually, we're kind of working on this project."

"We can finish without you," Marisol jumped in quickly.

"Besides," Patrice went on, "you're injured. You should take the rest of the evening off."

"Injured?" Ben asked, his smile fading and his eyebrows creasing.

I lifted the hand with the Band-Aid pasted in the center. "Scissor accident."

He made a clucking noise with his tongue. "You shouldn't be careless with scissors, Kate. Don't you watch horror movies?"

"I saw *Child's Play* when I was a kid, and that pretty much did it for me."

He smiled but didn't respond to my comment. "Walk with me?" he asked, reminding me that I hadn't actually given him an answer. A glance at the girls told me they were waiting patiently as well.

"Sure," I finally conceded. It wasn't like it would be difficult to spend time with Ben. I liked him, and he made me laugh.

"Great." Ben's smile got bigger, and he helped me up off the floor and into my coat before leading me out into the night.

"Have a nice time!" Patrice called from the doorway, looking as excited as if it was *her* going out with a cute boy.

Marisol catcalled, and I sent her a horrified look while Ben laughed.

"You know," I said when we were out on the sidewalk, "you could have just asked me out. You didn't have to plan this whole elaborate 'I was out for a walk' scheme." I made quotes with my hand, and he nudged me with his elbow.

"I know. But Marisol was having fun with it, so I just let her. But I would have asked you out eventually."

I smiled up at him, surprised by how comfortable I was with him. It felt like we'd known each other forever.

He stared down at me while we walked, until we'd reached the end of the street and turned onto another one. "I really like hanging out with you," he said.

I blushed. What gave him the confidence to just go around telling people he liked them and asking them out on *walks* without even so much as a stammer? I wished some of his confidence would rub off on me.

"Thank you" was all I could say.

"Have a lot on your mind?" he asked after we'd been walking

in silence for a minute, past houses and lawn statues and white picket fences.

I shrugged. "What am I supposed to talk about?"

He laughed. "Whatever you want to talk about." He pulled at the cuff of his sweater, straightening it casually, and there was something about the way he did it, something so sophisticated. He was like an Asian James Bond.

"I guess I'm just a little overwhelmed."

His eyebrows shot up. "Because of me?"

"No, not you." I ran my hand through a bush as we passed by, the leaves cool on my fingertips. "It's just everything, I guess." I was definitely not a conversationalist, and Ben was going to figure that out any second now.

"Why don't you tell me about it?"

We stopped in front of a house where a little fountain gurgled on the front lawn.

"Michael hasn't told you all my secrets yet?"

He sent me a strange look, holding my eye for a long moment, until I felt like he was looking right through me. "No. No secrets. Michael's not that kind of guy. I don't know if you noticed, but he doesn't even really talk about himself."

I nodded. "I noticed." We started walking again, and I could hear traffic passing on a nearby street, while ours was silent.

"Besides," he went on. "I want to hear your secrets from you, not someone else." There was something about the way he said it that made me sad. Maybe because it was obvious Ben was interested in me, and even though I really liked him, I didn't think I *like* liked him, and that tiny little fact was like an ocean between us. Because apparently I could only want what I couldn't have.

I scoffed. "Maybe I don't even have secrets." I tried to play it off as a joke, but when he glanced over at me, his eyes were serious.

"Everyone has secrets, Kate."

My stomach churned, and I became desperate for a subject change. "What are you going to study at Stanford?"

He smiled down at his folded hands. "Has everyone been bragging about me?"

"Something like that."

"Engineering. I want to be an astronaut."

It had been shocking enough to me that he wanted to go to Stanford, but for him to have such a huge dream, one that I could tell he was confident about achieving, was astonishing. "Wow. An astronaut. That's incredible."

He shrugged. "It's the only thing I've ever really wanted, ever since I was a kid. This just feels like the natural next step."

"What's it like, knowing exactly what you want to do with your life?"

He looked over at me, the side of his mouth quirking up just a little. "Cut yourself some slack. You're what, sixteen?"

"Seventeen in December."

"You have plenty of time to figure out what you want to do. You don't want to swim? Okay, great. You'll find something else that excites you. I'm certain of it. And that doesn't have to be now or before you graduate or even while you're in college. You'll figure it out."

I shivered, and even though I had on a coat, Ben stepped close to me as we walked and put his arm around me. I was really cold, so I let him. He smelled good, spicy and clean, like cologne and hair spray.

He held me close until we were standing in front of Marisol's house again, right at the end of her driveway.

"Thank you for the walk," I said, because what else was I supposed to say? I stepped away from him, but Ben stepped forward, and before I even realized what was happening, he was kissing me.

It wasn't a long kiss—his lips pressed gently to mine for just a second, just long enough for me to register how soft, how gentle, his mouth was, and when he stepped away, I wasn't sure what to say. I bit my lip. "Um . . ."

He sighed and moved away from me. "Yeah. I kind of got the feeling that this was one-sided."

"I'm sorry," I said. I knew I didn't have to apologize, and I knew that Ben wasn't expecting me to, but I still felt like I should. I'd flirted back and let him think he could kiss me, but it just felt *wrong*.

"Is it Michael?"

I was so surprised by his words that I jumped. "What?"

He smiled, like I'd confirmed his suspicions. "It might not be obvious to everyone else, but it's obvious to me. I thought I'd be able to win you over, but I guess not."

My pulse thundered in my eardrums. Ben had noticed. He knew how I felt about Michael. Was he right about no one else noticing? Or had Patrice figured it out, too?

"I was kind of hoping I was wrong." Ben nudged me with his elbow. "Look, your secret is safe with me, and I really don't think

———

anyone else has a clue. But if I'm going to be honest, I think you're wasting your time on Michael." He leaned against my car and crossed his arms. "Patrice has had a thing for him since they were kids, and I never thought he'd give in, but last year, he was so lonely, you know? He was spending all his time cooped up with his mom, and it was hard on him. So when Patrice finally made her move, he took her up on it. I honestly didn't think it was going to last as long as it has, and I think he's too nice to ever break up with her."

I didn't want Michael to break up with Patrice. It was obvious to me that she really cared about him. The last thing I wanted was to see her heartbroken. And yet, the idea that it might never be over made my heart ache a little.

"Even if he's more interested in someone else."

That ripped me out of my thoughts.

Ben's face was coated in a kind of sincerity I hadn't seen before. That charming lilt that he always had was gone, and he was looking at me like he knew me. Maybe he did. Everyone else seemed to know me better than I knew myself.

"He hasn't said anything, trying to keep it to himself like he does with everything else that's bugging him. But I know him pretty well."

I scowled at him. "But then why did you . . . ?" I couldn't bring myself to finish the question, one that slipped out of my mouth unbidden. If he thought Michael might like me, why had he flirted with me? And tried to kiss me?

But he knew what I was asking. "Michael's my best friend. I don't want to see him get hurt because he did something stupid. And I do really like you. So I thought if you dated me and got over Michael, this whole thing might just go away. Offer's still on the table." He smiled.

I smiled back even though I felt like someone had taken a melon baller to my insides. "I don't think I should be dating anyone right now."

He shrugged. "Fair enough." He reached out and squeezed my arm, and then he turned and walked off into the night.

I got in my car and drove home, and when I got to the third floor, I stopped in the hallway and looked over at Michael's door. I didn't know if he was home or not. Maybe after the girls had finished the project, Patrice had called Michael. Maybe he'd gone over to her place. Or maybe they were behind that door right now, sliding into home base.

I went inside my apartment and shut the door firmly behind me.

Fourteen

The next day on my way to lunch, I found myself staring at the trophies in the swim case at school. They had an entire case in the hallway outside the cafeteria. So did the football team and the track team and the basketball team. The swim team had trophies and medals and pictures of athletes and coaches. Some of it was from the previous year; some of it was from ten years ago.

Right behind a state championship trophy from 1996, there was a picture of a guy coming up out of the water during the butterfly that caught my eye. Whoever had developed the photograph had made all the colors too bright. The blue of the water was too blue and his skin was too peachy, but I stared at it anyway. The guy was almost smiling. He was coming up out of the water during a stroke, taking a breath of fresh air as he did so, and from the look on his face, you would have thought that was it for him: that was bliss. Maybe it was.

"Do you miss it?"

I jumped. Coach Wu stood beside me, a clipboard in her hand, like if she didn't constantly have a connection to her team, the whole world might fall apart.

It took me a second to process her question. "Do I miss what?"

She raised her eyebrows at the case. "Swimming. Competing."

I wasn't sure how to tell her that yes, I missed swimming, but no, I didn't miss competing. That was the problem, really. "I guess."

"Why did you feel like you needed to quit?" she asked, crossing her arms and watching me.

What, was she writing an article or something? People were starting to stare. If a student stood too long next to any teacher, people assumed they were getting in trouble. I was watching them instead of her, wishing I could jump into their midst and disappear. "Coach Wu, I know you think you're trying to help me," I said as kindly and respectfully as I could, "but swimming just isn't going to happen for me." That sounded so mature. I wanted to pat myself on the back.

"Is it because of your father?"

I clenched my jaw. My maturity threatened to jump out the window. I wanted to tell her that it was none of her business and that she had no right to even be asking me questions. She wasn't my guidance counselor and she really wasn't anything to me at all, not a coach, not a teacher, just another human being.

But I didn't say anything. I figured that was the best way to hold the anger in.

Coach Wu sighed. "Well, I can assure you that if you joined the swim team, you wouldn't have to deal with your father."

As long as I was swimming, I would have to deal with my

father. He would come to my meets, I would see him at District, and he would call to see how my training was going once he thought I had cooled down. What he didn't know was that I wasn't ever planning to cool down.

"No, thank you." I started to turn away to join the throng entering the cafeteria, but she stepped halfway in front of me.

"Listen, I know that things are difficult between you and your dad right now. It's hard having your parent be your coach. I've seen that situation happen on more than one occasion. It adds a lot of pressure, so I get that. But now that he's not your coach anymore, you could start to separate your personal life from your life in the pool. You could move on if you wanted to."

I felt my face flush. I felt my whole body flush. I felt every single capillary in my body come up against my skin and burst. "Excuse me?"

She blinked, clearly aware that she'd set off a reaction inside me. "Well, I just mean—"

"You don't know a damn thing about my father or me." I knew I was crossing so many different lines, but now that I had gotten started, I couldn't stop. "You met him a few times? Well, good for you. You must know everything. It wasn't swimming that *added a lot of pressure*, okay? It was the fact that he decided to forget that he had a team and a wife and a family and cheated on my mom, and I'm certainly not going to *move on* by joining your team so that I can win your sport some more financial support from the school board. So I would appreciate it if you would leave me alone before I report you for harassment."

I turned and walked right into Marisol. She and Patrice had

materialized out of nowhere, and Marisol put out a hand to steady me as we walked together toward the cafeteria.

"What was that?" Patrice hissed to me as we stood in line. My hands were shaking, and I couldn't hold my tray. Marisol took it from my hands. "Did you just threaten to report Coach Wu?"

"I said I didn't want to be on the team." My voice trembled. "And I meant it."

"I think she's just a little pushy," Marisol said from behind me. Patrice still had a hand on my elbow to move me along the line, even though none of us had grabbed any food. I reached out absently and put a piece of pizza on my tray.

"I think she has no idea what she's talking about. She thinks I can just *move on* now that my dad is out of the picture? I quit swimming because my father slept with one of the swim moms, and now every time I look at a pool, I want to vomit." Unless that pool had Michael in it, but I didn't think it was a good idea to say that in front of his girlfriend.

Both of them were quiet until we took a seat. I hadn't missed the looks they were giving each other, that weird telepathic facial conversation they had. I looked down at the food on my tray, but there was no way I could eat any of it.

"Well, the good news," Marisol said, "is that while you were with Ben, we finished cutting out all the letters for the blanket. All we have to do is hot-glue them on fabric and let Michael's mom sew it up." She leaned across the table and wiggled her eyebrows mischievously at me. "How was your *walk*?"

I took a bite of my pizza so I wouldn't have to answer.

—

Patrice and Marisol looked at each other.

"It wasn't good?" Marisol asked.

I shrugged. "I like Ben, but I don't think we're very compatible."

Marisol narrowed her eyes at me. "Wait. Do you like someone else? Because I really thought you'd be into Ben. Everyone's into Ben."

I felt my face go red, and I pretended to wipe my mouth on a napkin to hide my blush. "No, it's nothing like that. Ben is really nice, but I just don't think it's good timing."

"Sometimes it just doesn't work out," Patrice said. "We get it."

I couldn't meet their eyes.

○ ○ ○

"So, I heard a rumor that you physically assaulted Coach Wu in the middle of the hallway today. You're quite the celebrity."

The door to the roof hadn't even fallen closed behind me before the words were out of Michael's mouth. I shouldn't have been surprised. Of course it was all over school, and since Michael had had some sort of meeting with the school counselor that afternoon and hadn't ridden the bus, he hadn't had the chance to bring it up yet.

"Thanks for the reminder." I tossed my towel and change of clothes on one of the lounge chairs against the wall.

Michael went from sassy to concerned in one second flat. "Oh, hey. I was just joking. Are you okay?"

I scrubbed my hands down my face. "She's still trying to get me to join the team, and she came up to me in the hall and started asking all these questions, and then she starts telling me how I shouldn't let my personal life interfere with swimming and I should move on or something."

I was babbling, and now that I was replaying our conversation out loud, it sounded so juvenile.

Michael reached out to me, his fingers brushing my elbow, and I jerked away from him. I couldn't let him affect me like this. He wasn't being fair. He had a girlfriend. He wasn't allowed to touch me comfortingly.

"It doesn't matter." I jumped into the pool.

I pushed myself against the bottom. Through the rippling water, I could see the sky, the blurriness of the buildings rising on either side of ours, the bubbles floating from my mouth to the surface. I pressed my hands to the floor beneath me, feeling a lump form in my throat. I wanted to stay under until my lungs gave out and I dissolved into the water, but I could feel the panic rising inside me as I tried to push thoughts of Coach Wu away. I wanted it to be over. Couldn't it just be over already so I could love the water again? So I could be normal again? So I could be free?

My skin started to tingle with the anxiety and my chest was aching for breath, so I pushed away from the floor and came up to join Michael, keeping himself afloat in the center of the pool. His legs and arms moved in wide circles, sometimes not fast enough and he would slip downward, his chin slapping the water before bobbing back up.

"You okay?" he asked, but I couldn't talk about it. I couldn't even explain this confusing storm inside me.

I pressed myself against the wall and motioned for him to do a lap. He hesitated, but he eventually conceded, having trouble staying under the surface with his body while trying to keep his form perfect. But he made it from one side of the pool to the other without dying, which was technically a success.

"Make sure you're slicing in with your hands, not splashing down. And you're not kicking fast enough. That's why you're sinking."

He smiled like I'd just told him he was the greatest swimmer on the West Coast. "You gonna join me?" he asked after another lap, gasping between words. I knew he wasn't going to be able to do much more before the cigarette lungs took over. I crossed my arms and considered. I didn't want Michael to get discouraged, which is easy to do when you think you're doing amazing only to be upstaged by someone who just happened to do it better for one reason or another. I'd been practicing for almost ten years and didn't have a set of trashed-out lungs.

"Sure," I finally said. Michael seemed cheery enough to take the competition, but I still swam slow, keeping pace with him beside me as we went to one side of the pool and then to the other. Michael executed a surface-and-turn-around kind of maneuver when he reached the wall while I did a flip turn and pushed off the wall, giving myself significantly more distance than he had.

I waited for him at the other side of the pool, and when he got there, gulping in breaths and smiling like a little kid, I shoved him playfully on the shoulder. He floated away from me.

"You're amazing, you know that?" He pressed his head to the concrete lip of the pool and kept smiling at me.

Something about the way he smiled at me, like he didn't have a care in the world, made everything well up in my chest then.

I turned away from him, but I was too late. I was heaving in breaths that didn't feel like they were making it to my lungs. I covered my face with my hands, trying to stifle the sound of hyperventilating. I tried to find something solid to hold on to, but I felt like I was getting farther from the edge of the pool, unable to get a grasp on it. Any second now, I would drown.

"Hey," Michael said behind me. "Hey, what did I say?"

I wiped at my face with chlorine hands, trying to regain some sanity, trying to quell the dizziness. "What's happening to me?" The words came out raw and desperate.

I heard Michael treading water behind me. I felt the heat of his body along my back. "What are you talking about?"

I squeezed my eyes shut and gulped in a breath, focusing, *focusing* on not slipping away. "Swimming," I finally said, because what else was there? My whole world began and ended with swimming. "Why do I feel like this?"

"You're okay." His hands found my arms, and then he wrapped his arms around me until he'd pulled me against him, front to back. The heat of his skin and the feel of his heart thumping against me made me stop trembling. "Swimming is not all you are," he said. He pressed his mouth to my ear, like if he said the words directly against my brain, I might be more inclined to believe them.

I shook my head but couldn't speak. Slowly, I felt everything inside me begin to calm. The world came back into focus, and I felt his fingertips digging into my sides. I shivered, the air cold on my flushed skin. "How can I love something and hate it at the same time?" I asked, my voice weak. My whole body felt sore and tired.

"Life is complicated," he whispered.

And then I felt his lips on my neck, pressed and held there,

———

197

and the feeling of his hot breath made something break into my mind: Patrice. Patrice's sad face as she wondered what was going on with Michael.

I jerked away from him.

He looked as dazed as I felt, his eyebrows pulled down in confusion.

"I can't do this." The panic that he'd managed to coax away was back. Before he could stop me, before he could say something to convince me that his mouth on me had been something other than what it had seemed, I used the stairs to bolt from the pool, grabbing my clothes and towel as I went. He didn't call out after me, and he didn't follow.

o o o

I knew Michael could catch up with me if I took the stairs down to my apartment, so I took the elevator, closing my eyes and plugging my ears and focusing only on my breath as the elevator lurched, taking my stomach with it. When it came to a stop, I rushed out as fast as I could. There was no one in the hall, so I quickly put on my clothes over my wet suit in an attempt to feel more grounded before I opened the door.

When I let myself into the apartment, it didn't smell like dinner, like I'd hoped. Lily was sitting on the couch, and when she caught my gaze as I came in, her eyes were wide.

"What?" I was certain something terrible had happened, but she didn't have a chance to answer before my mother's voice cut her off.

"Katherine, if you could please have a seat." My mother was seated at the dining room table, her arms crossed tightly and her lips thin with disappointment. I knew that face. I knew it because it was one my father loved to use on me when he caught me doing something he didn't approve of: talking to a boy, slacking on my homework, staying up past my appointed bedtime.

I went into the dining room, but I didn't sit at the table. There could only be one reason my mother was looking at me like that. She knew.

"What's going on?" I asked, looking from her to Lily, hoping that maybe by some miracle I was wrong. Maybe I'd made some other huge mistake.

"Where have you been?"

This was potentially a trap. I could lie and say that I'd been at practice, but if she knew I wasn't, then I was busted. And if I told the truth, that I was with Michael, I was also busted.

Lily watched us with horror across her face, like I was currently burning at the stake.

I chose to stay quiet.

"I got a call from Coach Wu almost two hours ago."

I bit my lip. My mother's eyes had fire in them.

"She was calling because she's worried about the way you're adjusting to your new life. She really thinks joining the swim team would be best for you." Her words might have almost sounded sarcastic if they hadn't been so bitter.

"Did she also tell you that she harassed me in the middle of the hallway today?" I knew that jumping in with this bit of news was probably not going to help my case, but I was fairly certain it couldn't hurt.

My mother slammed her open palm on the table, and it felt like the entire building trembled. "You've been lying to me for weeks," she hissed. "What have you been doing with your evenings? Something could have happened to you at any point, and I would have had no clue where to find you."

"I've been giving Michael swim lessons after school."

My mother stared at me, not saying anything for so long that I had time to count the beats of my heart in my ears. "I don't understand. You're not joining the swim team? You're off with some boy you barely know without telling me—"

"You're the one that invited him to Lily's wedding!" I cut in.

"I'm not finished!" she shouted. "I thought I could trust you. I thought this move would be best for all of us, but clearly it was too much for you to handle."

"And we had another option?" I threw my hands in the air. "Oh, right, we should have just stuck around with Dad while he was sleeping with someone else."

"It wasn't like it was the first time," my mother said, flat and cold and so quiet I thought I hadn't heard her correctly.

On the couch, Lily sat up straight. "Wait. What?"

My mother shook her head. "I'm sorry. I didn't mean to say that. It's not important. What's important is that you, Kate, are grounded."

But my mother wasn't getting off that easy. Within seconds, Lily was standing beside me, and we were both staring down at my mother, who pushed her chair back and began pacing along the table.

"Dad cheated on you more than once?" I demanded.

My mother sighed and came to a stop in front of us. "Yes, your father cheated on me more than once." This version of my mother was so different from the one I'd seen just moments before, her eyes sad and her shoulders slumped, that I wasn't sure whether to feel completely outraged that she'd kept this secret from us or just feel sorry for her.

However, Lily didn't seem so torn. Her mouth fell open. "Then why the hell did you wait until now to dump his sorry ass?" My mother and I both stared at her. Her outburst gave me chills.

My mother's eyes flicked to me, for just a fraction of a second, and I knew what she was going to say before she said it. I knew that there was only one reason she would stay with my dad, even if it was killing her. I squeezed my eyes shut, all the fight draining out of me.

"What?" Lily said, but Mom didn't say a word.

I turned to my sister. "She stayed with him because of me. She stayed with him because of the swimming."

Lily's eyes slid to our mother. "Is that true?"

She still didn't say anything.

"So why now?" Lily asked. "Why leave him now?"

My mother stared down at the table. "Because it hurt too much. I couldn't do it anymore. I prayed that you would forgive me, and I did what I had to do to survive."

Lily and I were quiet. Hadn't we done the same thing, trying to survive, when Lily left Tom and I quit swimming? We were just trying to keep breathing.

I leaned my palms on the table and took a deep breath. "Lily's right. You should have left him the first time."

We were all silent for a long moment, the sounds of our breathing mingling in the small room loudly enough to hear.

"This doesn't change anything," my mother finally said. "You're still grounded."

I groaned. "We were just swimming. And we were upstairs!"

She shook her head. "You lied to me. You're grounded until the end of the year. No going out. Home and school, that's it."

Lily's eyes went wide. "That's a long time."

"Mom, come on," I said, trying to imagine myself cooped up in my room for the next two and a half months. "I wasn't out drinking. I wasn't doing drugs. I was literally in this building the whole time."

My mother drummed her fingers on the tabletop. "Fine. One month. But only because it's been a hard few weeks for all of us."

I thought maybe there was a chance I could get her to lower my sentence even more, but I really *did* feel bad for lying to her, so I took my punishment.

In my room, I stared at my phone. I wanted to tell Michael what had happened, that we'd been caught. But I couldn't. I couldn't go near him again, not until I'd figured out what was going on between us.

So I dialed Harris's number. We weren't exactly on speaking terms, either, but he'd always been there for me, whether we were fighting or not. He always answered.

But he didn't answer now. His phone rang and rang and rang and finally went to voice mail, and I wanted to cry, listening to his voice in my ear. When the beep came, I hung up.

———

Fifteen

I woke up to the sound of someone throwing open my bedroom door. When Lily rushed into my room, it was still dark outside my bedroom window.

"Kate, get up. Something's wrong." She latched onto my arm and pulled me up out of my bed. The front door hung open, and my mother watched from the entryway as people in uniforms went in and out of Michael's apartment. Everyone was talking, and there were so many lights, I was almost blinded.

"What's going on?" I asked Mom. She was holding her robe closed as she watched, and I finally realized that the people outside were paramedics, and they were rolling a stretcher into Michael's apartment.

I started to go for the door, but my mom grabbed my arm. "You should stay out of their way. It's Harriet. She's having some trouble."

We stood in the open doorway and watched as the paramedics

---

returned, this time with Michael's mom on the stretcher, an oxygen mask over her face. I could see the panic in her eyes, and it broke my heart.

And then Michael rushed out of the apartment.

"Michael!"

That time, when I lunged for the door, my mother didn't stop me. Michael was following close behind the paramedics, but he whipped around when I called his name.

"Kate," he sighed, his shoulders slumping slightly. "Mom's having trouble breathing. I think it's pneumonia again, but she said she had this headache, and I don't know what . . . ," he trailed off, his eyes wandering over my face before he hugged me. He was still in his clothes, even though it was the middle of the night.

"It's going to be okay," I said when his arms went around me. "Are you riding in the ambulance?"

He seemed to remember that he was in a hurry and gently pried me off him. The elevator doors were closing. "Yeah, I have to go with her." He turned back to me, and his face was so serious, so scared, that he didn't even look like the Michael I knew. "Will you meet me there?" he asked. "Please."

"Of course."

He held my eyes for a long moment, extended his hand out to me just barely, like he might just drag me along with him, but then turned and made a run for the stairs.

My mother's eyes were on Michael's back as the stairwell door closed behind him. She looked back at me, and I could tell that she wanted to argue, but how could she?

She reached back into the apartment to the hook by the door

———

and grabbed her keys. She handed them to me, and then she and Lily went back inside.

∘ ∘ ∘

Michael was sitting in the waiting room with his head in his hands. He didn't look like Michael. He looked like a shadow of the boy I knew, the one that was always smiling. This boy looked like he'd never smiled in his life.

"How is she?" I asked, taking a seat beside him.

He shook his head. "I don't know. They're trying to drain the fluid from her lungs."

"I'm sorry, Michael."

He was quiet for a long moment, and the sounds of the hospital infiltrated the conversation—beeping from far-off rooms, nurses talking at the front desk, footsteps rushing in and out of the hallway.

"I don't know what to do for her." His words were barely more than a whisper. "She just keeps getting worse, and I'm completely helpless."

I scooted closer to him, needing to feel his warmth to know that everything was real, hoping that maybe just my being closer to him would be enough for now.

He sighed and pressed his face into his hands again. "I just feel so alone." His voice broke.

"No. Michael, no." I reached out and took one of his hands, hot and limp in mine. "You're not alone. You've got me."

He looked down at our hands together and wrapped his fingers around mine. "Kate—"

"Michael!"

—

I ripped my hand out of his. Patrice rushed into the emergency room, her shoes clapping loudly against the linoleum floor. We got up to meet her, and she stood on her toes to throw her arms around Michael.

"Are you okay? What's going on?"

I stepped away from them, feeling like I was intruding on an intimate moment, even though I'd been there first. They finally separated, but Patrice held on to him, pressing her forehead to his. "I'm all right," he told her, and she seemed to accept it because she let him go and turned to me.

"Kate, I'm so glad you could be here with him. Thank you." She stepped forward and hugged me, and I hugged her back, keeping my eyes on Michael over her shoulder. I was afraid he would fall over. Patrice pulled away. "You look exhausted. Why don't you go home? I'll take it from here."

Michael's glazed eyes were on the floor. I wanted to stay with him, but Patrice was right. He wasn't mine to look after.

"Okay. Keep me posted."

She nodded, and I left the emergency room in a bit of a haze.

o o o

I woke up with the sun shining directly into my eyes and popped up in bed. The sun should not have been shining in my eyes. That meant it was late. The clock said it was after eleven, and I felt my heart squeeze. Mom was going to be so pissed.

I was struggling into a pair of pants that I'd found draped over my computer chair when I realized that one of two things had to be true: One, my mother knew I'd slept in and had chosen to go to work without waking me, letting me miss school. Or two, she had no idea how late I had slept and would therefore have no clue if I didn't go.

I finished getting dressed and sat at the end of my bed. I couldn't stop thinking about Harriet, the fear in her eyes when she'd been rolled out on that stretcher. I checked my phone, but I didn't have any messages, from Patrice or Michael or my mom. I walked out of my room and straight to Michael's apartment.

He didn't even look surprised when he opened the door. He just looked tired, his whole body ragged and thin. He stepped away from the door, silently inviting me in, and I went straight to the kitchen.

"Have you eaten?" I asked him.

He watched me, one hand slung across the bar. "Yeah, I had some coffee at the hospital."

"Coffee isn't food." I was already going through his fridge, pulling out edible ingredients to throw together. The one thing I could tell by looking at Michael was that he might have been taking good care of his mother, but he obviously wasn't taking good care of himself.

I shut the fridge, my arms full of sandwich supplies. "How long have you been home?"

He squeezed his eyes shut and ran a hand over his face. "Since seven." Almost five hours. I wanted to be sad that he hadn't let me know, but I could see from his groggy expression that he'd been asleep.

I turned my back to him and put the supplies on the counter. "How's your mom?" I focused on putting mayo on white bread, then adding lettuce, turkey, sliced tomatoes. If I stopped to think, I would start crying.

———

"She's fine. She's at the hospital with my uncle. She's sleeping. She'll be fine." He sounded like he was trying to convince himself, and I did my best to ignore how his voice made me feel. I didn't know this Michael, this guy who fell apart and forgot to eat and moved like a zombie. I piled turkey on the sandwich. He looked like he probably needed the protein.

Something brushed against my elbow, and I spun around with a gasp to find that Michael had come up behind me. He was standing too close, his arms held up awkwardly, like he wanted to put them around me but couldn't make himself move, even though he'd just slunk across the kitchen like a cat.

I was still holding the mayonnaise-covered knife, preparing to cut the sandwich. I opened my mouth to say something, not really sure what, when he spoke over me.

"Thank you for being there, at the hospital. I don't know what I would have done without you."

I twisted to snatch the plate off the counter. I put it between us. "Eat," I told him.

He took the plate and took a step back, looking vulnerable. It was like Michael was standing before me without a layer of the armor that I'd never even noticed was there.

I stood there, watching him, but he didn't eat the sandwich. He set it on the counter beside him.

"You don't have to look at me like that." He sighed and wrapped his arms around himself.

"Like what?" But I knew what he was talking about. I was trying not to look like I pitied him. I didn't pity him. I was worried about him. I was scared for him.

"Like I'm some little boy. Like you have to take care of me because I can't take care of myself."

I took a step toward him but stopped myself. "That's not it. I just . . ." My heart felt like it was going to burst. I felt like I needed to scream at him. Couldn't he see how much he'd done for me? That I just wanted him to be happy?

That I was falling for him?

"Michael, I care about you. I just—"

"I broke up with Patrice."

My brain seemed to short out, sputtering and stopping like a car out of gas. I grabbed the counter behind me for leverage. "What?"

He was frozen still, his eyes stuck on me. He licked his lips. "She was being so nice and so supportive, and she stayed at the hospital all night. She stayed with me until Mom was feeling better. But the whole time, all I could think about was how I wished it was you. It killed me when you left. I wanted to beg you to stay. I wanted to beg you to come back. I wanted to beg you to feel the same way about me that I feel about you."

My body went hot. I was standing in Michael's kitchen, and he was telling me things I definitely wanted to hear, and I couldn't say anything, couldn't answer him, couldn't think, couldn't breathe.

We didn't speak for a long time, too long, so long that I was afraid maybe I'd made the whole thing up. We held on to the silence, and he crossed the kitchen to me, coming close enough for me to smell the sleep on his skin.

The room was too bright and Michael was too dark, all shadows in a black shirt and his dark hair, and without thinking,

I reached out and grabbed his shirt. He leaned forward and kissed me.

His mouth finally on mine felt like coming up out of the water after a race, like triumph and fresh air. I let go of his shirt and slid my hands up to his neck, feeling his skin beneath my fingers while his tongue found mine. I grabbed his shoulders and felt him push me back into the counter, felt the ache in my skin as my jeans dug into me, and it felt incredible.

He pulled back and sighed my name. He pressed his forehead to mine, and I tried to breathe, but somehow I breathed better when he was kissing me. His fingers streaked down my face, and I finally opened my eyes to look into his.

"This is a terrible time to be this happy," he whispered.

I just nodded and wound my arms around his neck, pulling him back down to me. He tasted like peppermints, so much sweeter than I'd imagined. He tugged at my ponytail, and I finally stepped away from him, bumping into the counter behind me.

"You need to eat." My words were a little shaky, and so was his breathing.

He, regrettably, went back to his side of the kitchen and picked up his sandwich. I had never enjoyed watching someone eat so much. I leaned against the counter, feeling like I needed it to hold me up. My legs were still trembling.

He'd actually kissed me.

He'd actually told me he had feelings for me.

He'd actually broken up with Patrice.

My heart was beating impossibly fast, like I'd just swum the last split of a long-distance race.

Michael was smiling around his sandwich until his phone

beeped in his pocket. He pulled it out, setting the sandwich aside to send a text message. "My uncle."

Right. God. His mother. Guilt washed over me. I'd come to check on him, and instead we'd made out in his kitchen.

I tried to focus on other things, focus on anything but the way the curve of his mouth felt against mine. Dammit, why did he have to kiss me while we had so many other things to deal with?

"What about you?" he asked, tucking the phone back in his pocket. "Are you okay?"

"My mom found out about everything. She grounded me."

He pursed his lips and took another bite of the sandwich. "Yeah, I guess that makes sense."

"I'm not even really supposed to be here, but nobody was home, so . . ."

He finished his sandwich, and I thought he already looked more like himself, color in his cheeks and a slight smile on his lips. I wanted to kiss him again.

His phone beeped with another text message. "I'm just going to call my uncle. Check in on her."

He disappeared into his bedroom, and I went to his living room. It felt smaller now somehow, with only me in it. Even though I knew I should probably be going to class or at the very least respecting my mother's grounding, I wasn't ready to leave Michael. His apartment was warm and quiet, and, well, it had Michael in it.

Michael, who didn't have a girlfriend anymore.

I reached over and turned on the stereo. Apparently no one had touched the stereo since the lesson we had had in the living room because salsa music immediately flooded the room. I was

211

still fiddling with the thing when Michael appeared beside me. He put his fingers over mine, and my heart lurched in the most pleasant way.

He moved my hand out of the way and changed the song, letting the salsa music fade away and a slow guitar song take its place. He pulled me against him and let his hands fall to my waist. It was deliciously bizarre to be able to do this with him, to be able to slide my fingers up his neck and press my head to his shoulder. We could do this now.

His mouth found mine again, and this time, I let him kiss me because maybe if we stayed here, we could pretend the rest of the world wasn't flawed. He pushed me back until we were on the couch, our mouths sliding lazily over each other, until I was too tired to keep my eyes open, and we fell asleep pressed together.

* * *

We jerked awake at the sound of someone knocking on the door. As I pushed away from Michael, my mind went to all the people who it could be: my mother, catching me in the act and prepared to ground me further; Patrice, come to get back together with Michael; Michael's uncle with news on Harriet.

I wasn't expecting Lily.

"Are you trying to get yourself in even more trouble?" she hissed when I got to the door. I put my shoes on while she watched me. "Mom is on her way home. She just called me."

"Text me," I said to Michael before Lily dragged me into our apartment and shut the door. She stomped into the kitchen and started to rummage through the pantry.

"Are you mad at me?" I asked because she was certainly acting like it.

She sighed and dropped a pan onto the stove. "No, I'm not mad at you." She turned to look at me. "But my life would be significantly easier if you would stop doing things behind Mom's back that would get you in trouble."

I leaned against the counter. "Yeah, I know."

She stopped and looked at me, but after a second, she went back to what she was doing, and I was left to watch her, feeling the excitement of my afternoon with Michael slipping away.

Sixteen

The next night, I was back at Marisol's house, my blood pounding in my ears as I knocked on the door. Michael and I had agreed that keeping whatever we were doing secret for now was our best option, but the guilt was already eating at me. I hadn't seen Patrice yet, but I could only imagine how she felt. I knew how much she liked him. And here I was, swooping into their lives and stealing him away. I pressed my face into my hands.

How could I face her after this? When she found out, she was going to hate me, and I couldn't even blame her. I was an awful friend. An awful, awful friend.

Marisol's smile was bright when she opened the door, but as soon as it was closed behind me, she latched onto my elbow. She leaned in close, so close I could smell something salty on her breath. "Okay, so you heard, right? About Patrice and Michael? I mean, how could you not know? You live across from Michael. He told you, right?"

I opened my mouth to object to her assumption that Michael would have immediately told me, even though it was true, but before I could, she was steering me into the living room.

Patrice was sitting in the middle of the floor with a hot-glue gun in her hand. Since Harriet had been dealing with her health, Patrice had convinced her older sister to do the sewing on our elements blanket, and now we just had to glue into place all the letters and numbers we'd already cut out. Or more specifically, that Patrice and Marisol had cut out while I was busy with Ben.

"Okay, so tell me again exactly how it went down," Marisol said when we'd settled onto the carpet, and I felt my entire body tense up. She couldn't seriously mean for Patrice to reenact the breakup.

I hadn't even really had the chance to discuss it in full with Michael. He had missed another day of school, deciding to stay home and take care of his mother, and other than deciding not to tell anyone about what happened, we hadn't discussed what was going on between us.

"I already told you everything." Patrice was focused on hot-gluing a very large F on a blanket square.

"Right, I know," Marisol said, "but you haven't told Kate, and we definitely need a second opinion."

"A second opinion on what?" I busied myself with sorting things on the floor. We only had one glue gun, so there wasn't much to do while one of us was using it.

Patrice looked at me, her eyes steady and wet. There was something there. Suspicion? Knowledge?

I looked away. I was imagining it. There was no way that Patrice could know I'd already kissed Michael unless she had put a hidden camera in his kitchen. What I was seeing in her eyes was probably just plain devastation. I felt sick.

"Marisol thinks he's into someone else," she finally said. Her voice was tired and gravelly, and I felt a little disoriented by it. Patrice was usually cheery and kind, but now she had bags under her eyes, strands of her curly hair stuck to her face.

Marisol shrugged. "It just feels so out of the blue. Guys don't just give up regular nookie unless there's the promise of getting it somewhere else."

I felt like Marisol had punched me in the chest. Just the week before, Patrice had said they weren't sleeping together. Oh God, they couldn't have slept together, right? Did he sleep with Patrice days before breaking up with her and kissing me on his couch?

Patrice sighed. "Mar, you know we didn't have sex."

Marisol rolled her eyes. "Okay, fine."

Patrice's arms fell, like the tiny scrap of fabric and the mini glue gun in her hands had become too heavy to hold up. "He said we never really fit right but he'd wanted to give us a chance. And then he just decided he couldn't do it anymore, said he really liked me more as a friend."

I couldn't do this. In the story of Patrice's life, I had just become the villain. How could one moment make her so miserable and me so happy?

Marisol put her arms around Patrice and held her close. I took possession of the glue gun. I needed to get out of there as soon as possible, so I started gluing parts.

"So what do you think?" Marisol asked, and it took me a second to realize she was talking to me.

———

"About what?" The hot tip of the glue gun touched my thumb, and I jerked it back.

"Do you think Michael is seeing someone else?"

I shrugged. "I don't know."

"You live right across the hall from him. Have you ever seen any girls coming or going from his apartment?"

Both of them were looking at me, but I'd gotten so used to lying. I could lie to two more people. "No, I haven't seen anyone."

Patrice sent Marisol a *told you so* look.

"How's Jesse?" I asked, effectively changing the subject. Marisol's eyes lit up. Beside her, Patrice sent me a small smile that I took as a thank-you for changing the subject. Guilt roiled in my stomach.

"Oh, um." Marisol glanced at Patrice, who rolled her eyes.

"It's okay. You can talk about Jesse. It's not like I expect everyone to be miserable just because I am."

Marisol didn't seem too convinced, but she continued anyway. "Well, I was going to tell you the news later, but I'm no longer in the virgin category." She smiled at both of us. "It happened last night."

Patrice's eyes went wide. "Really? Wow. That's um . . ." Patrice and I glanced at each other, and I had to look away. There was too much trust and companionship in her eyes that I didn't deserve.

I did my best to get through the night with little talk about boys, instead talking to them about TV shows that I didn't watch and music I rarely listened to. At the end of the night, I walked out of Marisol's house with a mental list of their favorites to look into.

Watching to make sure the door closed behind me, I scrambled into the driver's seat of my mom's car and dialed Michael's number. I felt somewhat frantic by the time he picked up the phone.

———

"Hey." I could hear the smile in his voice. It was going to kill me to hear it disappear.

"Did you break up with Patrice because of me?" The obvious answer was yes, he had. But I needed more than that. I needed to know that I wasn't directly responsible for the end of their relationship.

I honestly expected him to hesitate. I expected him to trip over his words and try to convince me of something that I was already dead set against. But he didn't.

"No." Confident. Positive. Perfect. "There were a million and one reasons for me to end it with Patrice, but I didn't really care about any of them until I realized I had the chance to make it work with someone I was crazy about."

I set my head against my steering wheel and let out a breath. "Maybe this is a bad idea."

"What's a bad idea?"

"Us." I wasn't even sure *us* was a real thing yet. But it felt real. I put my car in gear, feeling twice as awful for having this conversation with Michael when Patrice was so close by. I pulled out of Marisol's driveway and headed toward home.

"Doesn't feel like a bad idea to me."

"You didn't see her, Michael. She's completely shattered."

"And that sucks. But we're all going to get through this. Patrice and I have been through worse together."

I opened my mouth to speak as I pulled up to a red light, but he spoke over me, like he knew I was about to argue.

"If you want to take some time, I understand. This didn't exactly happen in the best way. I shouldn't have made a move a few hours after breaking up with Patrice. But I've wanted to kiss you since we met, and it was the first time I was allowed to do it, even if it meant maybe upsetting Patrice. I've spent a lot of time worrying about upsetting her, and I think I need to do what feels right to me now."

Someday we'd have to tell her that we were an *us*, if that's what we were, and she would be even more devastated and confused, and she would know that her suspicions had been right. Why did Michael have to be such a good kisser?

"I don't want to take time. I want to be with you."

The smile was back in his voice. "I want to be with you, too. We'll figure everything else out."

"Yeah. We'll figure everything out." We hung up at that, and I felt just as heavy as I had before. Trying to juggle utter guilt and uncontainable happiness was already exhausting.

o o o

Not being able to tell anyone about Michael and me was like trying to contain fireworks inside my rib cage. We couldn't hold hands at school or kiss or do anything that anyone, especially Patrice, might see.

On the bus, we sat just a little too close and stared just a little too long, and when we separated to go to class, we lingered a little too much, and it was glorious.

Lunch with Patrice, on the other hand, was torture. She looked miserable, her eyes tired and her skin dull. It was in such direct competition with the sunshine that I felt sparking out of all my pores that I considered skipping lunch until we could get everything figured out.

But how long would that be?

I sat down next to Michael in American Lit and groaned.

"Lunch went well?" he asked, his mouth turned down.

I groaned again, louder. "This is awful. Are you not having this problem?"

He rapped his fingers on his desk. "Well, Patrice has kind of been avoiding me, so no."

I reached into my bag and pulled out my copy of *The Crucible*. "I feel like I kicked a puppy."

He reached across the aisle and massaged my shoulder. "I'm sorry." His fingers moved down my arm, and I shivered.

"Do you think there'll ever be a time when we can tell her without her freaking out?"

He seemed to seriously consider the question. "To be honest? I don't think so. But we can put it off until we're ready to deal with the consequences."

I groaned and dropped my head onto my desk. "How did I manage to get myself out of one problem just to get myself into another?"

"What was the first problem?"

I rolled my head to look at him. "I had a huge crush on my friend's boyfriend."

His face dissolved into a smile, and I smiled back even though I was really very screwed.

* * *

That afternoon, I met Michael at the bus stop, and it was strange how everything had changed. When the wind blew my hair in my face, he reached out and moved it out of the way, and then he left his fingers on the curve of my neck.

He bent down to put his mouth against my ear. "I wish I could be alone with you." It came out of him in a rush, like he'd been holding it in.

I had pushed up on my tiptoes to whisper in his ear when a honking horn caught our attention. The bus had pulled up and people were filing on, but my mother had pulled up beside it, just feet away from us. Her eyes went from Michael to me.

"I guess that's my cue," I told him. I hadn't been expecting her, but knowing my mother, she was probably here to check up on me, make sure that I was actually where I said I was.

Michael's mouth perked up in an imitation of a smile, and I nudged him with my elbow. "You want a ride?"

Michael glanced in my mother's direction and then back at me. "No, you go ahead. I bet you and your mom could use some one-on-one time."

I hesitated, mostly because I wasn't positive I *wanted* to be alone with my mother right now, when I was still feeling guilty about lying to her and uncertain about how everything had gone down with her and my dad. But I let it go.

"How was school?" my mother asked when I was buckled in. She maneuvered into the line of cars that was migrating slowly out of the parking lot.

"It was fine. Shouldn't you be at work?"

She glanced at me and tightened her hands on the steering wheel. "Some things were canceled today, so I left early. I thought it might be good for us to talk."

I picked at my cuticles and refused to look at her. What was there to talk about? Dad? Lily? The fact that I was becoming an uncomfortably good liar?

———

"I'm ungrounding you."

The shock of what she said felt like a jolt through my entire body. "What?"

"But I need you to be honest with me from now on." We weren't far from the apartment now, but the closer we got, the more obvious it was that we weren't going home. We drove right by. I glanced at the building as it passed.

"Okay," I said, hesitantly.

"Are you seeing Michael?"

I set my head back against the seat and closed my eyes. "Yes." No point in lying now.

"Okay, then, your grounding ends now, but there will be rules about the time you spend at his apartment and the time he spends at ours. There will be no unmonitored visits either way. I realize that you're almost seventeen, and that's a very tricky age to deal with, but there's a lot we haven't talked about where boys are concerned."

I groaned. "Mom, I don't need a sex talk."

We pulled into a shopping center, and she grabbed her purse from the backseat. "I am *not* having a sex talk with you right now. I know you know how everything works. But I want you to know that you can talk to me about anything if you need to." Her face seemed to lose some of its buoyancy then. "Maybe if I'd been more open with you, you would have felt like you could come to me about not being on the team."

"It's not that I felt like I couldn't talk to you. I just didn't want to make matters worse with everything that was going on."

She sighed and nodded, her eyes going watery. "I know I've

been distracted lately, but I promise I'm fine. You can talk to me about anything."

"Okay."

She wiped her eyes. "Okay, now. I thought it might be a nice time for a wardrobe update. Fewer swimsuits, more normal-teenager clothing. What do you say?"

"Sounds great."

◦ ◦ ◦

"Are you sure you feel comfortable going out?" I asked Michael as he locked his apartment door.

He smiled over his shoulder at me. "Everything's fine. I really want to take you out, okay? So let's just go."

We held hands all the way down to the parking garage and climbed into his mother's station wagon, and I tried not to smile at him as he drove us half an hour out of Portland, to a dance club off the highway. He knew I liked him, but I didn't need him to know that I was incapable of looking away.

"Are you sure I'm going to be allowed in?"

Michael pulled into a parking space outside the club. "It's all ages on the weekends. It'll be totally fine. It's not like we're going to try to drink."

He walked around the car and opened the door for me. I took a step toward the club, but he stopped me with a hand on my waist. He pressed his face into my neck, and I let him leave a kiss there before stepping away from me again, but I didn't miss the sweep of his eyes down my body. I'd felt self-conscious putting on high heels. Even though I liked wearing skirts and dresses occasionally, high heels had never been something I'd gotten used to. But if the way Michael was looking at me was any indication, he really liked them.

He spun me around and tucked me into his side as we moved toward the door. Nerves settled in my stomach. I'd never been in a club, and I'd certainly never been in a club where I was expected to show off the skills I'd only recently gained in front of a bunch of people who were probably going to be much better.

Inside, every inch of the place was packed with people, drinking, talking, dancing. Most people looked college age or older.

I thought we might sit down and get a soda, but Michael had other plans. He held my hand, pulling me into the riot of color that was the dance floor. It was orange and pink and had swirls that made me even dizzier than I already was.

"Hey," Michael said into my ear. "Don't be nervous. Nobody's paying attention to us. It's just me and you here, okay?"

He took my hands in his and started a step in time with the music, done so smoothly it was an art in itself, and I just watched him. I tried to remember the beats and where my feet were supposed to go as he was going, twisting his hips so effortlessly that I was jealous.

He dropped my hands for a second to put his hands on my hips, helping me move them loosely with the aid of his fingertips through the fabric of my skirt. I laughed and let him take my hands and spin me, bungling the turn and tangling our legs together.

When we'd straightened out, he pressed a kiss to my cheek, and we tried again. Around us, other couples were dancing beautifully, moving in circles and masterful moves that had them intertwining and coming apart in just a few steps.

Michael put his fingers under my chin and moved my face close to his. He bit his lip and turned in my arms, once, twice, three times, in different ways before getting me to do another turn. The trumpets were loud in my ears in a rhythm that was impossible not to move to.

Without warning, the music changed into something slower, something with drums and a romantic cadence to it. Michael slowed his steps slightly, pulling me a little closer to him and lacing our fingers together between our bodies.

I was caught in his eyes, dark with something I'd never seen in them before. He pulled me against him, moving our hips to the beat while our feet stayed glued to their places. His hands pressed into my hips, and I thought I might melt right into the floor. Then he slid them up my back and into my hair, and he leaned forward to kiss me, holding tight to me.

There was something intoxicating about being kissed there, in the midst of all those people, with the music loud in the air, both of us sweating and trying to catch our breaths. He sighed against my neck. He led me off the dance floor then, to a table where we drank soda and ice-cold water and laughed and kissed and held hands. I wanted to stay there with him for as long as I could.

"So, what do you think?" Michael asked, his hand on my knee underneath our table.

I sighed, happy and tired. "It's loud."

Michael laughed. "That's it? It's loud?"

I shrugged and moved a little closer to let him put his arm around me. "It's nice. But I'm definitely not good enough to dance with these people."

Michael smiled. "They're not professionals or anything like that. They're just people."

"Not sure I believe that."

He laughed again, and I was caught by the sound, low under the beating of the drums and the shout of the trumpets. "Are you ready to go home? I should probably get back to Mom."

I glanced out at the dance floor, at the colors and the lights and the couples dancing so confidently. "Just one more?"

He grinned. "Yeah, okay."

◦ ◦ ◦

Michael gave me one more long, heated kiss against the stairway railing between the second and third floors of our apartment building, then whispered into my ear about how beautiful I was.

At my door, he was leaning in for something a little more chaste when my phone rang. It was Harris.

Michael read the screen. "Answer it," he said, but I didn't want to. I wanted this night to be perfect. I wanted the happiness that had taken up residence in my chest to be allowed to live there for just a few more hours. So I silenced my phone and let Michael kiss me.

Seventeen

The next morning, I tried to call Harris, but he didn't answer, and I stared at my phone, hoping it would ring.

"Everything okay?" Lily asked, coming into my room and dropping down onto my bed. She had a box of chocolate-chip cookies in her hand, and I reached out and grabbed one before she could pull the box away.

I shrugged. "Harris isn't answering his phone."

She shoved a cookie into her mouth. "He's probably just busy."

"It's Sunday."

"Well, sure, but he's a busy guy. I bet he's just hanging out with his girlfriend." I didn't answer, and she nudged me. "Hey, what's the big deal?"

"It's never been like this with us, you know? He's my best friend. We should be talking on the phone and sending emails and figuring out how to visit each other, but it seems like I just keep getting blown off."

Lily blinked at me. "It's been a month. You guys are going to be fine. You're just going through an adjustment period."

"I guess." It didn't feel like an adjustment period. It felt like Harris was living a whole different life without me. It felt like he was turning into a stranger, and I couldn't figure out why. Was this just because of my dad? Just because I was gone?

"Dad called me yesterday."

I dropped my phone onto the mattress. "Are you kidding? Did you answer?"

She shrugged, her shoulders sliding along my comforter. "Yeah. He wanted to talk about school and Tom and stuff."

"What did you tell him?"

She scoffed. "I just told him that I was figuring things out and let him go at that. It wasn't like we had a heart-to-heart or anything. It was awkward."

I nodded.

"He asked about you."

My eyes shot to her, and I felt my pulse kick up. She munched away for a second, like she was afraid to tell me something. This was it. She'd told my father about me quitting swim and any second now, he was going to call and demand an explanation. I didn't want to care about my father's opinion. He wasn't controlling me anymore, and logically, I understood that. But I'd spent almost ten years trying to make him proud, and I wasn't ready to handle him after he found out I'd quit.

"Did you tell him I quit the team?"

She pushed herself up until she was sitting beside me on the bed. "Of course not. I told him that if he wanted to know what was going on in your life, he should call you."

I sighed, the tension going out of my shoulders. "Oh. Okay." I tried to sound relieved, but I wasn't. I tried to imagine what I would say if he took Lily up on her advice and called me. I wouldn't answer the phone. I couldn't.

"Kate?" She bit her lip, like she was nervous. "Do you think maybe you should talk to him?"

I shook my head so aggressively that my ponytail slipped a little. "Absolutely not. How can you even suggest that? Have you forgiven him for what he did to Mom?"

"No!" She practically shouted the word. "No, I haven't forgiven him, but it's different with me. We weren't as close as you two were, and if what he did to Mom is what made you want to quit swimming—"

"I would have quit either way."

She leveled a look at me. "If none of this had ever happened, and you were still living in Salem, you would have quit?"

No, I wouldn't have. Of course I wouldn't have. "That's not what I mean. I just mean even if I forgave Dad right now—which I couldn't do—I still wouldn't want to swim anymore. I think maybe that part of my life is over." I hadn't said the words out loud like that before, and it sent a little ball of panic into my stomach.

"Really?" Lily seemed just as surprised as I was by my words.

"Really." But maybe something better was starting.

∘ ∘ ∘

We were slated to present our elements blanket the next day. Even though I knew all I had to do was stand in front of our class while Marisol, who was way better at public speaking than I was, talked about it, I was still nervous.

The blanket was folded in the middle of our lab table, Marisol and Patrice huddled over it, picking off little glue strings that we hadn't caught the week before. I sat down next to Roger and neither of the girls seemed to notice me.

"Hey."

I jumped, startled. I hadn't actually realized that Roger was awake. He was looking at me now with a confused look.

"Do I know you?" he asked.

Across the table, Marisol and Patrice laughed.

"I doubt it," Patrice said, "considering you've been asleep since she enrolled."

I snuck a look at her, but she and Marisol were whispering to each other, and it took me a second to realize they were speaking Spanish, just like on my first day.

"Hello there," Roger said. He had green eyes, almost as light as jade. Who knew?

At his greeting, Patrice stopped talking and sent him a severe expression I'd never seen her use before, but before I could question the reason behind it, Dr. Stewart started class.

"Lab table number one," he called out. "Dazzle us with your creativity."

They'd chosen to depict their periodic table of elements using pieces of nature glued to a trifold board. It included twigs, leaves, rocks, feathers, and other miscellaneous items. Dr. Stewart inspected it closely while they gave a speech about being closer to nature because they chose twigs, and how they felt like it gave them a better understanding of science.

He *hmm*ed and the confused-looking lab group took a seat at their table, leaving the trifold board on the floor beside Dr. Stewart's desk.

"Lab table number two," he called out.

We all shuffled to the front of the class, including Roger. Dr. Stewart rolled his eyes when we unfolded our blanket, and my stomach knotted up. It was a terrible idea. I knew it was terrible. He thought it was awful, and he was going to fail us all.

But what came out of his mouth wasn't a criticism of the project. "Roger, I'll give you credit for this project if you can tell me your new lab partner's name."

Roger looked over at me, squinting in my direction like he might be able to telepathically conjure the correct name. "Beth?"

Everyone in class laughed, and Dr. Stewart crossed his arms decisively. "Have a seat, please."

Roger's shoulders sank, but he didn't argue. He walked back to the table, immediately putting his head down. None of us said anything for or against him. Dr. Stewart came close to us, like he had before, looking at every nook and cranny of the blanket as the three of us held it awkwardly unfolded against our bodies.

"Why a blanket?" Dr. Stewart asked.

"Well," Marisol said, gearing up with a smile. "We thought about doing food or plants or something a little more natural, but then we realized that it would be better to use a material that's made of more than one element. Most of these jerseys are polyester, and polyester is made of all kinds of chemical compounds." She started to tick them off on her fingers. "Terephthalic acid and monoethylene glycol. This fabric is made of chemical reactions, and so what better way to present the table of elements than to show it in multiple forms?" She grinned, and the whole room was silent.

I blinked at her. Where had that come from? I had no clue what those chemicals she mentioned were, but she knew them well enough not to stumble over them, so I was impressed.

Dr. Stewart seemed to be as well. He stared at Marisol for a second, his finger on his chin, and then nodded. "This was a nice idea." He pursed his lips. "And thank you, Marisol, for that insightful explanation. It's a little sloppy, but altogether it looks very nice. It's great to see the three of you working together on this."

Relief sang through my bones. I wasn't even sure what I'd been so nervous about. It was just a stupid project.

"Well, most of us worked together," Patrice said, and my eyes slid over to her, not sure what she meant. She didn't need to throw Roger under the bus when Dr. Stewart had already dismissed his participation. Marisol looked down at the floor, and Patrice was looking straight ahead at Dr. Stewart. "I hate to say this, Dr. Stewart, but Kate barely participated."

I was so shocked by what she said that I almost lost my grip on the blanket. I whipped around to face her and was very aware of the eyes of everyone in the class on us, even Roger. "What?"

"Is that true, Kate?" Dr. Stewart asked, rather patiently.

"No. What are you . . . ?" I looked at Patrice, trying to decipher why she was saying what she was saying, but she wouldn't look at me. "The blanket was my idea. I helped put it together."

At that, Patrice finally faced me, her eyes angry and wide.

"You mean when you skipped out on our work time to go on a date with Ben?"

My mouth fell open. "You guys made me leave." My chest was tight, and it felt like the room was getting smaller. I didn't understand what was happening. Had I stepped into an alternate dimension? Had Patrice completely lost her mind?

"Oh, and did I also make you steal my boyfriend?"

Horror washed over me, even as everyone in the class started to talk and make *oooo*ing sounds.

"I didn't—" I started to say, beginning to panic, but Patrice spoke over me.

"Oh, please," she hissed, her hair bobbing around her cheeks as she leaned close to me. To be honest, I was afraid she was going to hit me. "Sarah Miller saw you and Michael making out at some club on Saturday night, so don't even deny it. We became friends and then you stabbed me in the back."

I felt sick. And dizzy. My face was burning, and I tried not to focus on everyone talking around us, staring, laughing. "I swear, I didn't—"

"Okay, everyone, okay!" Dr. Stewart shouted over the din of the class.

I could hear Patrice saying something else, her voice loud and insistent, but I couldn't understand anything. I dropped my corner of the blanket and left, ignoring the sound of Dr. Stewart calling after me.

◦ ◦ ◦

I hid in the bathroom through the rest of first period, and when lunch rolled around, I hid in a stairwell by the gym that I rarely saw anyone use. I wished that Michael was with me, but I took comfort in the knowledge that I would see him next period. All I had to do was survive lunch.

Which was easier said than done.

I pulled my phone out and considered calling Harris, but what good would it do? He was in class right now, and I didn't think he would leave to take a call from me. I wasn't a priority to him anymore. He lived in a totally different world now.

I stayed there until the bell rang and then rushed to American Lit, where I only kept myself from throwing my arms around Michael when I saw the way everyone was looking at us. That settled it. Between Chemistry and now, everyone had heard what happened at the front of Dr. Stewart's classroom. I pretended I didn't see them.

Michael sighed, his face already looking tired. "Hey," he said. He'd heard. Of course he had. "How are you?"

I scoffed and took my seat. "Well, Patrice hates me and so does Marisol, and they humiliated me in front of our entire Chemistry class, which may or may not have cost me my grade on our stupid project. So, altogether, I'd say I've been better."

He scraped his chair over to me until his hands were on my arm. "I'm sorry. I didn't think this would happen."

I put my hand on his cheek. "It's okay. It's not your fault."

He closed his eyes for a second, and when he opened them again, he was back. "She'll get over it eventually. This isn't my first argument with her. We've had too many to count."

I shook my head. "It's different. This time, you broke up with her and then immediately started seeing someone else. And while

———

you might have had fights with her before, I haven't. She has no reason to forgive me. I'm no one to her."

"She likes you. She has since your first day. She told me. She'll get over it, I promise."

In the meantime, I would have to handle being a social pariah to the only people who'd actually liked me.

° ° °

"Are you okay? Are you feeling sick?"

I didn't look up at my mother. Yes, I was feeling sick, but not the way she meant. I pushed my food around on my dinner plate. "I'm fine."

Under the table, Lily nudged me with her foot. "Is it Michael?"

I pushed my plate away hard and looked up at them. "Could we just stop talking about Michael for one second?"

Beside me, Lily's eyes went wide. "I'm sorry. I didn't mean to upset you."

I buried my face in my hands. It wasn't Lily's fault, and it wasn't Michael's fault. It was my own damn fault.

"What's going on?" my mother asked me, her voice gentle from the other side of the table.

I sighed and let my hands drop. "It's nothing—just drama at school."

My mother's brow wrinkled. "Do you want to talk about it?"

I shook my head immediately. "It's nothing to talk about. Michael thinks it'll pass, so . . ."

My mother tried to smile at me, but it seemed to crumble a little when I looked at her. "Why don't you call Harris? You haven't been back to Salem in a while. Why don't you go down and visit?"

Because Harris had stopped answering my phone calls and started spending all his free time with the person responsible for this mess. "We're not really talking right now."

My mother's mouth popped open in a little O. "Well, what about those girls you've been spending time with? What were their names, the ones from your chemistry class?"

I squeezed my eyes shut. "Actually, I think I'm just going to get some of my reading for Lit out of the way, maybe go to bed early." I pushed back from the table, leaving my mostly full plate of food as I turned and went to my room.

But I was only there a second before my mother knocked on my door and let herself in. "Kate," she started, but I stopped her, putting my book down on my bed.

"Mom, I really don't want to talk about it."

"Actually," she said, coming to sit at the end of my bed, "I wanted to talk to you about something else."

I pushed myself up, my back against my headboard. "Okay."

Her index finger traced the design on the cover of my book. "I thought I was doing the right thing by coming here. I know I could have waited. You'll be a senior next year, and I could have held off longer, but I knew how it would be. I knew your father would insist on deciding what college you go to. He would try to get you to stay as close to home as possible so he could still be involved in your coaching. He never would have let you go."

She stopped and took a deep breath, and I thought maybe she was trying not to cry. "But then that practice happened, and I was so angry that he had let it happen and that he'd had such

236

terrible self-control, that I knew I couldn't stay anymore, and I guess it didn't occur to me that it would be this hard on you."

She looked up, and I was struck by how comforting her familiar features were.

"It's not your fault."

She gripped the spine of *The Crucible* and pressed it into my mattress. "Maybe not, but I still wish things were different. I wish you were happier here." She finally let go of my book and folded her hands in her lap. "I never meant for our moving here to make you feel like you couldn't swim anymore. I know it shook you up. It shook me up, too. But you don't have to give up swimming, if that's what's making you so sad. I just want you to have the right to choose for yourself."

I was shaking my head before she was even finished speaking. "It's not that. I mean, it's a little bit that. I do miss swimming. But quitting swim didn't make me sad." Empty, maybe, but I didn't think *sad* was the right word.

She pursed her lips. "Things are going to get better," she said quietly. "I know they are. But I don't want you to forget that you still have me, and you still have your sister. I'm sorry to hear that you and Harris aren't speaking, but he wasn't your only friend."

I knew that much. I still had Michael, even if he couldn't quite understand how I felt about hurting Patrice. "Thanks."

She smiled, a genuine smile this time.

o o o

Even though it had come at a cost, it felt great to be able to hold Michael's hand on the way to class the next morning. He curled his fingers around mine and talked to me about his mom all the way to school. We split up at the staircase, the way we did every B-day, and I rushed up to the third floor, where I had Health Science first period, but I hadn't even made it all the way up to the third floor when I heard crying.

I stopped, even though I was fairly certain whoever it was had to have heard me coming. It wasn't like I had anticipated someone needing privacy in the middle of the stairwell. Most of the students used one of the elevators or the main staircase in the commons, but I preferred this emergency staircase in the back of the building because it was usually secluded.

"It's okay," a voice came down to me.

"You can come up. Just ignore me." I recognized the voice. It was Marisol. I rounded the flight and stopped on the landing between the second and third stories to see her sitting on a step halfway up, a crumpled tissue in her hand and her hair falling out of its ponytail.

Oddly, there wasn't disdain in her eyes when she looked at me. "You know how it is. They get what they want, and they move on," she said. She scrubbed at her face with the tissue, but it wasn't doing much good. I thought the poor thing had pretty much reached its saturation point. She threw it over the railing, and I said nothing. "Why am I even talking to you?" she said, her voice raw. "You screwed over my best friend."

The fact that Patrice and Marisol thought I was the spawn of Satan had had enough time to really sink in that it didn't hurt like a knife wound when she mentioned it. "I didn't mean to screw anyone over," I told her, even though I was certain I was talking to a brick wall. "Michael and I weren't together before he broke up with Patrice."

I waited for her to argue. I waited for her to tell me that I was scum. But she didn't.

"You swear?"

"I swear. I mean, I've liked Michael since we met, but I did my best to back off as soon as I knew Patrice was in the picture. She's been so nice to me. You both have. I never meant to hurt anyone."

I felt like I was on trial. Didn't she need a spotlight or a gavel or something? She wiped her eyes. "Well, it doesn't matter. Patrice is my best friend, and Michael broke her heart, and you're dating Michael, so you're my enemy by association." She groped in her clothes, probably searching for another tissue, but she didn't find one. I pulled out the travel pack I carried and handed it to her.

"Jesse told me he loved me. It's such a freaking cliché." She pulled one of the tissues out and wiped her nose with it. "I shouldn't even be surprised. Isn't this exact scenario in some kind of manual that every girl has to read before giving up her virginity?"

"I wouldn't know."

She rolled her eyes. "God, what help are you?" As if to punctuate her point, she pulled the last tissue out of the pack and stared at the empty plastic as if waiting for more to appear. "I just—" she stopped and wrapped her arms around her knees. "What if no one else wants me?" She broke into sobs then, covering her face and gulping in air.

I sat down on the step beside her and put my arm around her because I wasn't sure what else to do. "Marisol, you're a freakin' catch. Jesse isn't the only one who's ever going to want you." I squeezed her arm, and she took a deep breath to try to regain her composure.

———

"You know, I really liked you. You fit right in with us."

Her words felt like a ray of sunlight. "Really?"

"Yeah." She pushed herself up off the step, knocking my arm away from her. "Too bad you blew it."

o o o

I braved lunch in the cafeteria that afternoon, but it was worse than I'd thought it would be. Before, everyone had just seemed to ignore me. Now, it felt like everyone was watching as I took a seat in a far corner, away from my usual table, where Marisol and Patrice were acting like I didn't exist.

I tried to focus on *Fahrenheit 451* while I ate my peanut butter and jelly sandwich, but I was distracted every time Marisol or Patrice shifted, every time they moved, thinking that maybe they were going to look over at me, maybe they would come and talk to me. But I knew that would never happen. I was alone, and I needed to get used to it.

And for the most part, I thought I had, until someone crashed into my table, knocking it just hard enough to jostle my tray, sending peas rolling across its surface. I assumed that it was an accident until I looked up into the face of the girl who'd done it. She wasn't alone, and I immediately recognized the girls surrounding me as the swim team. Their faces, the ones that had been watching me that day at the rec center, were burned into my brain, and now here they were, looming over me.

"Oops," the girl who'd rammed into my table said. "Didn't mean to disturb the greatest swimmer in all of Oregon. I know we're not good enough to even be breathing the same air as you."

My stomach started to roil, my lunch becoming unsettled. "It has nothing to—"

She bumped my table again, and it scraped across the floor toward me. "I don't care," she said. "If you think my team isn't good enough for you to swim for, that's just fine. Obviously, champions go around stealing other girls' boyfriends and then flaunting it in front of everyone. So, good for you. You're a gold-medal-winning slut."

Once, during freshman year, a girl on the swim team, Lizzie Bloom (short-distance breaststroke, red braces), was tortured relentlessly by a group of girls because she'd been caught by her parents having sex in her hot tub with a junior, some guy on the soccer team. The information went viral before first period the next day. I remembered all the names they'd called her: *slut, whore, tramp, dirty.* Each one had felt too harsh, like a paper cut, for someone so kind and undeserving. Now, this one word felt like a knife burrowing under my fingernails.

I felt my skin flush, and then, stupidly, I felt a tear run down my cheek. How to make a situation worse: Cry in front of everyone. More and more people were starting to stare.

The girls all backed away and then left, taking a seat on the other side of the room, all of them turning to look at me once they were settled. Every muscle in my body trembled, and I told myself to move, again and again. *Run. Run. Run.*

Patrice's eyes were on me, but they weren't mean or even curious, really. They were full of pity. I looked away from her, ashamed and mortified and just really, really sorry. Sorry for wanting someone who wasn't mine and sorry that I'd rejected the swim team and sorry that I'd ever moved to Portland.

———

∘ ∘ ∘

My phone buzzed on my nightstand and I rolled over to see the screen lit up. The time said it was a little after midnight, and I was still up finishing my assigned reading for American Lit.

There was a text from Michael.

Is now a good time for a swim lesson?

I glanced at my open bedroom door. My mother had never known about my late-night meetings with Michael, but now that she knew we were a couple, she'd been keeping a particularly close eye on me.

I stepped out into the hallway quietly, ready to tiptoe to the front door, but my mother's bedroom door was closed and Lily wasn't asleep on the couch, as I'd thought she would be. So I quietly and slowly opened the front door, grabbed my keys, and locked the door behind me.

It was so strange how quiet the world got at night. Even in a city as populated as Portland, there were fewer cars on the roads, fewer people walking on the streets, less music coming from some undetermined location. I felt like I could hear the stars twinkling.

"I thought we were having a swim lesson," Michael said from the pool, where he was standing in the shallow end, running his arms back and forth in the water to create waves. He wasn't wearing a shirt, and I was momentarily thrown by the situation. Things were different now. I could touch him, could look at him, could do whatever I wanted with him without feeling guilty because he was someone else's. He was mine now. I wanted to throw myself into the pool.

"We are."

He made a curled-up little shape with his lips. "*Hmm.* You're not really dressed for a swim lesson."

I looked down at my clothes, a sweater and a pair of jeans. "I was trying not to wake my mom. There was no time for a wardrobe change."

He nodded and walked toward the steps. "That's okay. We can talk instead. Talking is good."

I pulled my sweater off over my head. Michael's eyes went wide, and I tried to ignore him as I wriggled out of my jeans.

Except for the material and the underwire, underwear was no different from a bikini. Michael had seen me in a bikini, but standing in front of him now, you would have thought I'd stripped down completely. Maybe it was the unveiling of something that was supposed to be hidden.

His mouth parted slightly as I stepped into the pool.

I was barely all the way in before he pulled me against him and kissed me. I let my legs float up and around his waist, and he spun us around so that I was pressed between him and the pool wall. The pool was already warm, but every inch of my body went hot as Michael's mouth moved over me, from my lips to my neck to my collarbone.

"We're supposed to be swimming," I said, a little breathless as his fingertips found my rib cage.

"Aren't we?" he asked against my skin.

I laughed. "Not exactly."

He pulled away from me, and we drifted slowly to the deeper end of the pool. But once the water began to rise up to his shoulders, I saw some of the sense of ease filter out of Michael's eyes.

I pressed my hand to his cheek. "Just keep kicking your legs. I'm not going to let you drown." I wrapped my arms around him until we were pressed together from chest to waist, our legs tangling together under the water.

"I'm crazy about you," he whispered against my ear.

I pressed my face into his neck, smelling the pool water in his pores. "So when do we get to start our salsa lessons again?"

Michael shrugged. "Whenever you want. We could start right now."

I laughed as he pulled me into position and started counting off, our limbs dragging slowly through the water. He spun me around, and the water splashed out behind me as I spun back into his arms.

He kissed me again, but before I could get distracted, I pulled away. "I can't stay long. If my mom finds me up here, she'll murder me."

Instead of letting me go, he pulled me into him, holding me close in a kind of desperate embrace that made me nervous. "I feel okay when I'm with you," he said. "It's like nothing bad exists."

I pressed my forehead to his. "I know how you feel."

He held my face in his hands. "Are you okay? I heard about what happened at lunch."

I pulled away from him just a little. "How?"

He shrugged, splashing a little. "Marisol told Ben. Ben told me. I'm sorry it happened."

The kicking of his legs had slowed slightly, but I kicked

harder to keep us afloat. "I'm okay. It was a little surprising, but nothing I can't handle." The only really surprising part had been the fact that the attack had come from the swim team and not from Patrice, even if a part of me knew that Patrice would never do any worse than she already had.

"Okay," he said, his lips pressed to my cheek.

Getting out of the pool proved more than Michael could handle, as I was now not only in my underwear but in my wet underwear, and we spent another few minutes making out in a lounge chair before I got too cold to stay.

We shivered all the way down to our floor, and just as he was leaning in for a good-night kiss, the elevator opened and Lily appeared before us.

Her eyes went wide when she saw us, standing there in the hallway, dripping. "Kate? What are you guys doing out here?" She glanced at the door, like our mother might be there to catch us.

"We went for a swim." I tried to cover my almost naked body with the dry clothes that I hadn't bothered to put back on. Michael didn't have so much as a towel, and I could see the goose bumps on his arms.

Lily's eyes narrowed. "A swim, huh?"

I narrowed my eyes right back. "Well, where were you so late?"

Lily scoffed. "I don't have to tell you. I'm an adult. You're the one who's going to be in huge trouble if Mom finds out you were swimming with your boyfriend in the middle of the night."

I didn't let up. "Were you with your new boyfriend?"

Lily's joy seemed to dwindle slightly. "Um . . . no . . . I wasn't. I just . . . um . . . lost track of time." She was looking everywhere but at me, and my eyes met Michael's quickly before he excused himself to go inside.

Lily unlocked the door, and I left a trail of water behind me as we went in. "Lily, is everything okay?"

She hung up her coat and dropped her purse by the couch. "You should probably take a shower. You smell like chlorine."

She sat down on the couch, and I stood there for a second, debating whether to pry or not. Eventually, I took her advice and went for a shower.

◦ ◦ ◦

"So, she wouldn't tell you where she was?"

Michael and I had paired up for our American Lit worksheet, and thanks to the fact that neither of us had social lives now that our friends weren't speaking to us, we were far ahead of the rest of the class in our reading, making the homework far easier.

"No. And I know it's probably not a big deal. But there was something about the way she was acting. We've always been really open with each other, and I don't know, it's a little weird that she doesn't want to tell me. It kind of irks me."

"You didn't tell her about us at first." He popped a peppermint in his mouth and stuffed the crinkly wrapper in his pocket.

I wriggled a little in my seat. "Well, my dynamic with her has been a little off-balance since the wedding."

"I'm sure everything's going to be fine. She's going through a lot. She was probably out with one of her friends from school."

He was probably right, but I still worried about her. I just wanted to know that she was taking care of herself. If anyone deserved to be happy, it was Lily.

———

The bell rang, and Michael and I left the classroom, him heading to Pre-Calculus and me heading to Government, but before we went our separate ways, Michael prodded me in the direction of a quiet hallway and pressed his mouth into the crook of my neck, and I giggled, partly because I was ticklish there and partly because this wasn't the first time that Michael had gotten cozy with me in the halls.

Between us, my phone vibrated, two short vibrates that told me it was a text message. Michael pretended not to notice and continued to kiss my neck while I dug my phone out of my pocket.

Did you see this? the text from Lily read, and I put a hand on Michael's chest to get him to back up before I opened the article she had attached. Michael looked down at the phone now between us, his face immediately concerned when he saw the headline:

SALEM SWIMMER SENTENCED
AFTER STEROID USE

"Oh my God."

Michael took the phone from me when I was done reading the article and read it for himself while I stood there. I stared down at the tile that stretched between the girls' bathroom and the boys' and tried not to throw up.

"This is him, isn't it?" Michael asked after a long moment. "This is your friend; the one that stood you up?"

"Harris." This couldn't be real. Harris? Using steroids? The article said he'd been kicked off the team, been suspended, and could even face time in a juvenile detention center.

It was like reading about a stranger. In my head, I tried to reconcile the person that the article painted, a star athlete fallen from grace, with my best friend, the boy who skipped class to make out with his girlfriend, the boy who half-assed everything he did so he wouldn't look uncool by caring too much. Harris wouldn't do this. It had to be someone else.

"It's not true," I said just as the bell rang.

Michael watched for a second as a stray kid rushed to whatever class he was late for before turning back to me. He pressed his hands into my shoulders. "Kate, hey. We'll figure this out, okay? Whatever it is. We'll figure it out. Go to Government, okay? I'll come get you after."

I tried to focus on what he was saying, but everything was a little muffled, a little blurry. The world felt like it was opening up underneath me.

"Kate." Michael put his hands on either side of my face, and when I met his eyes, the world seemed to come back into focus. "Go to class, okay?"

I nodded, and he tucked my phone into the side compartment of my backpack before we separated.

I tried to focus in Government, but I couldn't think straight. Harris had tested positive for steroids, he'd been kicked off the swim team, he was facing real charges, and just thinking about it made me want to be sick.

I pulled out my phone and turned on the screen under my desk, but when I opened up a new text to Harris, I didn't know what to say.

Eighteen

fter school, I tried to call Harris. Not once, not twice, but seven times. He never answered. I'd heard his voice mail message seven times, and I was tired of the robotic tone of his voice. "Why isn't he answering his phone? What is he doing? How is this even happening?"

Michael's eyes followed me from one side of my bedroom to the other, back and forth while I tried to figure out how I was going to get more information about Harris. He hadn't answered his cell phone and neither had April, his girlfriend, and now here I was, completely unsure of what to do. I felt like a bird that someone had tossed into a cage, pecking at the bars. I thought about trying to call him again, but as long as I didn't call him, I could pretend he would pick up the phone when I actually did.

"Maybe you should sit down."

"I can't sit down." I knew Michael couldn't understand. I had to talk to Harris. I had to get the story from a reliable source, not some online newspaper that called Harris a star pupil. I needed to hear him deny it, needed to hear his voice.

I stopped pacing. Michael was sitting on my bed, his hands twisted in the comforter, his eyes full of concern.

"I have to go see him."

Michael got off the bed and came to stand in front of me, effectively blocking my path. "Wait, you're going to go?"

"I have to. I can't just stay here while this is happening. I need to see him." I went back to my phone, considering texting him to let him know that I would be coming to Salem but deciding against it. If he was going to run away from me, I would just have to catch him off guard. The article had said he'd failed the test the previous week. Days had gone by, and he hadn't told me. I wasn't about to let him get away with it again.

Michael's eyes fell to the phone in my hand. "Maybe that's not such a great idea."

The hand holding my phone dropped to my side. "Why not?"

His hands came up to grab my hips, and I tried not to be distracted by it. In the living room, through the open bedroom door, I could hear my mother and Lily talking about something in hushed voices. I wanted to curl up in a ball in my closet and not come out until this had all gone away. But I couldn't. Because I had to know the truth.

"You're not in a great emotional state right now. You shouldn't drive all the way to Salem like this."

"Michael, I can't just *not* go, okay?" I put a hand on his plaid-covered chest. The warmth of his skin beneath the fabric made the world quiet down just a little.

Michael's eyes shifted to the door and then to me. "Why don't you let me go with you?"

Bringing Michael along just didn't seem like a good idea. Michael was Portland and salsa dancing and the taste of peppermints; Harris was Salem and swim meets and childish jokes. They wouldn't mix well.

"It's okay. I should go alone. He's more likely to want to talk if it's just me."

"Kate." Michael caught my attention again. My mind was drifting in and out of the room, unable to stay grounded. "Maybe just sleep on it. Let things die down a little, and then you can go see whoever you want. Just take a breather, okay? This is a lot to process. You're too upset to drive all the way to Salem tonight. Especially alone."

I didn't meet his eyes, entirely certain that nothing he could say would keep me in Portland while Harris was suffering. But he was looking at me with those desperate eyes, so I said what I knew he wanted to hear. "Okay."

He leaned forward to kiss me gently, and his phone rang. He shut his eyes for a second. "That's Ben. I forgot I told him I'd hang out with him tonight. I'll cancel." He was already reaching for his phone.

"No, don't do that. Hang out with him. I'll be fine." I wasn't staying here, but I didn't want Michael to know I was going. He would worry about me, and I didn't want to be another burden on him.

He scowled at me. "I want to stay here with you. I can see Ben anytime."

Something stirred in my stomach. I'd never lied to Michael. Not even when it had probably made sense to. And lying to him now—it made guilt claw at my chest. "Hang out with Ben," I told him, pulling away to sit on my bed. "I'll probably just watch TV or something. No big deal. It's okay."

He stayed where he was, looking awkward in the middle of my room. "Are you sure?"

I nodded, feigning confidence. I just needed him to leave. I needed to separate him from this drama. "Yeah."

He hesitated still. "Okay. Then I'll see you tomorrow?"

"Of course."

He kissed my cheek and disappeared. I waited until I heard the door open and close, and then I went to find my mom and Lily in the living room. They were still huddled on the couch, in the same spots they'd been in since I came home.

My mother shot upright. "Are you hungry?" Without waiting for an answer, she turned in the direction of the kitchen, and I was forced to follow her. I knew she and Lily had heard Michael and me talking. It was written all over their faces.

"Actually, no. Do you think I could borrow the car tonight?"

My mother shut the fridge without taking anything out of it and came to stand in front of me. "Katherine, you can't go out there. I'm sure Harris and his family have a lot on their plate right now without you getting in the middle of it."

I ground my teeth together. "I need to know what really happened, okay? Harris will talk to me. I know he will. I just need to see him."

She chewed on her lip, her eyes flitting over her shoulder and back again. "If you think this is the right thing to do . . ."

Lily had joined us in the kitchen. She leaned against the counter. "Sis, I don't mean to be a bitch, but maybe Michael's right. Maybe you should sleep on it and—"

I cut her off. "I'm going."

o o o

Harris's family lived on a huge piece of land almost half an hour from the aquatics center, a gated estate that I'd coveted, even though we'd lived in a house almost as big. Even with enough square footage for the entire family to live out their daily lives without ever bumping into each other, Harris's house had always been warm and cozy, full of noise and light.

I pulled up behind Mr. Monroe's BMW and threw open my door. In the past, I might have stayed right there in their driveway, setting up camp on the roof of the car until Harris realized I was out there and came to join me. Or I might have bypassed the house altogether and gone for the pool around back, jumping in without invitation or permission.

But this time, I rushed to the front door and knocked before backing up and looking up at Harris's window. I couldn't see in, but I was hoping to see movement—anything that might indicate whether he was home or not.

I heard the front door crack open, but it wasn't Harris who stepped out onto the porch to greet me. It was his mother.

"He's not here." She wrapped her arms around herself against the chill and looked at me with tired eyes. Her face had lines of exhaustion mapped across it that she hadn't bothered to try to conceal with makeup.

I felt my heart squeeze at her words. "Do you know where he is?"

Her chin began to quiver and she shook her head. "He's barely shown his face since everything happened. He's been staying at friends' houses, taking off without telling anyone. I just don't know what to do anymore."

I wanted to sympathize with her. My heart ached for the kind woman who had always had encouraging words and a warm meal for me, but I didn't have time to console her. I had to find Harris, and if I had to scour the entirety of Salem, I would.

"He might have gone to the meet."

I had already turned to get back in my car, but I spun back around at her words. "There's a meet tonight?"

She nodded. "Do you think he would do that? Do you think he would go after everything that's happened?"

"I'm not sure. But I'm going to find out." I jogged to my mom's car and slammed the door shut behind me.

o o o

The aquatics center was packed. With competition season creeping closer, everyone wanted a piece of the action. I parked in the back and made a run for the entrance, knowing in the back of my mind that there was no hurry, but not finding Harris at home had only added to my anxiety.

Inside, the meet was already under way. The starting shot sounded, followed by splashes as the swimmers dove in, then cheering and whistling, but it all seemed to fade into the background as I walked into the room. My eyes went to the pool first, where a butterfly was taking place, a butterfly that Harris wasn't swimming in, but I couldn't help myself. I watched for a second as one swimmer pulled ahead, and just as the rest of the swimmers hit the wall, I saw my father standing on the sideline, shouting and clapping his hands in that loud, slow way that didn't mean a celebration of accomplishment. It meant *I'm in charge, and I'm telling you to go faster.*

I pulled my eyes away and walked by the starting blocks to get to the stands.

"Kate!"

I ignored my father's voice, louder than anything else in the room, even though some of the faces in the stands were turning toward us now. I looked at each of them, praying that I'd see Harris's face, even if it didn't make sense.

"Kate!"

I put a hand on the rail to step onto the stands, but a hand wrapped around my upper arm, pulling me to a halt. I spun around and yanked my arm away from my dad's grip. "What do you want?" I demanded, aware that more eyes were turning to us from the stands and the sidelines.

"I want to talk to you about why your name isn't on the roster for the 6A program."

"I'm not here to talk to you." I really didn't have time to discuss swimming when there were more important things to deal with. I turned back to take another step up into the stands, but he stopped me again.

"If you're looking for Harris, he's not here."

I sighed. Of course he wasn't. "Great." I rushed past him to leave. I wasn't interested in staying there so that he could make matters worse, but he followed me, waiting until I was almost to the door before calling out to me again.

"Kate, you need to talk to me about what's going on. I'm not going to just let you throw away all the hard work I've done—"

At that, I spun around, my hands in fists because I thought I might hit him. "The hard work *you* did? What about all the hard work *I* did?"

He clenched his jaw, and when he didn't say anything, with both of us watching to see who would break first, I turned to leave again. "I don't have time for this," I muttered, more to myself than to him.

"I'm your father," he said, following me out into the lobby. "You'll make time."

"Just leave me alone!" I shouted so loudly that the girls at the front desk stopped talking to watch us. "Why can't you just leave me alone? Will it help if I tell you I quit the team? Will you leave me alone then?"

His eyebrows furrowed. "That's a lie. You're just saying that to hurt me."

I growled, a frustrated sound at the back of my throat. I couldn't believe that I had been afraid to tell him, that I had been afraid of disappointing him. "Not everything is about you. I don't care about hurting you. If you don't believe me, call Coach Wu. She loves telling everyone that I'm a quitter."

His face was beginning to purple, the veins in his neck popping out to say hello. "Oh, I'll call her, all right. I'll call her to tell her you'll be training again before the month is out and that you'll be ready in time for District."

I laughed. "You don't have a say in it anymore, Dad."

"Is this because of Harris?" He planted his hands on his hips, and I could see his fingernails turning white. "That boy wasted my time, made me look incompetent, made this team take a hit that they didn't deserve, and now you're going to let his decisions derail your future?"

"This isn't about him!" I shouted. I didn't know how else to make him listen. "This is about you. This is about the fact that you took everything from me: my life, my home, my friends. You're toxic to everything you touch. I trusted you, and you threw me and Mom and Lily into the dirt. You're nothing to me now, and I'm not going to let you drag me back into your one-man show and pretend you're doing it for me." When I was done shouting, the lobby went silent, the girls at the desk watching us with wide eyes and my father's chest heaving like he'd just run a marathon.

He shook his head, his face now something akin to pale. "Kate, I didn't mean to—"

I put up a hand to stop him. I didn't want to hear him. I had let him manipulate me for so long, sacrificed everything I wanted to make him proud, and I was done. "Doesn't matter." I inched away from him toward the door. "Doesn't matter anymore. It's over."

o o o

I didn't know where else to go. I drove up and down the highway, trying to imagine where I would go if I were in Harris's place. My body was starting to ache from being curled up in the driver's seat for so long, and my head was hurting from my brain moving a million miles an hour.

And then, as I was driving down a strip of service road a few miles from Harris's house, I spotted the park. Harris and I used to jog to that park, which was mostly just a jungle gym, a grassy hill, and a baseball field. Sometimes we'd take his dog, Boomer, with us and let him off his leash to run circles, always getting a home run.

The park was completely empty, the sun pretty much gone, and the sky bleeding from blue to pink. The lights shone brightly down onto it, and I could see straight across the hill to the houses on the other side, the lights in their kitchens on, preparing dinner.

I walked to the dugout and sat down, pulling my feet up onto the bench with me. I tucked my arms tight around myself and set my head on the chain-link fence beside me. I breathed in the cold air and wished I'd never come here. I could have been at home, watching dancing shows with Lily or acting as the third-wheel on Ben and Michael's man date. I could have been in bed, reading *Fahrenheit 451*. But instead, I was here, miles away from home, alone in the dark with no clue where to go next.

But as I was staring out at the field, I realized that the meet had to be over by then.

Which meant the after-meet party had begun.

o   o   o

It took half an hour of calling around to everyone I knew on the team to figure out where the party was. I had called Harris half a dozen times, but of course he hadn't answered. I didn't even know for certain if he was going to be there tonight, but if he wasn't, I could almost guarantee someone at the party would know where he was.

I had been to plenty of after-meet parties over the years—the ones my father allowed me to attend because he thought I'd worked hard enough to earn it. The swim team used the parties to blow off steam.

The party was at Rex's house. Rex (breaststroke, nose plugs) used to be the team geek, but if the success of his party was any indication, he was coming up in the world. People I recognized and some that I didn't were packed into the living room, where pop music screamed out of the speakers so loud that the hardwood floor was vibrating.

No one noticed me as I walked through, bypassing people pressing in on every side. I made it into the living room and around to the dining room, where there was a game of spin the bottle going on, people gathering around a Ping-Pong table. When I stepped in, Rex was being devoured over the top of the table by Clarissa (individual medley alternate, black lipstick). When they parted, Rex's lips were smeared with black. Everyone cheered, and then, while I was pushing toward the door to the kitchen, someone yelled my name.

I saw Cal at the head of the table, and then everyone else at the table turned, and they all started shouting my name, like any second they were going to hoist me onto their shoulders and start singing "For He's a Jolly Good Fellow." Cal stumbled out of his chair and came to wrap me in his arms. I hadn't seen any alcohol around, but he was very clearly drunk. He planted a wet kiss on my cheek and moved in close until I was stuck between him and the wall behind me.

Everyone else went back to their game.

"Hey, you should join." His breath smelled like gasoline. "Maybe me'n you can finally swap spit."

I tried not to grimace. "Cal, have you seen Harris?"

Cal clearly wasn't paying any attention to me. He slid around to my side and pressed his face into my neck. "Harris?" he mumbled. "Nah." I elbowed his side, and he flinched away from me, his eyes finally clearing up a little. "Damn it, Kate. Come on. What is it?"

"I'm looking for Harris."

He threw up his hands. "I dunno where he is. Been gone for days." His shoulders sagged then, and I saw the second that the realization hit him. "You here 'cause of the drug test?"

I grabbed Cal by the wrist and pulled him behind me into the kitchen, where the light was so bright, I actually flinched, and I wasn't even drunk. There were a few girls giggling over something by the bar. I kept pulling Cal until I found a walk-in pantry. I shoved him inside and shut the door behind us. I pulled a string and the light came on.

Cal bit his lip and took a step toward me, but I put up a hand to stop him. "We're not hooking up," I told him. "I need to know what's going on with Harris."

He frowned and leaned back against the shelf behind him that housed cans of green beans and corn. He crossed his arms and shrugged. "Okay. Whattaya want me to tell ya?"

I wanted to roll my eyes as he slurred the words. It was barely nine o'clock. "It's true? He got kicked off the team?"

He sent me a look like *duh*.

"Harris has been doing steroids?"

His eyes roved over my head. He reached past me and came away with a tin of cheese puffs. He popped it open and tossed a handful in his mouth. "Aren't you, like, his best friend or sumthin'?" he mumbled around the puffs.

I reached out and pinched his arm, right above the elbow.

"Ow!" Chunks of cheese puffs flew out of his mouth. "Shit. What's your problem?"

"Tell me what's going on."

He rolled his eyes and slammed the tin of cheese puffs onto the shelf next to him. "Yeah. K? He's been juicin'. And he would've gotten away with it too if it weren't for April."

"What the hell does that mean?"

He leaned in, until his lips grazed my ear, and whispered, "She snitched."

I groaned. I guess it shouldn't have surprised me that April had known. She was his girlfriend. Apparently the only one who hadn't known was me, his best friend, if I was even that anymore. "I can't believe you all knew the whole time. You are such an asshole. That shit can mess you up. And even if it didn't, you and everyone on the team should have known better than to let him do that."

"I'm not his babysitter!" he shouted.

Just then, the door of the pantry opened, and Alexandria (50-yard freestyle and a wingspan of over six feet) smiled in at us. "What is this, seven minutes in heaven?"

I shoved past her. Halfway through the kitchen, I looked back over my shoulder. "Alexandria, have you seen April?"

She was still standing in the doorway of the pantry, but now she had one hand on Cal's chest and a cheesy smile on her face. "The snitch? Last time I saw her, she was running upstairs, crying."

Crying?

I felt my phone vibrate in my pocket. Michael. I stared at the screen for a long time. His picture was one of us, sitting on the edge of his bed acting chummy, and I stared at it until the screen changed, notifying me that I'd missed his call. There was no way I could talk to him right now. If I did, he would know where I was. He would know that I'd ignored his advice. So I shut my phone off. Michael and our rooftop pool felt a lifetime away.

It took quite a bit of shoving before I finally made it up to the second floor. I checked the bathroom first, since that's where I would go if I was crying, but it was empty. From there, I moved to each door, knocking before entering and leaving the door shut if it sounded like there was an enthusiastic couple inside. Finally, in the last room, empty enough of personal belongings for me to assume it was a guest room, something caught my eye. The closet door was closed, but golden light seeped out onto the carpet.

I walked over to it and knocked.

"What do you want?" a voice—April's voice—came from inside.

"It's Kate. Could I come in?"

When she didn't answer, I pulled the door open. She was sitting inside, with her back against the wall and tears streaming down her face. Completely alone. I stood in the doorway, just staring at her, until her head came up, and she saw me, her face halfway covered by her hair.

She laughed, a wheezy, completely humorless laugh. "I guess I should have known you'd come looking for me."

I didn't feel like I'd thought I would. I'd thought I would be angry. I'd thought I would go in and yell at her like I had at Cal for letting something like this go on. Or maybe for getting him kicked off the team. I couldn't even decide which. But now, looking at her, I felt the dread in my stomach. Because I knew it was true. Without even asking her the questions I'd planned to.

I went into the closet and sat down on the carpet across from her. Her eyes and nose were red. I pulled the door shut behind me. With both the closet door and the bedroom door shut, the only indication that there was a party going on was the rhythmic thumping of the floor beneath us.

"Are you okay?" I asked her.

Her head tilted back, and she stared up at the light above her. "Not exactly."

I'd always considered April my friend. We'd been on the swim team together since freshman year, and we'd gravitated toward each other when I didn't always get along with the other girls. And then, almost a year ago, she'd started seeing Harris, and I'd started seeing a little less of both of them, but I'd still always really liked April. She was nice and not overly competitive, and she was good to my best friend. Looking at her, I almost didn't even see the girl I'd always known.

"Why are you hiding in a closet?"

She took in a deep, shaky breath. "Because I'm the snitch, and everyone hates me."

"That can't be true."

"When it got out that it was me who told Coach to test Harris . . . ," she trailed off, shaking her head. "No one would even look at me. At practice on Tuesday, they trapped me in the locker room and told Coach I started my period and couldn't come to practice. And tonight at the meet, someone hid my cap and goggles, and I got disqualified. When I got here, everyone started chanting *snitch* until I came up here, and now I can't go back out there." She pressed her forehead to her knee. "As if it isn't bad enough that my boyfriend probably isn't my boyfriend anymore."

"Harris will forgive you." I couldn't say whether that was true, but I wanted to say something to comfort her.

She scoffed and wiped her nose on the back of her hand. "I just wanted my boyfriend back. I found him passed out in his room last week. I was terrified, but Cal told me not to call the police or tell Harris's parents or anything. I shouldn't have listened. He'd just snap at me for no reason—fine one minute and screaming in my face the next. I just wanted it to stop. I knew he would get in trouble, but I thought it was a small price to pay for him to get clean."

I'd seen Harris help little old ladies put groceries in the trunks of their cars. He adopted Boomer from a shelter because they were going to put him to sleep. He'd talked to me while I sat in a tub full of ice after a particularly grueling workout. I couldn't imagine that man, the one I'd seen go from a boy to a scrawny teenager to someone I respected and looked up to, doing drugs to get ahead.

I watched her, wrapped around herself in the mostly empty closet. "You did the right thing," I finally said, and she let out a tiny breath. She shouldn't have had to be the one to speak up, but I was glad she had. "Can I ask you a question?"

She looked directly at me, her eyes wet and unfocused, like she hadn't really meant to say any of those things at all. "What?"

"How long has he been doing this?"

She shrugged. "A few months. Since the beginning of the summer." The tears had started to seep from her eyes again.

———

Since the beginning of the summer. He'd been doing it while I was still in Salem, and I hadn't even known. Harris was already slipping away from me, even then.

"Did he call you? Is that why you're here?"

I thought I heard a little bit of hope in her voice. I hated to dash it. "No. I read about it online."

She sighed. "I thought so. No one can find him."

"He's probably sleeping in his truck somewhere." Harris had once said that his truck was more comfortable than his bed because he didn't have to listen to his parents snore in the next room.

I was angry about the idea that I might have to go back to Portland without seeing Harris. But what was I supposed to do, drive all over Salem until I stumbled upon him?

"Drive you home?"

She frowned. "There's no way I'm going back out there."

"Well, you can't sit here all night. And I don't think you're going to be able to climb out the window. We're on the second floor."

Her eyes went to the closet door, like any moment someone might whip it open and throw eggs at her face. "I don't know, Kate."

I pushed myself up off the carpet. "I have to drive back to Portland. I'd be happy to walk you out and give you a lift."

Her lips curled warily, her eyes full of fear. "Okay," she finally whispered, and we emerged from the closet together. The closer we got to the door, the louder the music got, and I could feel my heart pounding along with it.

We made it all the way downstairs without anyone noticing us, and I thought going through the kitchen might make it easier for us to slip out unnoticed, but I'd forgotten about the game of spin the bottle going on just outside the doorway.

We'd barely taken a step by the crowded Ping-Pong table when someone shouted. "Look, it's the snitch!"

And then it started.

"Snitch! Snitch! Snitch!" I could think of worse names they could have been calling her, but with everyone's attention on us, every mouth in the room open to attack April, I started to feel her terror, too.

Without thinking, I grabbed her hand and pulled her through the room, rushing past people booing and shouting, until I threw the front door open and we raced down the driveway.

By the time we made it down the block to my car, huffing and trying to catch our breaths, the party was just a distant rumble of bass in the night.

I pulled open the driver's side door, but April didn't climb in, and when I looked at her over the top of the car, she was leaning against the passenger side, her hand on her stomach, laughing.

She saw me watching her and laughed harder. "Oh God," she said when she'd caught her breath. "I'm so screwed." Her mouth hung open in exaggerated misery, and I laughed at the sight of her, pressing my forehead to my cold window, fogging it up with my breath.

We laughed until there wasn't anything else to laugh about, and then we got in my car and I drove her home.

*   *   *

April didn't live far from the Monroes, in a little house that I'd always thought was cute. She waved to me from her front lawn, and I waited until she was inside and the porch light came on before pulling away.

I was just going to go home. Maybe in the morning things would look different, as people were so fond of saying. I could go home and swim with Michael or watch TV with Lily or just do homework, and maybe I would feel better when I opened my eyes the next day.

But when I drove by the baseball field again, farther away on the other side of the hill than where I'd been before, I saw a figure down there, under the streetlights along the main road, pressed against the fence like a proud father watching his kid play T-ball.

I pulled over to the side of the road and parked, barely remembering to turn my headlights off before rushing down the hill to meet him.

"Harris!"

He hadn't seemed to notice me running toward him, didn't realize I was there until I was right beside him, he was so zoned out in the dark. "Kate?"

I was the slightest bit out of breath from the run, and Harris watched me until I found whatever it was I was going to say to him. "Where have you been?"

He turned away from me to look back out at the red dirt on the baseball field. "Here and there. Doesn't matter. Guess you heard what happened."

"Yeah."

He sucked both of his lips inside his teeth and shook his head. "I really fucked up. I fucked everything up."

I reached out to put my hand on his arm, giant with hard muscle, but he jerked away from me, turning to face me and suddenly so aware, so focused on me, that it was a little frightening.

"What are you even doing here?" he demanded, his face all sharp lines and edges. "I thought you didn't want to have anything to do with us anymore."

So many different emotions bounded through me all at once: fear, hurt, worry, and anger, and eventually the anger won out. It wasn't the right thing to do in that moment, when Harris obviously needed comfort, but I was so angry at the world, and especially at him, and that anger got the best of me.

"What are you talking about? You're the one who chose my dad. You're the one who never shows up and never answers my calls. You're the one who did drugs and got thrown off the team and *didn't even tell me about it*." It was the wrong time for it, the wrong time to point the finger at him. But once I started, I couldn't stop. "You're supposed to be my best friend. I've been sitting around wondering what happened to you, and you were here, ignoring your life to do something as stupid as steroids."

He shook his head, silent, looking out at the baseball diamond, and I realized that he was crying. He was actually crying, right in front of me, so hard that his cheeks were wet in seconds. I'd never seen him cry before. All the anger in my chest evaporated. "I just wanted to be as good as you. I just wanted to be good at something for the first time in my fucking life, and all I did was fail even harder, and now I have nothing." He scrubbed violently at his eyes with the heels of his hands.

"You don't have nothing. What about April? What about school? What about me?"

He crumpled even further, bowing over slightly, his arms

———

wrapped around himself. This couldn't be healthy. Could he be going through withdrawal? Was he about to pass out right in front of me? Maybe he needed to go to a hospital. He shook his head, over and over. "I'm so tired."

I moved toward him again, reaching out to him. "Let me take you home. Your mom is worried."

He threw himself away from me. "Don't touch me! You haven't been here, Kate. You left, remember? You left me here."

"Harris." I didn't know what else to say. How could I tell him he was right or wrong or anything when he was like this? How could I tell him that he wasn't the only one who was hurt? How could I tell him that he had so much in his life without swimming? But I knew how he felt. I knew what it was like to find meaning in something only to have it taken away, only to have it turn on you, and I knew nothing I said was going to make that hurt go away.

He focused on me again, his eyes clear and steady in the darkness, his face still shining with undisturbed tears. "You don't belong here anymore. My world is fucked up enough without you coming back and trying to fix everything."

I took a step toward him, but he moved away just as fast.

"Just go," he pleaded with me.

"Harris, please. Let me help."

He shook his head. "I'm done." And like he needed to prove it to me, he turned and walked away fast. I took a step to go after him, but he disappeared so fast that all I could do was drop down on the bench behind me and bury my face in my hands.

Maybe he was right. I had no idea how to put him back together. I gripped the bench and tried not to cry. Harris and I had

———

been best friends since third grade. He was the big brother I'd never had, and up until a month ago, he'd been the person who knew me better than anyone, and now I didn't know if I'd lost him or not.

I walked back up the hill to my car, dejected and helpless, and sat in the driver's seat with the door open, my head pressed into the seat while cars drove past on the road beside me. I pulled out my phone to check the time and realized that it was still turned off. It had been off that whole time. I turned it back on and called Lily.

"Hey," I said when she picked up. "I'm on my way home, I promise. It's a long story, but I—"

"Thank God. Where the hell have you been?"

I tucked my phone into my shoulder to start the car. "What are talking about? I've been in Salem."

"Yeah, and not answering your phone. Michael and I have been trying to get in touch with you for hours."

"Michael? Why? What's going on?" I felt dread travel from the back of my neck to my fingertips as I pulled onto the road.

"His mother is in the hospital. It seems like it could be serious. I didn't tell him where you were, but he's been trying to reach you. He called me a few times to see if I could get ahold of you."

I pressed harder on the gas pedal, sending the car rocketing toward the highway. "I'll be there as soon as I can."

"You should probably go straight to the hospital."

Nineteen

It took me forever to find Michael once I was at the hospital. I called him a few times when I got close, but his cell phone went straight to voice mail. I finally got his mom's information, but she was in the ICU and I wasn't allowed anywhere near her. There was no one in the waiting room, and I sat out there, listening to the hum of the coffee machine and the sound of the toilet flushing somewhere down the hall, for what felt like forever. It was cold, and I sat in a chair, rocking back and forth to keep myself warm and awake.

Finally, somewhere around two in the morning, a door opened, and Michael came into the waiting room. He was looking around, probably trying to find the bathroom I'd been listening to all night, when his unfocused eyes landed on me. He stopped walking, and the hand that he'd been using to rub his sleepy eyes fell to his side.

I moved toward him, crossing the room to put my arms around

him, and I was amazed at how warm and soft he was. I wanted to keep him there and pretend that everything else didn't exist. I wanted to pretend that the last twenty-four hours hadn't happened. He was the only good thing left.

He said my name softly, and I felt him pushing me, his hands on my upper arms, until they fell away.

"How's your mom?"

He didn't quite look me in the eye, his gaze moving over my head and down at the floor. "She's not doing so great. One of her lungs collapsed, and they're having to drain fluid again. Things are really tricky right now."

"I'm sorry."

He nodded, still not looking at me.

And then he did. He met my eye, and I knew what was coming before it was out of his mouth. "Where were you? I killed my battery trying to get ahold of you."

"My phone was off. I forgot I turned it off."

"You went to Salem, didn't you? After you said you wouldn't?"

I stared at him. I could feel something bad coming, like you do getting ready to walk into the dentist's office when the ache has already become unbearable. I didn't say anything. He knew, and I knew, and there was no point in confirming what was already out in the open for everyone to see.

He shook his head. "Of course. You've lied to everyone else. Why should I assume you wouldn't lie to me?"

"That's not fair." I crossed my arms, suddenly very thankful for the distance he'd put between us.

"I don't really care what you think is fair right now."

I closed my eyes against the anger in his voice. It had never been directed at me before, and even though I knew I probably deserved it, it hurt anyway—a sickness that burrowed down deep until I thought I might scream.

"My mother is in the other room fighting for her life, and I needed my girlfriend here with me."

My eyes came back open, and he was looking at me with harsh accusation. "I had to go. You would have done the same thing."

"And did it work out for you?"

I was still trying to figure out what I was going to tell him when he spoke again.

"You should go home."

"But—"

"You can't come in to see my mom anyway. Family only. So you should just go."

I stepped toward him, putting out my arms. I wanted to hold him again. I wanted everything to be okay. I wanted to sleep in this waiting room if it meant I was closer to him. But he put up his hands. "I think I just need some time alone."

"Michael, please. I want to stay with you." I tried to keep my voice steady when I just wanted to cry.

He shook his head, looked up at the fluorescent light above us, and his skin looked translucent beneath it. He didn't need to say anything else.

"Okay." I could feel it coming on, like a cold. "I'll call you later today."

"I don't think you should call me."

The tears stopped. What hit me then was worse than tears. It was panic and hurt and . . . nothing. All of a sudden, my body and brain were numb. I didn't know what to say. He had been mine

———

for two weeks, and that was all it had taken for me to screw it all up.

He wasn't even looking at me. His eyes were everywhere but my face, but I didn't want to look away from his because I'd already lost so many people—Dad, Patrice, Marisol, Harris—and I didn't want to lose him, too. But he still wouldn't look at me.

"Okay." I turned and left slowly, hoping maybe he would come after me and beg me to stay. But he didn't.

∘ ∘ ∘

When I woke up, the sun was shining afternoon bright through my bedroom windows. I was still in my clothes, on top of my blanket, and I smelled like hospital. My clock said it was well into the day, almost two in the afternoon, and I'd slept straight through.

I checked my phone, hoping that Michael had decided to call, but he hadn't. I considered staying in bed for the rest of the day. And then I considered going back to the hospital. Michael had been upset. What if I just went back to make sure that he was okay? I wouldn't mention our relationship or how much I desperately needed him. I could just see if his mom was doing any better.

When I walked into the living room, where Mom and Lily were watching TV, I knew something was wrong. My mother muted the TV. I wasn't sure how, but they knew what happened last night. They knew that Michael had broken up with me, if that was what he'd done, and based on the way they were looking at me, they knew just how pathetic I was over it.

"Do you know if Michael came home at all this morning?" I asked them. "Have you heard anything about his mom?"

———

My sister and mother looked at each other. I hadn't realized until then that they were both in their pajamas.

"Sweetie," my mom finally said, apparently after they'd exchanged some sort of silent agreement. "Michael's mother passed away this morning."

All the air went out of my lungs. I sank down into the armchair. I thought of Michael's mom: long hair and kind eyes and a bright smile. A woman who used to dance with her husband and laugh with her son. I felt something crack in my chest, and I didn't know if it was for Harriet, for Michael, or for myself.

"Where's Michael? Is he home?" I wasn't sure how these things worked. I'd never lost someone close to me. I'd never lost someone I shared a home with. I started to get up out of the chair to go see him. He had to have gone home. Would he want to see me? Would I just make it worse? Selfishly, I was prepared to find out.

"Kate." My mother got up off the couch to follow me to the door.

"What?"

"He's gone. Michael's gone."

I had this horrible moment when I thought she meant he was dead, too. It took me looking at Lily, to seeing her wide eyes, to understand that that wasn't what my mother had meant. "Where is he?"

"He's in Vancouver. He didn't even come home. His uncle came this morning to get Michael's stuff. I only spoke to him for a minute."

I heard what she was saying. I heard it very clearly, but I still walked to the door, I still put my hand on the knob. "He's gone?"

I'd never closely examined the odd color of our front door, somewhere between turquoise and honest-to-God green.

"He needs to be with people who can take care of him. He can't stay here. He's only seventeen."

I wanted to scream at her, as if that was the most reasonable solution to this miserable situation, so instead I went into the hall and stared at his door. I pressed my forehead to it and remembered the way Michael had come out of it the first time we'd spoken to each other. It was silent inside. It felt like everything had changed, been turned on its head in the last ten minutes. I heard my mother come into the hallway, and I knew she was watching me, but I didn't know what else to do, so I turned and walked away from her, away from our apartment, away from what used to be Michael's home, away from everything.

I threw open the door to the roof, and I didn't wait for it to close behind me as I rushed toward the pool, slipped my shoes off, and plunged in, jeans and all. I let the water close over me and listened to my pulse in my ears as I sank to the bottom. My body felt like a paperweight, sinking until my butt hit the floor.

I sat on my bed, my hands pressed to my ears, trying to block out the screaming. No matter how hard I pushed, I couldn't seem to quiet them, only block out some words. But I could still make out most of it.

"You're disgusting!" I heard my mother scream before I finally decided to leave. It felt like the house was going to shake to the ground around me, and maybe I would shake apart with it.

I could hear my breathing in my ears as I crept into the hallway. Even with my parents' voices attempting to drown it out, every breath was loud in my own head.

"You gave up on us years ago," my father shouted. "You think you

can just paste on a smile and tell yourself it's okay and that's going to fix everything?"

I slammed my hands back over my ears and raced down the stairs, the lump that had settled in my throat hours before threatening to surface. I reached out for my mom's keys, and with my hand away from one ear, I realized the fighting had stopped.

My hand dropped, my body hesitating for just a second. Maybe I'd imagined the whole thing. Maybe it hadn't really happened. The house was so silent that I could imagine my mother in bed, reading a book, my father lacing up his tennis shoes for an evening run. For a heartbeat, everything felt normal.

And then their bedroom door flew open.

I lunged for the keys and had the door open by the time my dad made it down the stairs to me.

"Kate," he said, the sound of his footsteps coming close. "Wait. We need to talk."

I stepped out the door. I thought maybe if I just kept going, he would let me leave. I could walk away from him and go somewhere else to try to breathe. I unlocked the car with a little beep-beep, fully intending to leave the front door wide open if it meant getting away from him faster.

"I know you're mad, but we need to talk about this." I felt his hand curl around my upper arm, pulling me to a halt. "I didn't intend to—"

I wrenched my arm from his grip and spun around to face him. I wanted to say so many things: that I hated him, that he was horrible, that I regretted every second I'd spent looking up to him, trying to make him proud. But I couldn't say anything.

He was standing there, his mouth hanging open, his hand still stretched out toward me, and I couldn't say anything. I backed away *from him until my legs hit the car's front bumper. He stood there until I got into the car and drove away—a figure in the open doorway with nothing to say.*

I scrambled to get my feet under me and catapulted upward, breaking the surface and gasping for air seconds before the tears kicked in. I covered my face, breathing in the smell of chlorine on my skin like a balm. It didn't help.

The water was like acid on my skin, and I scrambled to get out, trying to get away from it as fast as I'd wanted to get to it in the first place. I sat on the edge and shivered, looking down at the water like it would come up out of the pool to get me.

I wanted to lay on the bottom until the world ended, I wanted to swim laps until my muscles burned and the rest of the universe ceased to exist, I wanted everything to stop. I didn't want this life where everything good was eaten up by something awful.

I pounded my fist on the ground beside me, pounded it again and again until my bones started to ache, and then screamed into my open palm until I felt like I could breathe again.

o o o

I went downstairs to take a hot shower, pretending I didn't see the looks my mother and sister sent me when I told them I didn't want to eat dinner. I showered and changed into pajamas before climbing right back into bed. I held my phone against my body while I stared out the windows so in case I didn't hear it ring, I would feel it vibrate against me. I called Michael, but it went to voice mail again and again, and I cried into my sheets until I felt empty and dried out.

I fell asleep when the sun started to go down and woke to the soft clatter of ceramic smacking together. I couldn't see if it was my mom or Lily in the hazy dark. I pushed myself up and turned on the light. Lily was looking down at me, a glass of water and a peanut butter and jelly sandwich in her hands. She put them on my bedside table.

"You should eat." She took a seat at the edge of the mattress.

I just nodded. I was starving, but the idea of eating was highly uninteresting. "Thanks." I pressed my back to my headboard and wrapped my arms around my legs. My back was starting to hurt from being in bed for so long. But at least the other pain had subsided, the hurt, the shock, the sadness. It had all faded into the background, letting numbness take over, like a virus that I wouldn't be able to kick.

"I'm sorry about what happened." She pressed her hand to one of my feet in an awkward way, though I knew she was trying to be comforting. "I never met Michael's mom. What was she like?"

A ball of tears settled hard in my throat. "She was really nice." I pressed my forehead to my knees.

"He found out that you went to Salem, didn't he?"

I nodded a weird, stilted nod. "I told him I wouldn't go, but then I did."

"I know how it feels, you know. It hurts so much to lose someone like that."

I brought my head up, and somewhere inside, something poked out from behind the wall of numbness. A little anger demon. "You have no idea how I feel. You're the one that walked away from Tom, remember?"

She looked at me like she had no idea who I was, like I was

a stranger on the street who'd shoved her down onto the pavement. Then she shook her head and got up.

"I'm sorry," I said before she'd taken a step. "I'm sorry. I shouldn't have said that. I don't know why I . . ." Maybe if I saw my face in the mirror, I would look at myself the way Lily had looked at me. Maybe I wouldn't recognize myself anymore, either.

"I never should have asked you to help me ditch my wedding." She turned back to me, and I saw that her eyes were wet. She reached up and rubbed her knuckle across her cheek.

"Lil—"

She put up a hand and shook her head. "I've been thinking about it a lot lately. I broke up with Jack."

My mouth fell open. Jack, the hunk. "Wow. That's, um . . ."

"When he asked why, I couldn't really give him a reason, except, you know . . ." She trailed off, but she didn't have to say it. Lily wasn't over Tom. And how could she be? If I felt like this after only knowing Michael for a month, how did she feel after being with Tom for almost three years?

"Anyway," she went on. "It wasn't right of me to ask you to bail me out like that. It was selfish for so many different reasons, and I should have . . ." She sighed. "It doesn't matter. The point is, I'm sorry."

I couldn't figure out how to answer her. But she didn't wait for me to. She turned and left me there, alone with my peanut butter and my own guilt.

o o o

The last time I had gone to a funeral, I was eight years old, and the funeral was for my father's grandmother, whom I'd never met.

All I remembered was sitting in the almost empty room with my father on one side and Lily on the other, thinking about how I didn't know the woman inside the casket, and how I hoped they wouldn't open it.

It was Wednesday, and Lily and I had skipped class to make the drive out to Vancouver with our mother for Harriet's funeral. I hadn't spoken to Michael or Patrice or Marisol or anyone who could tell me how Michael was feeling, and it was like an itch under my skin.

I was nervous. Not only because it had been so long since I'd been to a funeral, but also because I was going to see Michael again. I had no idea what would happen. I might not even see him. He might be so surrounded by family members that I couldn't get close to him. Maybe that was for the best. After all, this wasn't for him. It was for Harriet.

We pulled up in the cemetery, behind a line of cars, and I didn't take my seat belt off. Everyone else started to get out of their cars, but I felt like I was suffocating. I had known this woman a fraction of the time that everyone else had, but everything that happened that night, even Harriet's death, felt like my fault. I knew that was irrational. I knew it didn't make sense. But nevertheless, it made guilt settle on my chest, bearing down so hard on me that I couldn't breathe.

"Maybe I shouldn't—" I started, but Lily leaned into the car and tugged me out. She put her arm around me, and we all pressed in together until we stopped halfway up the aisle. We scooted into three seats and sat down. I looked around, but I didn't see Michael, and I didn't see anyone that I recognized.

"Do you see him?" Lily whispered in my ear, but I didn't have a chance to answer before someone dropped down into the seat beside me. I turned and felt a little sigh escape my mouth when I saw Ben's face.

"Hey." He put his arm around me. "You okay?"

I nodded. I hadn't even noticed Marisol and Patrice hovering over us until I heard Patrice's voice.

"Ben, come on, we're not sitting here."

It took Ben a second to respond, his face moving slowly up until he was squinting into the sun, up at the girls. "You can be mad at Kate if you want, but I'm not. I'm staying."

I swear Patrice growled. "No, you're not." Her eyes flitted to me, but I was much too emotionally exhausted to feel intimidated.

"You don't own me. Sit wherever the hell you want, but I'm sitting with Kate."

Marisol rolled her eyes and gave Patrice a little shove toward the seat on the other side of Ben. I focused down at the grass beneath our feet while they settled in and then leaned in close to Ben. "You should just go with them," I told him. "It's not worth it."

Ben shook his head. "I'm happy you're here. Michael will be, too."

Did he know that because he had always been particularly perceptive about my relationship with Michael or because Michael had told him so?

A beep came from Ben's phone.

Marisol reached over to smack him on the shoulder. "Turn that down," she hissed, even though nothing had happened yet. People were still settling, and the podium that stood next to the

———

empty platform hovering over the grave was empty. I forced my gaze away. I thought perhaps the less I focused on the fact that I was currently at a funeral, the less likely I was to cry.

"It's Michael," Ben said, and even though I wasn't a particularly nosy person, I read over his shoulder. Ben didn't seem to mind. In fact, he seemed to twist his body to give me a better view.

Out by the hearse. Come over. Alone.

My eyes immediately flew to the hearse parked directly behind us, on the path that traveled in a circle around the cemetery. It was at the bottom of a steep hill, and I had to sit up as straight as I could in my chair, but I saw him. He was standing on the other side of the car, so that its large hood separated him from everyone else, smoking a cigarette and talking to a man I didn't recognize. When I analyzed the man's features further, I realized that he looked a lot like Michael, with dark hair and a thin body frame, and a slight hunch to his shoulders.

I hadn't been sure until that point what Michael meant by the one word *alone*. But when I saw him talking to that man, who I assumed was his uncle, I realized it didn't mean he was currently alone. He wanted Ben to see him alone. So I stayed seated while Ben got up and went to join them. Michael stamped his cigarette out, sticking the butt in the pocket of his coat when Ben approached. They hugged, and Ben said something that made Michael glance over in our direction.

I turned around in my seat, completely unable to handle his eyes. The one thing I loved about Michael more than anything else. I pulled my coat close around me as the wind blew in, sending

———

the flowers on the podium and around the grave site fluttering, some of the petals flying away to land on graves farther down the row.

There was no barrier between Patrice and me now, and I made an effort not to look over at her, not to let the sounds of her sniffling and digging around her purse for something catch my attention.

Beside me, Lily was looking at the program, a picture of Harriet printed in color on the front of it. "She lived quite the life," Lily said quietly, and my mother met my eye across Lily's lap.

Everything went still then and quiet. Ben took a seat beside me, and then the casket was coming down the aisle, being carried by Michael, his uncle, and four other guys I didn't know. Michael stared straight ahead, and they lowered the casket onto the platform before taking seats along the front row. Beside me, Ben laced his fingers in mine, and I wasn't sure if it was for my comfort or for his.

A priest stood up behind the podium and said a prayer and some kind words about Harriet, talking about her family and Michael's father and the things she'd accomplished in her life that I knew nothing about. I stared at the grass underneath my black shoes. It was starting to brown from the cold, dry air.

When I looked up, Michael was standing at the podium, clinging on to the edges tight, like they were holding him up. "I don't have much to say." He stared down at the podium and cleared his throat. "My mom was amazing. When my dad died, she raised me like she was two people. She worked twice as hard as she should have to make sure I got everything I needed and wanted. She loved me, and that's all I ever needed." His eyes shifted to the coffin but immediately returned to the podium. "Thanks, Mom. I love you, too."

I could hear Patrice crying, and Ben shifted to put his arm around her.

It was a closed-casket ceremony, and after Michael sat down and his uncle said a few words, they started to lower her into the ground while some of the more religious members of the audience sang old hymns about meeting one another in heaven.

When it was over, we all got up, and I knew that this would probably be my only chance to talk to him. But what was I supposed to say? We hadn't spoken in over a week. The last time I saw him, he was standing in a hospital waiting room, breaking my heart over a lie that felt so important at the time. I wanted to go back to that night and refuse to leave his side, even if he hated me for it.

I hovered in the back while Michael hugged Marisol, a quick half-hearted hug—it was the only time I'd ever seen them touch—and then hugged Patrice, who clutched at him tight. I tried not to be bitter that she'd forgiven him but not me. And then his eyes traveled over her shoulder and met mine.

But they weren't Michael's eyes. Michael's eyes were full of life and intensity and humor. These eyes were dark and cloudy, and something about them was oddly unfocused.

"Hi, Michael."

He pulled away from Patrice. "Kate. Hey."

I wanted to hug him, but I stayed where I was.

"We're going to catch up with your uncle," Ben leaned into Michael to say. "We'll see you at the apartment?"

Michael nodded, distracted. "Yeah, I'll see you over there."

———

Lily squeezed my elbow sweetly. "We'll wait in the car."

Most of the cemetery had emptied out as people went back to their lives or moved on to the small get-together being held at Michael's new apartment. We were mostly alone in the cemetery, while workers still cranked the casket into the ground.

"How are you?" As soon as the question slipped out of my mouth, I was sorry I asked. It was a stupid question, but I needed to know. I could see it all over him that he wasn't okay. He held his body in a weird way, all of him sagging under some imaginary weight. I wanted to put my arms around him and cry with him and feel everything he'd been feeling for the last week.

"I'm okay." He took a deep breath and looked over his shoulder at the headstone that was already waiting for Harriet. "I'm kind of glad it's over, you know? She was always in pain, always sick. She deserves peace."

I nodded like I understood, but I just couldn't. I wasn't as strong as he was. I was too selfish to understand such a sentiment. "She does."

But then his face changed. There was no more calm; there was only misery. "I should have taken better care of her."

I took a step toward him, no longer caring if he wanted me to or not. "You took amazing care of her. There was nothing you could do." I started to put an arm around him, but he stepped away from me so fast, my arm landed on nothing.

"You don't know that." His wet eyes met mine, but then he shook his head, as if he could shake off the whole situation, as if he could shake off everything he was feeling.

"I'm the one that didn't do enough. I should have been there with you." It didn't come close to the guilt I felt, but I needed him to hear it. I needed him to hear that I knew I'd done wrong.

He shook his head. "No. This isn't your doing."

"But if I hadn't—"

He put his hand up, and I could see that his fingers were trembling. "I'm really happy you came. Mom loved you. But I really can't talk about *us* right now, okay?"

I wasn't even sure how to take something like that. I didn't think he meant to hurt me, but that was what it felt like. Like I was nothing but a distraction.

I took a step toward him. "Michael, I just—"

"Stop trying to help me, okay?" He looked right at me, right through me, his eyes full of tears and anger. "Just go away. Please."

I wasn't sure what I was expecting. I supposed a part of me was hoping he would find my presence comforting. I hoped he would see me and realize how much he missed me, how much he needed me, that he would put his arms around me and cry on my shoulder. But that was all a fantasy.

"But I . . ." I loved him. That was what I wanted to say. I wanted to tell him that I loved him. Because even if it didn't make him feel better, I thought it might help soothe whatever was dying inside my chest.

I took a step back, but Michael wasn't even looking at me. He was watching his mother being lowered into the ground. The look in his eyes made me think the Michael I knew was being buried along with Harriet.

I turned and rushed down the hill. By the time I got to the car, Lily and Mom were settled in. But I couldn't go through with the rest of it. I couldn't go to Michael's uncle's apartment and eat finger sandwiches and sit there while I wanted to be sick to my stomach.

"Can we just go home?"

I saw them exchange a glance but ignored it.

"Are you sure?" Lily asked, craning to look over the seat at me.

I nodded and looked up the hill at Michael, but he hadn't moved from his spot. There was only one change: He was now bent over, crying.

Twenty

I stared down at the pool, which was rippling just slightly under the light breeze. It was so cold outside, and even though I knew the pool was heated, I stood at the edge, clad in only my bathing suit, looking down at it. Every muscle in my body was ready for it. I wanted to feel the slickness of it along my skin, the weightlessness of my body in the midst of it, the pull of my lungs as I pushed myself.

But I couldn't do it.

It'd been a month since Michael moved to Vancouver, since the funeral, since we had last spoken. I'd thought about calling him a million times, staring at my phone and typing out elaborate text messages that I immediately deleted. I'd thought about sending him a letter, but I was too embarrassed to ask Ben for Michael's new address.

I was too afraid. I didn't want to hear him say he didn't want me again. Most of the time, I was able to distract myself enough to forget about it. Ben and I had taken to meeting at least once a week for dinner and homework. We sat in Ben's living room and ate pizza while we quizzed each other for tests and helped each other outline essays.

But then there were times, like now, when I had too much time with my thoughts. I looked down at the water, and it felt like I could jump in and drown. I had never been so scared of it before. I put my face in my hands and tried to breathe, but the panic was rising in my chest. I gulped in air, cold and clean and painful.

When I was seven, I fell into the community pool and sank to the bottom. I wasn't scared as I held my breath and watched my father's shadow dive in after me. The world underwater was something unexplainable, and there was no substitute for the way it made me feel, alive and full of magic.

Six months later, I was in a swim program, and it didn't take me long to figure out that when I swam hard and excelled above all the other swimmers, my father seemed to love me more. And my unquenchable desire for the water was just a bonus.

But after ten years, the only time my father showed me affection was when I made him proud in the pool, and the only thing that kept me going was my need for his approval and my need for the escape of that underwater haven.

But all the hard work had gotten me nowhere. I was still here, without my father's favor. Nothing I did was ever enough.

But maybe it was enough for me.

Since coming here, I'd fought for myself and for what I wanted even when it was the hardest thing I'd ever done. I'd never fought for myself before, but now that felt like all I'd done. I might not have gained anyone else's approval. But I gained my own, and that felt good.

I was free.

I wiped my face and steadied my shaking limbs. I had to let the old me go. I wasn't going to be scared, and I wasn't going to lie, and I wasn't going to let this world dictate who I could or couldn't be.

I took a deep breath and dove into the deep end.

I came up out of the water with a gasp and pressed my back to the wall. I looked up at the sky, feeling calm, feeling steady.

I set my head back against the concrete and closed my eyes, breathing in the chlorine and the cold night air. I picked up my feet and let myself float on the surface, my stomach and shoulders going cold while I stared up at the sky, the stars twinkling bright to battle the city lights.

My feet hit the wall on the other side, and I pushed off, flipping myself over and starting to swim.

* * *

I had been visiting O'Dell's pretty regularly since Marisol and Patrice had taken me there over a month ago. Since Lily had found her own place and Mom had been getting more and more hours at work, I had become accustomed to spending evenings alone if I wasn't with Ben. I had had more than one lonely evening when I didn't think I could do my homework in our silent apartment, and I found that the atmosphere at the coffee shop helped.

That Saturday afternoon however, I wasn't there for the homework atmosphere.

"Just a small mocha cappuccino, please," I said to Leo, the guy behind the counter I'd come to know from my many visits.

He rang me up, and I pulled off my gloves to pay him. It wasn't nearly as cold as it could have been, as it would be in a month, but my fingers and toes were sensitive to the weather, so I stayed bundled if I could.

I watched Leo mix the cappuccino behind the counter. "Doing okay today?"

"Yeah, I am. Thanks." I took the proffered cup and turned to head back out, where Lily's car was waiting. I'd borrowed it for the weekend. I was so busy stirring my coffee that I didn't even realize there were people in front of me, between me and the door, and that those people were Marisol and Patrice.

For a second, my heart leaped, the way it did every time I saw them, thinking maybe everything had been a dream, and they still liked me, and we could still be friends. But then they would snub me, completely pretending I didn't exist, the way they did in Chemistry and lunch, and I would be reminded that in the world inside Lincoln High School, I was completely alone.

Standing before me, their eyes at least were on me, so they weren't pretending they couldn't see me at all, but they said nothing, just stood there in my way, like Greek statues.

"I was just leaving." I moved around them and headed for the door before they had a chance to say something insulting, like they had on occasion when they were feeling particularly wounded.

But when I reached for the door, I stopped. I didn't want them to feel wounded. I didn't want them to hate me. Even if we couldn't be friends, I didn't want to be enemies anymore.

"Patrice, could I just—"

Marisol moved to step between us, but to my surprise, Patrice reached out to stop her. Their eyes met, and I saw the tension in the way Patrice gripped Marisol's arm.

"It's okay," Patrice said, her voice soft even while her face was hard. "Get us coffee?"

Marisol eyed me for a second, and then she turned and walked to the counter, leaving us alone.

Patrice turned her stern eyes on me. "What do you want, Kate?"

"I just want to apologize."

She stood there, silent, her hands tucked into the pockets of her jacket.

"Patrice," I started again, a little more confident since she hadn't walked away yet. "I want you to know that I didn't mean to hurt you. You were so nice to me when I got here, and I liked you so much, and I didn't know that Michael was your boyfriend at first, and I swear, I didn't mean for it to go down the way it did."

Someone shuffled past us to get to the door. Patrice reached out a hand and pulled me out of the way in such a companionable away that it was unbearable. I wanted to hold on to her, but she pulled away. "Marisol said you told her nothing happened while Michael and I were still dating."

"That's true." I felt desperate now. She was listening to me. She was letting me talk. She was letting me apologize. "I know we crossed a line, and I know I was awful to you, but I never wanted you to get hurt."

She sighed, and for a second, I saw the old Patrice, the one who'd befriended me on my first day and invited me to this coffee shop and been heartbroken when Michael broke up with her.

"Look, I'm not stupid. I know things weren't working out between Michael and me. Things weren't great before you came along. I knew it wasn't going to last. It felt that way since the beginning. It always felt like Michael just said yes because I was already there."

She wasn't getting angry at me, and she wasn't telling me how I ruined her life, and that alone was enough to make a lump form in my throat.

Her eyes met mine then, focused laser beams that made me want to back away from her. "I know it's not all your fault. I should be mad at him, too. But I've loved him for so long, and I guess it felt like you ruined my shot even if you really didn't." She shrugged. "All this time, I think Michael was just a little lost."

I thought of that first day, Michael bent over his mother in the parking garage, the fear and worry on his face, the way he was so good at hiding it with his smiles and his charm. He was so good at not talking about himself that I didn't know he was falling apart until it was too late. Or maybe I was just blind to it. I felt something burrow into my chest: tears, anguish, desperation.

"I really screwed up," I choked out.

She didn't deny it, which oddly made me feel better. I was tired of people saying they understood. I was tired of not feeling the consequences. I should have to pay for not being there, and every day without him felt like a punishment.

"Maybe, but I don't think it matters anymore."

Her words made me cry, hot tears that made me feel like an idiot. "He's gone."

"He's not gone because of you." There was absolutely no malice in her voice, and then she was reaching out and rubbing my back the way my mother did when I was sick. She pulled me in the

———

direction of the hallway until we were in the girls' bathroom, which was painted pink and red, like Cupid had vomited on the walls.

"Yeah, he's gone because his mother died. His mother *died*, and I wasn't there for him. I was off breaking my promises, and he was *alone*. He was there for me, and he counted on me, and I wasn't there for him. Why wasn't I there for him?" I wrapped my arms around myself, trying to keep my insides in even as they felt like they would explode out of me.

After a little while, I could breathe again. She ran a paper towel under the faucet and pressed it to my swollen eyelids. "Everything's going to be okay."

"Why are you being so nice to me?" I could smell the brown paper of the tissue over my face.

"Because you've suffered enough."

I laughed and hoped that it was true.

She pulled the paper towel away from my eyes. "Plus, I'm pretty happy these days." A smile crept slowly but surely across her face. "I thought I needed Michael to be happy. I thought I needed him to love me. But I don't. I'm doing okay alone."

I nodded, understanding her point. But wants and needs were different things.

She tossed the paper towel in the trash before pushing open the door. "Hey, do you want to stay and have coffee with us?"

Out in the shop, Marisol was leaning her elbows on the counter and laughing with Leo.

"I can't. I already have somewhere to be, but thanks."

She watched me for a second, her made-up eyes shifting from my hair to my eyes to my chin, probably assessing my level of post-crying puffiness. "Okay. Well, we'll see you in Chem on Monday."

———

"Yeah."

I watched her join Marisol before I left with my own coffee.

◦ ◦ ◦

Ever since that night I drove down to Salem, I'd been making the drive almost every weekend. A few weeks in a rehab facility was enough to help Harris through the withdrawal symptoms, but it still sometimes felt like visiting a ghost. That morning, I sipped at my coffee on the hour-long drive, my heater on full blast.

Harris's bedroom door was open when I got there. I stood in the doorway and waited for him to notice me while he played a video game. His eyes flitted quickly to me, but he didn't pause the game. He was wrapped in a fleece blanket, his skin pale and his face a little sallow.

He'd lost some of his bulk over the last month, but he'd made it through the worst of everything: the muscle aches, the insomnia, the nausea. These days, he was just quiet.

"How are you?" I asked, sitting down on the bed beside him and watching while his character on the screen hid behind a school bus to take out someone on the opposite team.

"Tired." I knew he meant it. The skin under his eyes had begun to sag when he came back from rehab. Everything was out of his system, but he still seemed to be exhausted all the time.

He made exaggerated movements with his arms, as if that would help him win the game. "What do you do when you can't sleep?" he asked.

I tried to think of an honest answer. Sometimes the answer was hot tea, sometimes it was staring at the ceiling with the lights out, trying to force myself to get drowsy. And then it was Michael, sitting by the pool at two in the morning.

Sometimes I still went up to the roof by myself and swam or watched cars drive by. Sometimes I read for class until the sun came up and then caught an hour of sleep before I had to rush to catch the bus.

But mostly I lay in bed and thought about what Michael was doing in Vancouver, wondering if he was awake, too.

"Sorry. Can't help you there." I looked over at the TV, watching the shooting and the dizzying landscape for a moment. "What's the point of this game, anyway?"

He glanced at me. "To kill more people than the other team."

I just nodded. "Classy."

He nudged me with his elbow, and I watched him shoot at computer characters until my eyes started to drift closed. When something exceptionally loud exploded on the screen, I jerked my eyes back open, but eventually, I let myself sink down onto Harris's bed and fall asleep to the sound of his gun firing.

When I woke up later, the TV was silent and Harris was lying beside me on the bed, his arms tucked around himself, like he was trying not to touch me accidentally. For just a second, it felt like it used to, when we would spend hours together after school, talking and playing games and swimming, until we were exhausted and took a nap before I had to be home for dinner.

But nothing was the same. Harris was worn out, and so was I, and a nap wasn't going to fix this. While I watched him, his eyes opened slowly, finding me across from him, and he smiled.

It had been so long since I'd seen that smile that it sent a

———

shock wave down to my stomach, and I smiled back, reaching out and pressing the back of my hand against his.

"Is it over yet?" he asked.

I thought of all the things that *were* over: my relationship with Michael, our time with the swim team, my time here in Salem, my parents' marriage, whatever I had with my dad.

"Maybe," I said because I thought he was talking about him, the drugs and the pain he'd been going through, physically and emotionally, since he'd lost his spot on the team.

He nodded, like I'd given him the right answer, and took a deep breath before closing his eyes again. I let him sleep, but I stared out the window while the sun moved up higher and higher in the sky, until it reached in to warm my skin.

*   *   *

When I got back to Portland, I drove straight to Lily's apartment to drop off her car.

I trotted up the stairs to her apartment, using her key to let myself in. I didn't know if she was home, but when I walked inside, the apartment was quiet, so I didn't think so. She shared the apartment with a girl named Sherry, who was always in class or at the library or studying off campus somewhere, so I almost never saw her. I couldn't even remember what she looked like.

I tossed Lily's car keys onto the bar and went into the kitchen to get a quick glass of water before I left. I gulped some down and then heard a noise from Lily's bedroom. Maybe she was home after all. I chugged the rest of the water and left the glass in the sink.

"Lily?" I called out from the kitchen, and while there was no clear answer, I heard shuffling and a voice, Lily's. I figured she was probably on the phone, so I pushed open her bedroom door, and it took me a second to process the scene before me. Two people, one of them Lily, both of them mostly naked and struggling into their clothing. I clapped my hand over my eyes and rushed back to the living room.

"Oh God," I groaned. "That is so much more than I ever needed to see." I scrubbed at my eyes like I could erase the image from my brain.

Lily came out into the living room with her shirt all disheveled and the button on her pants undone. "I'm sorry. I didn't think you'd be back so early. I'm sorry."

And then the guy rushed out behind her, and the first thing that I noticed was that his shirt wasn't buttoned correctly.

The second thing I noticed was that he looked a lot like Tom.

He smiled bashfully at me. "Hey, Kate."

I was suddenly no longer embarrassed. I didn't care that I had just seen my sister half-naked because my sister had been half-naked with her ex, and that made something akin to hope bloom in my chest.

Lily must have seen the pure joy in my eyes, because her whole face lit up. "I was going to tell you, I promise, but we just weren't really sure what we were doing yet, you know, and with everything—"

"How long have you been seeing each other?" If Tom and Lily were trying to figure out what was going on between them before telling anyone, I could understand that.

Lily shrugged, and she and Tom exchanged a glance. "About

a month," she said, and I saw some of the light in her eyes dim at the answer. It was like this now. Talking about what had happened a month ago always felt like it was off-limits, even if no one mentioned Michael.

But there wasn't room for despair here. "I'm really happy for you."

Lily smiled, and it traveled all the way up to her eyes.

"I'm going to make some coffee," Tom said, leaving us alone in the living room, even though Lily's apartment was so tiny that there wasn't very much privacy anywhere you went.

Lily guided me over to the couch and pulled me down beside her. "Hey, are you okay with this?"

"Um, yes. Why wouldn't I be?" I'd known we made a mistake the second we got in the car that day, and all I'd wanted was for Lily to know what it felt like to have someone care enough not to give up on her.

"I just meant because . . . ," she trailed off, but she didn't need to elaborate. Was I okay with my sister being this happy even though I'd had my heart shattered?

"Of course I'm okay. I mean it. I'm so happy for you."

She smiled, but I could tell she didn't believe me.

I was happy. Of course I was. But a part of me was devoured by jealousy. I knew what it was like to find someone who would help you find your way when you were lost, talk you through a panic attack, hold your hand when everyone else was turning away. I wanted that again. But I didn't want it with anyone else. I just wanted it with Michael.

◦ ◦ ◦

—

I unlocked the door to my apartment, but when I threw it open, I was met with silence. "Mom?" I called out, the door still open in my hand, when the door across the hall opened.

It was a strange feeling, hearing it open again, like watching a lamp get thrown across the room by a ghost. I hadn't heard that door open in so long that it was almost frightening. Like a hopeless idiot, I turned around, half expecting to find him there, leaning against his door like he was that morning before school, looking at me under his messy bangs like he was afraid to show himself.

But it wasn't Michael coming out of his old apartment. It was my mom and some guy that I didn't recognize.

"Dinner will be ready at seven," she was saying. "I'll make lasagna." She smiled over her shoulder at him as she crossed the hallway, not even realizing I was standing there until the man's eyes moved to settle on me.

"Oh!" she said when she turned around and saw me. "I'm so glad you're home. This is Patrick. Patrick, this is my youngest daughter, Kate. Patrick and his wife, Laura, just moved in across the hall."

Patrick, tall and thin with square-rimmed glasses, nodded at me from the other side of the hallway. "Hi, Kate. It's nice to meet you."

"Patrick works at the nursing home with me. I invited him and Laura for dinner tonight. We'll see you a little later," she said to Patrick, and shut the door between them.

And then her smile dimmed a little. "Is it okay that I invited them?"

I laughed. "Of course it's okay." I didn't want to ask why it wouldn't be, but I thought I knew. Making friends with the people across the hall, letting go of the former tenants, letting the world keep turning after everything had come to a halt.

She sighed, her shoulders relaxing a little. "Okay. I know it's been hard, honey."

I waved her off, and she gave me a sad little smile before going into the kitchen to get dinner ready.

I watched her from the table, as she moved around, humming to herself. I'd noticed the change in her that I never thought would come. She'd been a little cheerier in the past few weeks, looking more weightless than I'd ever seen her. And even now, there was a hint of a smile on her face.

Some days it felt like the water was closing over my head, but I wasn't grasping for the surface anymore. Maybe no one could keep their head above the water, and we were all just being pulled under, learning how to breathe while life pressed in around us. And if they could do it, I thought I could, too.

It was time to move on.

Twenty-One

No one was surprised when Lily and Tom announced they were getting married. Things had gone from unsure to serious so fast that they were planning another wedding by February.

The guest list was reduced to a quarter of the original size, and what before was something large and extravagant became something intimate. We were lucky that Tom's parents were such respected, long-standing members of their church, or Lily and Tom would have been trying to fit the small wedding reception into the meeting room at their apartment complex. As it was, the congregation was happy to prepare the church for another weekend wedding. They seemed optimistic despite the previous failed attempt.

Lily decided to wear her dress, the same dress from months before, but she'd done a few alterations. I had a feeling she was being superstitious about the whole thing, but I was willing to

---

go along with anything that would get her wearing a wedding ring by the end of the day.

When we were back at the church, anxiety had set up a fort in my stomach. It wasn't exactly like it was before. There weren't fresh flowers everywhere or caterers setting up in the hall. Only family and close friends had been invited, and the church was quiet, the sanctuary barely buzzing with the noise of their conversations.

I moved through the building, making sure everything was going smoothly. Most of the guests were seated, with a few stragglers signing the guest book on the front table. At the end of the hall, I stopped by Tom's dressing room and peeked in.

He was inside, perched on a long wooden table, reading from something that, from where I stood, looked like a Bible, while his best man stared at himself in the mirror, flexing almost imperceptibly.

When Tom saw me, he smiled. "Everything good?" he asked, and I was surprised not to hear any fear or hesitation in his voice. Even after all that had happened, he was completely confident in Lily. He was confident in *them*.

"Everything's great. Are you all set?"

"Yep." To punctuate the point, he ran a hand across his slicked-back hair and tugged on the ends of his bow tie.

Inside Lily's dressing room, Mom was helping Lily pin her hair back. In the mirror, Lily smiled at me.

"Doing okay?" I asked, coming up beside her.

She laughed. "You mean, should you go ahead and pull the car around?"

"Har-har." I knew Lily wasn't going anywhere, but it was a

relief to hear her joking about it. We weren't pretending that everything was perfect. "Just want to make sure your feet are nice and toasty."

My mother laughed but didn't say anything. She'd been all too happy to hear that Lily had refused to let Dad come to the wedding, but she still seemed distracted as she gathered their prep stuff and packed it away in a large tote bag.

Lily snatched up her bouquet and moved her shoulders in a little happy dance that made me laugh, but then I remembered that I'd stuck Tom's wedding ring, in its little box, in the glove compartment of my mom's car late last night before Lily and I had our ballroom dancing finals marathon, so that there was no way I could forget it this morning.

"Damn. I left Tom's ring in the car. I'll be right back." I ducked out and rushed down the hallway toward the exit, the same exit Lily and I had escaped through that day so long before. The fact that the whole world was different now was both a relief and a point of terror. It was a world I didn't recognize anymore, but I thought maybe I could live with that.

It was freezing outside, and I had little protection from it, as my dress was knee-length, strapless, and I was wearing open-toed shoes. I bounced around on my tiptoes trying to get the door unlocked and then leaned down to rummage through the glove box.

With the ring box in hand, I turned back to the church, ready to make a run for it, but stopped when I saw the figure against the side of the building, my body completely forgetting the chill in the air.

For a second, I thought maybe my mind was conjuring some strange déjà vu image from all those months ago because there he was, standing in the same spot he'd been in then, watching me. But everything was different. His hair was longer, curling around his ears, and there was no cigarette in his hand. He was in a slightly wrinkled button-down and black slacks, and seeing him there was somehow the greatest and most confusing thing that had happened to me, it felt like, ever.

He wasn't smoking. He wasn't doing anything. He was watching me with his hands tucked in his pockets as if he'd been waiting for me, as if he knew I would come out of that door at any moment. Maybe he was out here because he wasn't sure if he wanted to go in and see me at all. Maybe he'd been ready to bolt.

I walked toward him slowly, but with his eyes on me, I suddenly couldn't remember how fast I normally walked. Was I walking at a normal pace?

"What are you doing here?" My hands were shaking so much that I dropped the ring box, and Michael hurried to pick it up for me. He held it out to me, but I couldn't focus enough to take it from him. I needed to steady my hands.

He held on to the box and met my eye. "Lily invited me."

Of course she did. Lily, the greatest sister that ever lived. I didn't even know what to say. This was all I'd wanted since the second he left, just to have him standing here in front of me so I could tell him how sorry I was for everything, but now here he was, and I had no idea what to say. He was looking at me, too, saying nothing.

Then the church bell rang so loud that I jumped. The bell ringing meant that it was noon and time to start the wedding. I snatched the ring out of Michael's hand. "I have to go inside. You should get a seat." I rushed inside, oddly happy for an excuse to get away. I wasn't prepared for this. I wasn't ready to say all the things I'd wanted to say, all the things that ran through my mind again and again in the middle of the night when I was trying to sleep. I had never expected to run into him here, today.

I shut the door behind me when I made it to Lily's dressing room. Mom was already gone, and Lily was waiting by the door for me to come.

"Are you okay?"

I sighed and slumped back against the door. "You invited Michael."

She bit her lip. "Is that okay? I just wanted—"

"It's okay." I popped open the ring box and took out Tom's band, a plain white gold band with Lily's initials engraved on the inside. "I just don't know what to say to him."

I reached for the door, but she put a hand on my arm. "Why don't you tell him that you've been miserable since he left?"

I gripped the doorknob. "Because that would be pathetic. Tell him I've been pining for him for months?"

She shrugged. "Why not? I can't be happy if you're not happy."

"I *am* happy. I am."

She kicked the heel of my shoe with the toe of hers. "Never hurts to have good things in your life." All day, her eyes had had a smiling curve to them that made her even more beautiful than normal, but when she stood there in the open doorway, her eyes lost some of their luster. "It's weird, isn't it, not having Dad here?"

"Lily," I said, as close to a warning as I could get. She was going soft now that she and Tom were back together. Where was my angry sister who was furious with my mother for not leaving Dad sooner?

"What?"

"Even after everything he did?" I asked her. For me, it wasn't weird that Dad wasn't here. I had learned to live without my father in my life, and I thought I could be perfectly fine without him in it forever.

"Even after everything," she said softly and reached out to hug me. She didn't say anything while she did it, but I didn't have to hear the words to know she was thinking them: *We should forgive him, we should let it go, life's too short to be so broken.*

I took her hand and we walked down the hall together to the open doors of the sanctuary. I could hear the music playing inside, and I turned to smile at her before walking in. I stared straight ahead, at the stained glass window above the baptismal as I walked down the aisle with Tom's ring in one hand and my bouquet in the other.

My entire body trembled through the whole ceremony. I knew Michael was there, but I didn't know where he was sitting, couldn't see him as long as I was looking ahead of me, at Tom and Lily. But I thought about him the whole time. While they exchanged rings and said their vows, all I could think about was Michael at the graveyard, bent down on the ground, crying.

○ ○ ○

"Ladies and gentleman, I'm proud to announce, for the first time ever, Mr. and Mrs. Thomas Murphy!"

I was sandwiched between my mother and Lily's empty seat as Lily and Tom twirled into the middle of the makeshift dance floor for their first dance. The room was mostly dark, and I couldn't bring myself to scan for Michael's face. I stared down at my plate, full of food from a home-style restaurant that could cater with little notice: potatoes, chicken, and a roll. A plastic flute of champagne fizzed in front of me. My mother was already sipping from hers.

As the dance ended, Tom put a hand on Lily's waist and escorted her to the table, where she took a seat beside me. The music played and people ate, and Lily leaned over and smacked a kiss onto my cheek. I could feel the weight of her lipstick as it stuck to my skin.

"This is absolutely perfect." When she picked up her fork to dig into her own food, people started to line up against the table to talk to her and Tom. She put her fork down, and I tried to smile at the people who also wanted to drag me into the conversation, but I was distracted by my thoughts.

"Oh, my lovely nieces! Look how beautiful you both look!" My aunt Marie leaned down and planted a kiss on my cheek, right beside where Lily had already left a mark. As soon as she was gone, I dipped my napkin in my cup of ice water and scrubbed at my cheek. Lily winked at me.

The man up against the table now was apparently a work associate of Tom's, and when he turned sideways, I saw Michael behind him, sitting alone at a table with a group of Lily's college friends. He fiddled with his water cup while I watched him, and I saw the differences in him now from the last time I'd seen him. He was here, really here, sharp and purposeful, like he hadn't been at the funeral. That Michael was a shell, an intruder taking over. But this was my Michael. I could see it in the way his eyes moved around the room, the way he took a bite of salad, the way he smiled when one of Lily's friends leaned over and shook his hand.

And then he got up and walked out.

I felt everything in me seize up in protest. He couldn't be leaving. I couldn't lose him again.

"I'll be right back," I whispered to Lily and skirted the dance floor, where people had already started to huddle and dance to the music, to get to the hallway. By the time I got there, Michael was gone. I rushed to the exit, but I didn't see him in the parking lot. But in a parking space right by the road, the very far left corner of the lot, was his mother's old station wagon. I turned and went down the hallway. He was probably just in the bathroom, and I was probably acting like an idiot. The bathrooms were at the very end of the hall, where it opened out into the foyer of the church, and I leaned against the wall outside.

I suddenly didn't care if I came off as pathetic because I *had* been pining since he left, and I wasn't about to let him leave without at least talking to me.

A blond in a cocktail dress sent me a kind smile when she walked out of the bathroom and disappeared into the meeting hall.

I stood there for another minute before I realized that Michael probably wasn't in the bathroom. I moved down the hallway, back to the meeting hall, but then I heard something, a strange shuffling noise coming from the sanctuary around the corner.

Inside, the room was dark, but I could still make out the shape of him in the light of the stained-glass windows, sitting halfway back from the front podium, staring down at a hymnal that he'd produced from I didn't know where.

"I was afraid you'd left."

Michael twisted around in the pew to look at me, closing the

———

book in his hand. His lips tilted up a little, like he wanted to smile, but he didn't. My body stuttered. "No. I was just looking for someplace a little quieter. You were busy, so . . ."

I grabbed hold of the doorjamb beside me. I wasn't sure how to start. What if this wasn't why he was here, to hear me say I was sorry? What if this was good-bye? Before I could decide how to start, he broke the silence.

"I'm sorry, Kate."

I waited for him to say he was over me, that he could never forgive me. He shook his head and turned away.

I wanted to see everything. I wanted to see what was going on in those eyes that I'd been dreaming of looking into again. I walked around him, facing him from the front of the room. He looked sad, and I was afraid that I was losing him, and that any second now he would go back to the shell.

"Why are you sorry?" I asked him, guiding him along. If he was going to walk out of my life, I needed it to happen fast, like ripping off a Band-Aid.

"I was such a jerk the last time I saw you."

I grimaced, remembering what he'd said, how his words had felt like a knife. "You were grieving."

He nodded in a distracted way. "Yeah. I was really messed up. I was messed up for a while, actually." When he impaled me with that steady gaze of his, his mouth was the furthest thing from a smile I'd ever seen it. "It was like I was asleep, and when I woke up, you were the only person I wanted to see, and you were so far away."

Something caught in my throat: my breath, my heart, my vocabulary.

He went on. "I wanted to call you. That's all I wanted. But

it'd been weeks, and I didn't even know if you wanted to hear from me."

"Of course I—"

Heels *click-clack*ed into the room, and my mother stopped in the doorway, not much more than a silhouette. Her eyes went straight to Michael, and I expected her to greet him, but she didn't. She looked from him to me, and as if my pain had traveled all the way to her, like radiation that blanketed the room, her face crumpled a little. "It's time for your toast."

I was terrified to let Michael out of my sight. I looked down at him, still sitting in his pew, his hands gripping the back of the pew in front of him. "You won't leave?"

He shook his head, looking up at me out of the corner of his eye. "I won't leave."

The promise made it possible for me to unglue my feet from the ground and follow my mother back into the reception hall. I took my seat at the table while the best man finished his speech, which had apparently been funny because laughter was still tittering through the hall. He raised his glass with the traditional salute and everyone followed.

I hadn't really considered my speech. I'd been so focused on getting Lily down the aisle and through her vows that my brain hadn't made it all the way to the reception. But as all the eyes in the room turned to me, I picked up my champagne glass for something to do with my hands just as Michael came into the room. He didn't take a seat but stayed in the doorway, like he was standing watch, waiting for something.

My eyes moved around the room. I didn't know most of

the people in it, but they were looking at me like they knew every secret I'd been hiding.

The champagne was quivering slightly in my glass.

"Maybe I'm not supposed to say it, but the last time we were here, it seemed like maybe today wasn't going to happen."

I wasn't sure what to expect, but it wasn't the complete silence that greeted me. It seemed that not a single soul in the room was breathing. I glanced down at Lily, and her eyes were steady on me.

I wrapped an arm around my middle, feeling so exposed with everyone's eyes on me, and tried not to look at Michael. "When I think about who you were before, I think maybe you're not that person anymore. You're braver, and you're more confident about what you want, and you're not scared to take a chance even if it might turn out to be wrong."

There was a little murmur in the room. "Um, I'm not saying that you're making the wrong decision. The exact opposite. I saw how miserable you were without Tom, so I know how much you want to be sitting exactly where you are right now. I just mean that getting married, falling in love, opening yourself up completely to someone else is scary and it's risky, and it doesn't always work out. But taking the jump is worth it. I'm just really, really happy that you're taking that jump."

I sighed out a shaky breath and pulled the microphone away from my mouth so everyone wouldn't know how hard I was fighting to breathe. "Lily, I'm so happy for you. You're my big sister and my best friend. When I needed you, you were my rock, and every single day, I'm glad you finally made it back here. Congratulations, Lily and Tom. I love you guys a lot."

———

I set the microphone down and everyone clapped as Lily and Tom shared a kiss and Lily rose to hug me, rubbing my back even as the music started and the DJ asked everyone to go out onto the dance floor.

"Thanks for inviting him," I said when I pulled away.

She squeezed my hands. Her eyes went over my shoulder and when I turned, he was there behind me, where my mother had been moments before, holding his hand out and looking so beautiful in the lights off the dance floor that it was enough to make me want to cry. His skin against mine when I put my hand in his was bliss, our fingers wrapping around each other so easily and naturally. I let him lead me to the dance floor, where he pulled me against him, and I died a little.

I'd spent so much time wishing that I could feel Michael against me again that the reality was almost painful, the nerves rising under my skin until his touch felt severe in the best way.

We didn't say anything for a long time. He moved his hands up from my waist and twisted a lock of my hair around his index finger as we swayed. "I missed you."

My answer was something like a whimper. His hand curled around my jaw, and he pressed his head against mine.

"I didn't want to leave."

I pulled back to look at him. "Then why did you? Because of me? Because I lied?"

He shook his head. "It wasn't really about that. Sure, it hurt at the time, but that was only part of the problem. Everything was falling apart, and I was just falling apart without you."

I gripped his shoulder, keeping us moving through the slow, jazzy dance. "I should have been there with you."

His thumb stroked my cheek. "It wouldn't have kept her from dying."

My heart ripped when he said it. He was so resigned to it. But of course he'd been living with the reality for months.

"I went to Vancouver because I had to. My uncle wanted me to go with him, and I wasn't in any condition to fight him on it. But I wanted to be here with you. It's all I've thought about, getting back here. I—" He stopped, and his eyes landed on me like a question.

"I love you," I said. Maybe it wasn't what he was going to say, but it didn't really matter. I'd felt it when he was here before, in those quiet moments on the roof and those brief glances that made me feel like maybe someone else understood me. But I didn't really know it was love until I was losing it. I didn't know until Michael was gone and he'd taken a part of my heart with him.

He smiled, like maybe he was relieved. "I love you, too."

My heart felt wild then, like it knew better than I did that there'd been a chance he didn't feel the same way, not after all this time and all the ways he'd been hurt.

He moved in closer to me, but before he could kiss me, before his lips could find mine, the music changed. I waited for him to kiss me anyway, but he pulled back and looked down at me with eyes that were sparkling. "Ready to dance?" he asked.

I was under the impression that we were already dancing, but when my brain processed the salsa music that sparkled through the room and the sound of Lily cheering loudly, I groaned. "Michael, not here."

He pulled me into formation, with not much more than his fingertips touching mine, and we started to move. I still didn't

———

know very much, as we'd only had a few lessons. He spun me around and pulled me in again. I let him lead me, even though I didn't really know the steps.

We weren't the only ones on the floor attempting to salsa and doing a clumsy job of it, and after a minute, Lily and Tom joined us, and Michael and I reverted to a more basic step so that Tom and Lily could follow.

When the song was over, Lily high-fived me like we'd just won some kind of competition, and I let Michael lead me back to a table so we could share a piece of cake.

◊ ◊ ◊

Michael stood beside me and cheered loudly as Lily and Tom drove away, and while the guests began to file out to their cars, we turned to go back inside. There were still plenty of people who wanted to stay and dance, and we had the church until six. Michael held the door open for me, but I stopped when I felt a hand on my arm.

My mom pulled me off to the side of the entrance, out of the way of the door. "Why don't you go on home?" she asked.

I pointed over my shoulder at where Michael was still holding the door open. "You don't want us to stay and help wrangle any drunk family members?"

"Kate." She lowered her voice, and her eyes went over my shoulder to Michael. "I'll take care of this. You go."

Maybe a better daughter and a better sister would have argued with her, but I was selfish, and I wanted all the time I could get with Michael, so I grabbed him by the hand and pulled him through the parking lot. He didn't object.

———

I'd ridden with my mom, so I couldn't exactly take the car, but I knew where Michael had parked his, so I pulled him behind me, toward the street and away from my mother. I heard her go back inside, and I stopped on the far side of Michael's station wagon. I turned and pressed my back against the car, pulling him against me. I wanted him to kiss me. I wanted it more than anything.

He leaned in, gripping the collar of the jacket I'd put on, but I pulled back, catching sight of a shadow of a figure across the street, standing shaded beneath a row of trees lined against the sidewalk.

Even from far away, I could see that it was my father. He was staring down at his feet as the sun beat down on the pavement between us, his hands in his pockets and dressed in a suit, like at any moment he was fully prepared to go inside and crash Lily's wedding.

Michael saw him too then. "Is that your dad?"

I nodded, unable to take my eyes off him. He raised his head and saw us, but I didn't see any kind of reaction in his expression. Just emptiness.

"Do you want to go and talk to him?"

My first instinct was to say no. My instinct was to turn tail and run, forget that my father existed and move on with my life.

But looking at him standing there, I felt bad for him. I'd never pitied my father before. He'd always made me feel like I had to please him, even if it meant letting myself down, and that had hurt. But he was my dad. And he was standing on the sidewalk like he was begging for it to open up and swallow him whole.

I squeezed Michael's hand. "I'll be right back. Don't go

———

anywhere." I'd said it almost as a joke, but when I saw him standing there, beside his mother's car, I suddenly meant it.

"I won't." He had a smile in his eyes.

I forced myself away from him and across the street, where my father kept his hands in his pockets and looked up at me from under his lashes like he was in trouble. "Did you have a good time?"

"Yeah, I did."

He kicked a rock with the toe of his best leather shoes. "She didn't invite me. She told me I wasn't welcome."

"Well, you were half the reason she ran out on the last one."

He nodded, and when he lifted his head, his eyes were glistening with tears that he was obviously trying to hold in. He reached up and tugged on his hair, ruining the time he'd obviously spent styling it.

His eyes went back to the church. "Who's that guy you were with?"

I crossed my arms. "A friend." I wanted to be angry with him, but there was something about the hunch of his shoulders that made him seem three inches tall, and I couldn't bring myself to get mad at him. Every cell in my body had been so filled with hate and anger for so long, but I was too exhausted to be angry now.

I looked over my shoulder and caught sight of Michael in the parking lot, still leaning against his car, watching us. I took a deep breath and turned back to my father.

"I just wanted you to be happy," he said, the words spoken uncertainly, completely without the arrogance I expected from him. "I woke up one day, and I realized that I'd spent most of my life being unhappy, and I didn't want that for you and for your sister. I was trying to be a good person."

I closed my eyes for a second and took a deep breath. How could he think that cheating on his wife would make him a good person? But I knew it was more than that. He meant with swimming. He had been trying to be a good dad by pressuring me to swim, by pushing me so hard.

"I guess I don't believe in good people and bad people anymore." After everything that had happened between Michael and me, and Michael and Patrice, and Lily and Tom, I meant that. "I just think there are people who make good decisions and people who make bad ones."

He blinked at me like he didn't recognize me. "I know I made bad ones."

I nodded. "Yeah, you did." And then I looked him in the eye. I'd been so afraid to tell him all the things I needed to, but now, with him here in front of me, shrinking, I wasn't sure what I'd been so afraid of. That he might be disappointed in me? That he might sit around and wish he'd had a better daughter? "You pushed me too hard. You took control of everything that should have been mine. And you hurt Harris. I loved swimming, but you made me feel like it was what I had to do to earn your respect, and that wasn't fair."

"This might be hard to believe," he said, his breath heavy, puffing out into the cold air. "But I never meant to hurt you."

I shook my head. "It's not hard to believe. It just doesn't matter. You hurt me anyway."

His chin wobbled, and in a weird way, it made me ashamed of him. I had done my best to be strong after he hurt me, and he wasn't being strong for me, hadn't been since I'd walked away from him. He just acted like a child and tore me down in hopes that it would make me need him. But all it did was make me need him less.

"I don't know if I'll ever be able to forgive you for what you did to Mom and for ruining everything that I worked so hard for. But I'm trying to figure things out. I just have a lot of other things to fix before I try to deal with what happened between us."

His hand came up, like he was going to pat me on the shoulder or something. And then it fell to his side again. "Just call me when you think you're ready to talk, okay?"

I wasn't sure that day was ever going to come, but I nodded anyway. I could at least promise that if I was ever ready, I would reach out.

He turned and walked away, his shoulders hunched and his walk slow, like someone who'd just lost a fight.

I crossed back to Michael, relieved as soon as he was close enough for me to touch.

He raised one eyebrow. "You think he'll be okay?"

I shrugged. "As okay as the rest of us, I suppose."

*   *   *

Back at my building, once *our* building, Michael and I went up to the roof. It was quiet so far up above the city after the commotion of the day. We stood side by side against the wall and stared out at the pink sky between the buildings.

"So what do we do now?" I asked him.

He rubbed my back, sending shivers through every inch of surface area I possessed. "What do you mean?"

I turned and pressed my back to the wall, and his hand

immediately came up, his fingertips against my chin. "I don't want you to go back to Vancouver."

"I don't really have any other option. It isn't that far. And, to be honest, it's been good for me, being away from here."

That stung.

He must have seen the hurt in my eyes. He pressed his thumb against my bottom lip. "Not because I'm away from you. Just because it would have been hard, being in the apartment without her."

He stepped closer to me. I ran my hands up his warm arms and gripped his shoulders. "I'm here," he whispered. "I'm always here. We're going to be okay, right?"

I nodded. I believed it. Michael had never really left. I was always thinking about him, thinking about what I would say when I saw him again, how it felt to be with him and then without him, what my life would be like if we were ever where we were right now.

He kissed me, his lips cold from the evening air and his skin smelling like winter. Even as the rest of me got cold in the wind, our mouths were hot, full degrees hotter than the rest of my body.

The concrete wall dug into my back, but I could barely feel it as my nerve endings were screaming everyplace Michael touched me. His fingers had found their way to my ribs, and it felt like CPR. It felt like oxygen after holding my breath for so long.

My brain had been so clouded with all the doubt and hurt and fear that I might never feel like myself again, but when I had him here, holding me like he wasn't going to let go even if the world ended, I remembered who I was and who I'd been since he'd left, and the two seemed to come together perfectly.

———

After a long moment, I pulled away to catch my breath. "What's that flavor?"

He laughed against my mouth, his full lips wet, and his dark eyes shining out at me. "The peppermints made me sad. So I started eating fruit candies instead." He pulled a crinkling package out of his pocket, ripped it open, and popped the candy in my half-ajar mouth. It tasted like grapefruit. He produced another and put it in his mouth. "They help. After I moved up to Vancouver, I started smoking again. A lot. Kicked the cigarettes a little over a week ago."

I reached out and squeezed his arm. "You're going to do great."

He slid his hand along my arm until his fingers wrapped around mine, and he clasped my fingers so tight that I thought he might never let go. He reached up and stripped my coat off, letting it fall at our feet and then did the same to his.

Before I had a second to ask him what he was doing or feel the cold wind across my bare arms, he grabbed my hand and we ran, jumping into the pool, our fingers still tangled.

We collided beneath the water, wrapping around each other like eels, until we were one creature coming back up to the surface. I held him close as we shivered in our wet clothes and closed my eyes, letting the smell of chlorine and grapefruit mix in my senses.

He pressed his forehead to mine. "I've been practicing," he said, his lips almost close enough to kiss. His legs were kicking, and I wasn't holding him up under the water. He was holding himself up.

"You're a natural." I smiled against his mouth, and then we slipped back beneath the surface, the world going silent against our ears.

Acknowledgments

I have to thank, first and foremost, my Father, King, and Savior, who blesses me with things I could never deserve.

Special thanks to Jean Feiwel, for taking a chance on this book and making my dream come true, and to Kat Brzozowski and Lauren Scobell for helping me make this the story I always wanted it to be. A huge thank-you to the team at Macmillan and Swoon Reads for the many ways you've made this experience amazing for me.

Thank you to the amazing people that make up the Swoon Squad, the kindest and most welcoming group of people out there. So happy to be in this with you guys. And, of course, the biggest of thank-yous to all the Swoon Readers. This book wouldn't exist without you, and all your comments meant so much to me.

Thank you to my writer friends who supported me through this process, especially Kathy Berla, my beta reader and guardian angel. Thanks to Mom and Meghan for listening to me complain week after week. Also, the YA Forum at writing.com, for teaching me everything I know. Thank you, Yoon and Christina, for being my first readers and my first fans.

It wouldn't be right not to thank Michael Phelps. You weren't the Michael in this story, but you were an important one nonetheless. Thank you for being passionate about swimming and being my hero since I was thirteen.

I have to thank all the people who inspired this story: Matt, for going away and making me miss you so much that I wrote a book about you coming home; Kristina, for taking me on an ice-cream adventure during the worst summer of my life; Christy, for *not* ditching your wedding; and Jeremy, for being one half of the greatest love story I've ever known.

Check out more books chosen for publication by readers like you.

DID YOU KNOW...

readers like you helped to get this book published?

Join our book-obsessed community and help us discover awesome new writing talent.

1

Write it.

Share your original YA manuscript.

2

Read it.

Discover bright new bookish talent.

3

Share it.

Discuss, rate, and share your faves.

4

Love it.

Help us publish the books you love.

Share your own manuscript or dive between the pages at **swoonreads.com** or by downloading the **Swoon Reads app.**